THIS CURIOU   ⎯MAN
PHENOMENON

*An exploration of some uncommonly
explored aspects of BDSM*

First Edition

Peter Masters

THIS CURIOUS HUMAN PHENOMENON

PHENOMENON

*An exploration of some uncommonly
explored aspects of BDSM*

First Edition

Published by The Nazca Plains Corporation
Las Vegas, Nevada
2008

ISBN: 978-1-934625-68-2

Published by

The Nazca Plains Corporation ®
4640 Paradise Rd, Suite 141
Las Vegas NV 89109-8000

Cover, Blake Stephens
Art Director, Blake Stephens

Table of Contents

1. Introduction

The hope I have here is simply summed up: To stir your imagination, awaken your interest, arouse your curiosity, enliven your spirit—all with the purpose of bringing you to ask, as young Maxwell put it, "What's the go of it?"—or, as Kepler had it, "Why things are as they are and not otherwise". Or, more simply in my own phrase, why is it so? Julius Sumner Miller (preface to *Millergrams*, 1966)

I wanted to start this book with a few introductory words on what BDSM is so that everyone—be they experienced practitioner or merely idly curious—has a chance of understanding what is to follow. The problem, unfortunately, is that introducing BDSM requires far more than a few simple words to do it justice.

But, being someone who doesn't know the meaning of the word "defeat", I'll try anyway. Let me begin with a few of the terms—and in particular, "BDSM"—and see where we arrive.

"BDSM" is a compact acronym standing for:

- Bondage & Discipline,
- Dominance & Submission, and
- Sadism & Masochism (or Sadomasochism).

Most commonly it's associated with sex, women wearing latex cat-suits, men in leather vests and chaps, riding crops, floggers, chains, and half-naked people tied to furniture being continuously whipped into erotic frenzies.

But much more than this, it's about relationships between people, even if these are only transient relationships between between people who meet a BDSM party, do a little exploring together, and then go their separate ways.

The people who engage in BDSM practices often describe themselves with labels such as top, bottom, dominant, submissive, switch, master, mistress, and slave. Commonly these give a clue as to who is doing what to whom, such as tops, dominants, masters and mistresses doing "things" to bottoms, submissives and slaves. Exactly what these "things" are, and the effect they have, varies. This is something I'll be looking a little later when I struggle with the thorny issue of actually defining these labels.

Some terms

A *scene* is a BDSM activity which has a clearly defined start and end. For example, a bondage scene might begin when the ropes are first applied, and end when they are removed. A master/slave scene might begin when the slave gives over control of themselves (and what they do) to the master, and ends when the master gives control back.

Play is not about games, but instead usually refers to a group of related activities. For example, "impact play" encompasses hitting someone with a riding crop, whip, flogger, ruler, paddle, or a bare hand (i.e., spanking). "Pain play" includes all those activities which specifically focus on applying pain, such as caning, whipping, piercing, cutting, and pinching. "Rope play" has to do, naturally enough, with rope, and can include both bondage (tying someone up) or suspension (dangling them from a convenient hook, usually while they're tied up). There can be some overlap between different types of play as, for example, using a riding crop might be seen as both impact and pain play.

Sadism & masochism or *S&M* generally refers to the use of pain and suffering to add to sexual excitement.

D&S or *D&s* or *D/s* generally refer to dominance & submission, a branch of BDSM where the activities include a strong focus on one partner (the dominant) asserting and using control over the other (the submissive) rather than just on physical play. The lower case "s" is suggestive of a difference in rank—namely that the Dominant has authority or control over the submissive.

Master/slave or *M/s* refers to a type of BDSM which may involve no whips, chains, floggers, or whips at all, and instead be focussed on the exercise of authority by the master (or mistress) over the slave. It usually has the the slave serving the master or mistress.

A *flogger* is an implement used to hit someone. It has a thick handle, and many short tails. The tails are fairly thick, and the feeling of being hit by a flogger is often more of a thud than a sting.

24/7 is short for "24 hours a day, seven days a week". It suggests a BDSM relationship between two people which continues for the participants beyond activities or scenes. Typically this has to do with one person recognising and accepting ongoing authority or power over them by their partner. In such a case, for example, the dominant partner might be able to contact their submissive partner at any time and expect obedience.

Vanilla is an adjective used to describe the bedroom activities, and sometimes the attitudes, of people who don't engage in any form of BDSM. For example, *vanilla sex* would be sex without using ropes, canes, or riding crops; and a *vanilla relationship* would be one where the two people involved strive diligently to conform to the respectable standards of society, and where neither attempts to take charge of, or assume power over, the other.

White-bread land is a term used by some BDSM practitioners to refer to people who, while they may be true experts at various aspects of BDSM—such as the practical aspects of bondage, caning, pain-play, and so on—don't explore any of the more profound or spiritual aspects of BDSM.

Sub-space is a floating or detached feeling some BDSM people get while being subject to their partner's whims—for example, while being tied or flogged, or while being spoken to firmly.

BDSMer: someone who practices some form of BDSM.

A *safeword* is a word or action used by someone to indicate to their partner that they'd like to slow down or stop whatever is going on. For example, when someone is being flogged—and really enjoying it, of course—and the intensity is getting a bit too much, instead of needing to explain how they feel to their partner, they just say the word, "red", to tell them to slow down or stop. This shortness of the signal helps them keep their state of mind. A safeword can also be an action, and is commonly used when the person needing it can't speak—such as when they've been gagged. In such a case they might hold something (such as a ball), and the signal is when they drop it.

The abundance of how

When people write about leather, S&M, D&s, and BDSM, they generally talk about the practical and mechanical aspects. These are easy to address, can lead to quick thrills, and as a result are common and popular themes. For example, if you want to know how to tie someone up, then it's easy to find a book which will tell you:

- What sort of rope to use and where to get it,
- How to do a variety of knots,
- How to make sure that blood continues to circulate once you've tied up your partner,
- How long you can safely leave them tied up,

- How to make sure they don't faint due to holding a particular position too long,
- How to release them in a hurry if there are problems,
- Where to place the knots so that they don't press on nerve bundles or joints,
- Et cetera, et cetera, et cetera.

Likewise, if you're keen on torture and feel inclined to:

- Pinch your partner with your fingers, or to place clamps on their sensitive bits, or to
- Pierce parts of their anatomy with needles, or to
- Inscribe sensual designs on their flesh with razor-sharp knives, or to
- Cane them or whip them into an erotic frenzy,

then there are plenty of guides to tell you how to do these things reasonably safely without causing nerve damage, infections, or permanent harm to non-replaceable body parts.

And, if wearing an elaborate collar, or being lead around on a leash, makes you hot-to-trot, or if being manhandled by an attractive partner gets your juices running, or if being treated as a servant by one or more delectable members of the desirable sex is your idea of an evening of bliss, then there's plenty of published material available to give you most of the tips you need.

The scarcity of why

So, there are lots of books on how, but if you're keen to know why, then useful literature is rare.

But why is the *why* important?

Isaac Asimov, a famous 20th-century science fiction author, said that any technology sufficiently advanced appears to be magic. A primitive tribesman seeing an electric light for the first time will think it's magic. It will be amazing to him. He will be able to learn to control the light via the light switch, but the technology is incomprehensible to him. If the fuse blows, the light bulb breaks, or a wire becomes disconnected, he won't have the understanding to make things right again. All he knows is the magical gesture which makes the light go on, and the magical gesture which makes the light go off. Once either of these gestures stop working he is lost.

In desperation he can pray, or try other incantations. The light bulb, though, still won't glow.

But, he can study. He can learn what makes the light bulb glow, and he can then become adept at making his light bulb, and the light bulbs of others, work again when something breaks.

It's really not that dissimilar to what happens with BDSM.

Isn't sub-space, that often detached, floating feeling—experienced and sought by many submissives—magical? The first time you experience it, or your partner experiences it, it's amazing. Where did it come from? All your life you never knew that you (or your partner) had this inside! But how the hell do fluffy handcuffs cause such a thing? Or who'd have thought that a few taps with a riding crop, or having your hands tied, could get such an awesome reaction?

So maybe you proceed to look closer. You learn what buttons to push to get a particular reaction. You learn to wave your magical flogger, or to do the magical incantations which get the responses you want.

But why do they work? Maybe you change partners one day and your trusty, hard-learned incantations don't work any more. Or maybe you push the buttons which used to work with your previous partner, and get some entirely different—and possibly unfortunate—reaction. Why is this? Is your new partner broken in some way? Where has the magic gone?

More to the point, how do you work out what's wrong when you don't know why it worked in the first place?

When you know and understand, when you are aware of which wants and needs are in play, and why some things satisfy them and other things do not, then making things happen, or making things happen *better*, becomes less hit-and-miss (pun intended) and more a matter of simply deciding to make it so.

Hence this book.

It isn't always about sex

It's true that many people use BDSM activities as a way of leading into super hot sex, and this is certainly an admirable goal. But as a consequence, many people tend to see it as *only* about sex.

This is unfortunate. Perhaps this is a sensational view of BDSM. Certainly, viewing BDSM as a spiritual journey, or even as a way of unwinding after a busy week, is not going to sell as many newspapers or magazines, or get as many bums on seats, as an article or movie about "deviant" sex.

We shall see that sex may be merely incidental to BDSM for a lot of people, and that the goal of super hot sex may not be anywhere near the top of their BDSM agenda. For example, gay masters can have deeply satisfying BDSM relationships with female slaves where never a cunt their cocks shall meet.

A note about references

Rather than bless you with only my words of wisdom and insight, and then leave it up to you to go and find your own sources to either confirm or deny what I've written, I have included throughout this book references to many of the sources I've used.

Where there is a reference it will be something like a surname and a year enclosed in square brackets like this: [FORDHAM1991]. Possibly there'll be a page number or range of pages after it in round brackets. You can find the full details of each reference, such as the full title, publisher, ISBN number, etc., in the bibliography at the end of the book.

Culture

It's worth mentioning that two of the references I tap into are Desmond Morris and Nigel Barley, both of whom being respected and well-published anthropologists. Anthropology is the comparative study of human societies and cultures, and one of the approaches which I'm taking in this book is that BDSM is not just a quirk of mind in one person, nor is it simply limited to the behaviour between two consenting adults in the privacy of their own bedroom. Instead BDSM exists in a complex mesh of intersecting cultures, subcultures and micro-societies.

The top-most culture is our western culture. On one hand, it expresses the view that BDSM, and the behaviours associated with it, should be confined to the smallest minority possible. It attempts to educate us, both directly and indirectly, that parity and equality are goals to seek, that always conveying our thoughts and feelings through calm and rational speech is a good thing, and that hitting others is a no-no.

But within this western culture operate other subcultures, and even micro-cultures. A small sampling of these which are of interest to us BDSM-ophiles are:

- Personal behaviours between two people,
- On-line BDSM communities, chat groups, and message boards,
- Gay/leather communities,
- Hellfire-type social/play parties,
- Swinger clubs, with a hint of BDSM,
- Fetish, with a taste of BDSM, and

- Authority-based or control-based social groups, or hierarchical structured BDSM groups (see chapter 17, *Structured groups*).

We might look at these and say, well, some of these things are strictly between a tiny number of consenting adults, and such a small number of people don't make a culture. This is true, but all of these things are done in a context which is strongly influenced by the cultures which surround it. Even the execution of the horizontal mamba is heavily influenced by what's "right" and "wrong" with sex as seen by our own western society—e.g., don't talk about it with others, absolutely women should orgasm, don't do it in public places (even when no one else is around), it's only done to create new Catholics and not for straight-out pleasure (Catholic church view), "nice girls don't", multiple partners means you're a slut, etc.

Likewise, BDSM can be coloured (even literally) by cultural expectations and limitations. For example, why does everyone need to be either naked, or dressed in black? What's wrong with a bit of colour, e.g., Hawaiian shirts?

Trying to consider BDSM in isolation without taking into account these influences is like trying to model something while viewing only a small portion of it.

The two surveys

The next two chapters are, respectively, a survey of many of the common physical and psychological activities which BDSMers get up to. As BDSM is mostly about people doing things to other people, I want to establish a reference in these two chapters to which I'll be referring in the rest of the book.

The rest

In the rest of the book, I'll be looking—as promised—at the *why* of BDSM. I'll be talking about different ways of seeing BDSM, at the different ways in which people use BDSM, and at the psychological and spiritual mechanisms in play.

Because BDSM is not mainstream, it isn't bound by many of the social and ethical conventions which limit other activities and therapies, and we'll see how this can provide interesting and very effective opportunities for self-exploration and self-satisfaction. But this same lack of social oversight can also potentially create serious problems, and I'll be looking at some of these as well.

2. Survey of physical activities

Popular images of BDSM often contain whips, chains, bondage, or leather cat-suits; or maybe a half-naked beauty chained to the wall in a darkened dungeon, being whipped by a hulking masked protagonist until her skin is raw.

In this chapter I want to survey many of the purely physical BDSM activities in which practitioners engage. These include a number of things in the popular images, such as the use of whips and chains, plus many which aren't quite so spectacular and therefore rarely make their way into mainstream representations of "the art".

Bondage and discipline

Bondage is about physically tying up or restraining someone. It can be done with ropes, chains, cling-wrap, superglue, hand-cuffs, cable-ties, cages, or anything else which restricts movement. Sometimes it includes blindfolding or the use of a hood.

Discipline is about pain, usually inflicted in a way associated with punishment. Canes, floggers, whips, and bare hands (for spanking) are common, with buttocks, breasts, and shoulders being common targets. Most types of discipline are a subset of what is sometimes also called "impact play" though being required to sit in a corner, or being locked up in a cage as punishment, might also satisfy some people's definition.

Bondage and discipline (B&D) are mostly seen as mechanical exercises. You tie someone up, then you untie them. Or you "warm someone up" with a light flogger or riding crop on their back or buttocks, preparing them for more intense experiences to come, and then move on to heavier floggers or canes for the rest of the scene. Or instead of using implements, the discipline might come from an old-fashioned, but eminently rewarding, hand-operated spanking.

With both bondage and discipline, there's a lot more actually going on than just what you see. There are issues of trust, boundaries, authority, and control at play, even in a casual, clothes-staying-on bondage engagement at a public BDSM party.

It'd be a careless, desperate, self-destructive, or gullible person who'd let themselves be tied up by someone they don't know without being able to trust that some form of safety net—such as a friend in the same room—is in place. Even when there is a safety net in place, or the person involved is someone they know well, for at least the duration of the scene someone else is going to have control of their movements (or lack thereof). They must surrender control of their physical freedom, at least for a time, into the hands of another.

Certainly there will be boundaries set to what can be done during the scene. These boundaries might be sexual—e.g., no fucking, or may be related to physical marking—e.g., no marking, bruising, or tattooing, or to do with words which can be used—such as no name calling, or to do with medical or health issues.

The point here is that with bondage and discipline, the physical acts are the defining features. Because the activities have a fairly clear start and end, B&D tends not to overflow into everyday life or to be thought of something that can be done 24/7.

Impact play

Impact play is basically about hitting someone with something. There are two common scenarios:

1. Applying discipline, such as in playing out a punishment scene (e.g., naughty schoolgirl/schoolboy), or
2. Creative application of particular implements to instil and modulate different sorts of pain.

Note: impact play is distinct from *percussive therapy*. Percussive therapy is the hitting of a poorly-behaved household appliance to get it to work again.

Discipline

With discipline-type impact play, it's common for participants to act out something such as a naughty schoolgirl/schoolboy scenario with one person being the teacher or schoolmaster punishing the other. The implement used is often a cane or bare hand, mostly often applied to the naked derriere (backside, bum, or ass).

For the truly dedicated, it's not uncommon that they kit out the room where they do this with old-style school desks and blackboards.

To stay *in character*, these sorts of scenes are often played out clothed, and with the victim either lifting their skirt or dropping their pants to receive the punishment.

Creative

Going beyond a bare-hand spanking, or the basic cane, there are a wide range of hitting tools available. Indeed, often a variety of implements are used, on a range of different body parts, during a particular scene to create very particular sensations, and to create a very particular experience. Here are a few of the different types of implements:

- Floggers—usually fairly short, up to maybe 60cm (24"), with a thick, rigid handle and a bundle of flexible tails. The width of the individual tails varies from flogger to flogger, as does the material from which they're made—flat leather strips, or sometimes narrow rope or rubber cord. The tails usually strike as a bunch to give more of a thud than a sting.

- Whips—often quite short, but mostly with rigid handle, and a single, narrow, flexible tail made of braided leather. These will sting or even cut.

- Crops—based on a riding crop, these are usually stiff rods of up to 60cm, made of fibreglass with leather braided around them. These sting.

Floggers, whips, and crops are mostly used on the back, or derriere. Small floggers and crops are sometimes used on the breasts, or on the balls and cock.

- Paddles—similar to table-tennis paddles, these have a short handle suitable for one hand, and a flat paddle for striking. The paddle can be finished and polished wood, or can be made of flexible leather in some cases, and can have short rivets or studs across the surface to add to its effect. Paddles are mostly used on the derriere.

Bondage and restraint

We can think of this form of BDSM activity as physically immobilising, restraining, or confining someone.

- It can be done with ropes, chains, cable ties (plastic ties), or plastic wrap— otherwise known as Saran™ wrap, Glad™ wrap, cling wrap, or the clear plastic stuff you use in kitchens to wrap up and seal food.

- Fully immobilising someone usually means tying them firmly to something fixed, such as a bed, a low table, a chair, or a specially-crafted piece of furniture which may also leave the person sexually exposed (i.e., with their legs spread apart).

- Partially immobilising someone, such as by firmly binding only their wrists together or their ankles together, or by tying them in a hog-tie—i.e., with their wrists and ankles together—still leaves the person with the ability to wiggle or resist. Unlike with the Borg, resistance is not necessarily futile as it can provide both a physical outlet for their experience, as well as requiring the partner, to some extent, to overwhelm the person tied up.

As we'll see later, the feeling of being overwhelmed or overpowered is sometimes a key goal.

- Restraining someone with handcuffs and/or legcuffs, a locked collar on a leash, or with spreader bars, limits their movement without actually immobilising them. A spreader bar, by the way, is a short, rigid rod with cuffs on each end. The cuffs can be attached to the partner's wrist, or more often, to their ankles or knees to keep their legs apart, and thus keep them sexually exposed.

- Placing someone in a cage confines them, but doesn't restrict the physical movement of their body as the previous cases do.

- The above can be combined. For example, placing someone in handcuffs, and then putting them in a cage, or handcuffing them to the bars of the cage; or tying someone's feet and ankles to anchor points without restraining their torso, etc.

- A notable and extreme restraint is nailing a guy to a post or wooden board by hammering a nail through a part of his scrotum. Not recommended.

- Another dubious, but not uncommon, strategy is to place someone in the boot of a car and then drive somewhere with them. This is dubious for two reasons: 1) they might suffocate if there is any sort of leak in the car's exhaust system, and 2) the front engine compartment of a car, and the rear boot are crumple zones, intended to collapse and absorb the shock of an impact with something (such as a tree, wall, or another car). Anyone in the boot in an accident is also likely to crumple, and the driver will probably face manslaughter charges.

- Very sensitive bits of the anatomy can also be the targets of bondage. For example, thread or very thin cord can be tied around nipples, or fine cord can be used around the base of a man's cock or around his testicles.

Any form of bondage or restraint is accompanied by health and other practical management concerns, such as overheating or dehydrating concerns with plastic wrap, blood circulation issues with long-term rope bondage, toilet management, quick release in case of emergency (e.g., fire, light-headedness, etc.).

The health and well-being of someone who is bound or restrained is in the hands of the person who restrained them.

There's more about health and well-being scattered through this book. And there's also a specific chapter on the subject—chapter 13, *Health concerns*—later.

Self bondage

This is tying or restraining oneself, often in such a way that you can't free yourself straight away. One guy I knew used a combination lock for this. He'd tie or chain himself up at night with the last link being a combination lock. He'd have a timer on the light so that it would go off, stay off for a preselected time and then turn back on. While the lights were out he couldn't see the numbers on the combination lock and thus couldn't undo himself. In case the timer failed and the light didn't come back on as planned he had the Sun as a backup, i.e., the Sun would come up in the morning and he'd be able to see the numbers on the combination lock again. Other practitioners use a padlock, and freeze the key to the padlock in a block of ice so that they can't get the key until the ice has melted.

Nipple clamps

These are delightful little gadgets which, as their name suggests, clamp on to nipples. They come in a variety of styles, typically in pairs connected by a short chain, and are usually adjustable so that how tightly they squeeze the nipples can be changed to suit the needs of the people using them.

The primary purpose of nipple clamps is to cause pain, often extreme pain which is exacerbated by movement. Thus, they can be used simply for torture. Or, because they're on a chain, they can be used to lead someone—i.e., someone wearing nipple clamps will tend to follow when the chain is pulled because of the extra pain involved if they don't.

Labial clamps

These are similar to nipple clamps, but instead attach to the cunt lips of a woman. With labial clamps the woman is frequently restrained or bound in such a way that her legs are held apart.

Weights can be attached to the clamps to exert a constant pull on her lips. Weights can also be attached to nipple clamps, but in this case they are, like labial clamps, usually used when the person is immobilised, often in a leaning-over position so that the weights hang free.

Piercing

Instead of being done to create holes for ear-rings, navel-rings and the like, piercing in the BDSM sense is generally done using a number of sterile hypodermic needle tips to create decorative or symbolic designs and patterns—such as a snake across the chest, or a star or flower around a nipple; or to act as anchor points for fine bondage, or simply to create interesting pain.

Hypodermic needles are designed to cause as little pain as possible, and not to leave scars or marks when removed, so often their use is mainly psychological. The needles are typically left in only for relatively short periods of time, and are placed to avoid major veins or arteries so that there's a minimum of bleeding.

Multiple needles can be used as anchor points for a fine bondage exercise. For example, a row of needles perpendicular to and along the top of a cock, can be used to tie it to the victim's likewise-pierced stomach with ribbon or fine cord.

Piercing is usually done to the the penis, nipples, breasts, chest, stomach, arms and thighs. It should be noted that piercing probably has most effect when done on a private part of the body, e.g., penis or nipples, rather than arms.

For many devotees of this activity the result is, apart from the design or pattern, a deep sub-space.

Cutting

Cutting, like piercing, is usually not intended to leave permanent marks. It is the use of razor-sharp blades to cut fine designs into the top layers of the skin, without cutting so deep as to cause bleeding, and without leaving permanent scars.

Parts of the body where this might be done include the back, chest, breasts, upper arms and thighs.

Similar to piercing, the result of this is often, apart from the design or pattern, a deep sub-space.

Branding

Branding, as opposed to piercing and cutting, does leave marks, and can be done either hot or cold.

Hot-branding is done by heating a flat metal design, often to red heat, and then pressing it to bare flesh (such a a breast or buttock) to leave a scar in the shape of the brand. This is not something you should try without training, as it can lead to major infection.

Cold-branding is done with a flat metal design cooled with dry ice, which is then pressed against naked flesh in the same way as hot-branding.

Thin sheet metal, such as from a tin can, is often used for the design in both hot- and cold-branding. Because it's thin it doesn't retain enough heat to do as much damage as a real, heavy cattle brand would do.

One of the key ideas behind branding is that of *ownership*. Branding is, effectively, a permanent mark by one person on their partner to indicate ownership and control.

Fisting

Fisting is inserting a hand into one of the larger bodily orifices below the belt, of which women have two and men have one. This usually involves lots of lubricant, lots of time, and plenty of patience.

Apart from stimulating various opportunely-placed nerve endings, fisting is big in the area of symbolic penetration.

Waxing

Waxing in a BDSM context isn't [primarily] the process of removing unwanted body hair, but is actually dropping molten hot wax, such as from a candle, onto someone who is usually blindfolded and restrained on a bed or table face up.

By adjusting the height of the candle, i.e., its distance above the victim, the temperature of the wax when it reaches the skin can be controlled.

Suspension

Suspension typically involves tying someone up in rope, and then lifting them off the ground with a winch. Most commonly, they are first "woven" into a harness made of rope which supports at least their whole torso. Anchor points are created in the harness to which the winch can be attached, and which cause the load to distributed safely as the person is lifted off the ground. The person is usually horizontal.

Variations include using special boots and hanging the person upside-down, and tying someone by their hands or wrists to a horizontal beam and lifting the beam so the person is hoisted off the ground.

This can be combined with a blindfold to add a fear element, i.e., so that the person might think that they're quite high off the ground when they're only a centimetre or two above it.

Fireplay

Fireplay, when done safely, involves finding a relatively hair-free part of anatomy, such as a [shaved] chest or stomach, laying the person on their back, applying a small amount of a highly volatile alcohol mix, and then igniting the vapour.

Note that rather than burning *on* the person, the vapour burns *above* them. This is not recommended for beginners. It can be spectacular and have a strong psychological fear effect.

Bad things can happen if the bit of anatomy is not free of hair, as hair can burn and the flames can make their way back to the skin.

Iceplay

No prizes for guessing that iceplay has to do with ice or icy water. This is sometimes done with ice phalluses for penetration, or ice-water for enemas. Being splashed with ice-water can also be a surprise for someone who is bound and blindfolded, and having ice-cubes run over the skin or dropped into underwear can also be part of the sensations a top gives their partner during some forms of play.

Iceplay, waxing and fireplay are sometimes grouped together and called temperature-play.

Sensation-play

Some BDSM practitioners do what is called sensation-play. This is exposing their partner to a range of different physical feelings or sensations. Contrasting feelings are often a focus. Iceplay and waxing can be part of this, as can:

- Fingernails—for light scratching,
- Feathers—for light stroking or tickling,
- Satin or silk material,
- Breathing on or blowing on the partner,
- Heavy chains versus soft ribbons, and
- Shaving—to expose previously protected-by-hair skin.

Breathplay

Breathplay is one of the riskier BDSM activities. It involves one person limiting or restricting the breathing of their partner. This can be done in various ways, for example:

- Suffocation—stopping the person getting fresh air. This can be done by directly placing something in or over their nose and mouth, like clamps or gags, or by placing the person in something like an old-style gas mask and blocking the air flow, or by putting their head in a plastic bag which is tied around their neck, or

- Constriction and strangulation—blocking the flow of air by tying something tight around their neck, or by applying pressure to the front of their neck (trachea).

The person whose breathing is being restricted is usually tied or restrained in some way so that they can't prevent what's being done to them. This is obviously fairly dangerous, and there have been a number of high profile deaths over the years due to this practice.

Catheterization

This is inserting a sterile tube into and through the urethra. It is usually only practised by BDSM enthusiasts who are also medical professionals—e.g., doctors or nurses.

The key ideas with this are extreme penetration, and loss of control of a bodily function, namely peeing.

Vaginal and anal stretching

Continuing along the penetration line, doctors commonly use various implements, including speculums, to spread open lower abdominal orifices—like the anus or vagina—for examinations. These same implements are also employed by some BDSM enthusiasts, in combination with lots of lube and a lot of patience, to stretch their partner's holes—often well beyond the point strictly required for an inspection.

Fisting

Closely related is fisting, where—also with lots of lube and lots of patience—a hand is inserted into either the vagina or anus.

Butt plugs

Also closely related are butt plugs. These are cone-shaped, and are made of rubber or similar. They are inserted into the butt (read: rectum) and have a groove at the base to stop them popping out. They are individually available in different sizes; and sometimes come as "training" sets in different graduated sizes, a bit like measuring cups in the kitchen.

CBT

CBT is *Cock and Balls Torture*. Fairly obviously, this is something done specifically to men. Because there's quite a lot of hardware available between a man's legs, there's also quite a lot which can be done there; and because there are lots of nerve endings in the area, quite a lot of interesting and varied pain and suffering can be inflicted.

Symbolically, too, this general geographic area has a strong association with a man's idea of his sexual power, and limiting what he can do with his cock can be very powerful.

Bondage (including using specially-made cock cages), flogging, pulling, stretching, piercing, enforced chastity, and so on, are some of the activities which can go on in this relatively small area.

Electric play, or electroplay

Electroplay is, as you may have guessed, the use of electricity in some BDSM activities. Electroplay isn't the use of electrical appliances—such as toasters, vibrators, or winches—as incidentals. but is directly using electricity flowing through the submissive's body to get a reaction of some sort.

There are two main sorts of electrical gadgets used for this.

- The first is the TENS unit. This stands for Transcutaneous Electrical Nerve Stimulator. It is a common piece of medical equipment which generates low-voltage electrical pulses to stimulate nerves. In normal use two electrodes are taped to the skin and the pulses flow between them. These pulses can cause mild to strong involuntary muscle contractions or vibrations.

  In BDSM use, it's not unusual for one of the electrodes to be taped to the skin and the other to be inserted into a convenient lower-abdominal orifice, such as the anus or vagina.

- The second sort of gadget comes from yesteryear. It's called a violet wand, and contains a very high voltage, but very low current, generator.

Originally developed by quacks (read: dubious medical practitioners) in the early 1900's, these also had two electrodes, one of which attached to the patient, and the other of which took the form of a wand which was applied to the patient. The wand typically had an insulated handle, and ended in a hollow glass tube, probe or comb which was filled with an inert gas. When the probe was brought near the patient, current began to flow through the gas into the patient and the gas would glow (often violet, but also other colours depending on the gas in the tube). There might also be blue sparks in the air between the probe and the patient.

In reality, this just produces a tingling effect, and on very sensitive bits of the anatomy it can feel like mild pinpricks.

It can look very impressive.

3. Survey of psychological activities

The previous chapter mentioned some of the less visually spectacular activities in which two BDSMers might get involved. Waxing and cutting, for example, or anal stretching, are never going to make good theatre no matter how many bright lights you use or where you shine them. But for the people actually doing these things they may be the absolute emotional or primal highlight of their week.

What's good about these things is less the external razzle-dazzle and more the *internal* experience. This brings us to this chapter, and to activities which have much less of a physical aspect, and more of a psychological aspect to them. These activities consist of creating states of mind or psychological experiences which inspire similar sorts of *goodness* to what things like piercing, cutting, bondage, and caning can cause. In later chapters I'll be talking about exactly what this *goodness* is.

The fact that goodness can be attained without whips or ropes doesn't mean that everything in this chapter is interchangeable with what was in the last. Just as some people incomprehensibly don't like science-fiction, prefer baseball to football, or can pass up an excellent cheeseburger, not every BDSM activity is going to resonate with every BDSMer. It is much, as they say, horses for courses...

Humiliation

Humiliation can involve a whole range of activities, but generally needs to be specifically demeaning or degrading to the individual being humiliated. The same act is not going to be equally degrading for everybody. For example, being paraded naked on a leash in front of strangers might be humiliating for some people, but not for some exhibitionists.

Humiliation activities can include being dressed as member of the opposite sex (cross-dressing), or being made to behave as an animal—e.g., a dog, being pissed on, or being verbally abused. Sometimes the humiliating acts are done in front of one or more other people for better effect. I'll write more on this *effect* later).

Generally, humiliation isn't used to psychologically destroy someone and leave them in permanent emotional tatters, but is instead done to pierce their external barriers and, if nothing else, let them feel that they're exposed and vulnerable to their partner.

Annihilation

Although not necessarily specific to humiliation, the idea of annihilation or suppression can make an appearance here. Humiliation can be seen as attempting to dismantle, suppress or diminish one or more of the submissive's identities. *Identity* is something I explore later in chapter 5, *Identity maintenance, management, and role-play*, but for the moment it is hopefully enough to say that humiliation sweeps aside or penetrates the persona of the submissive, passing completely through their defences.

In this sense, humiliation may led to partial and temporary annihilation of their sense of self, thus stripping them of an important self-defence.

In other words, a person uses their sense of self as an anchor, or as a guide to determine their feelings, thoughts and reactions to what's going on around them. When this sense of self is pierced, they're left without this anchor and are much more exposed to, and subject to, the influence of their partner; particularly in the area of self-worth for example.

Orgasm control and denial

Orgasm control is where one person limits or prevents their partner from reaching orgasm. More generally this is a form of *sweet torture* where a person is not permitted to orgasm for hours, days or weeks, until the moment of the big release chosen by their partner. Sometimes, there are sessions along the way, conducted by the person imposing the control, where the victim is repeatedly aroused close to the point of orgasm, but is then left to cool off unsatisfied.

In the case of male submissives, this can be very powerful—effectively it is their dominant partner taking control of the symbol of their manhood.

Nudity and nakedness

BDSM can involve a lot of nudity. This can include serving drinks or food while naked in front of one or more masters or mistresses, pissing in front of others or while being watched, or being posed or positioned in such a way that the person is sexually exposed.

The important idea is that of *being seen*, or being exposed without barriers to hide behind. Also it's a state of having no defences, and being unable to shield one's self. This doesn't suggest that the person is in any way attacked due to this nakedness, just that they are completely uncovered.

There can be some similarity between this and *humiliation*. Both attempt to uncover or expose the person, though the method used is different in each. We'll see much more about this in chapter 7, *Penetration*.

Fear

One of the common themes in all of this, and one which I'll talk about much more in the next chapter, is that BDSM commonly has little to do with any of the so-called higher-level brain functions. There's no problem-solving involved, no looking for cleverness, no debating or having involved discussions, no solving crosswords, and no trying to work out IQ test-type puzzles.

Fear is a psychological tool used in BDSM which operates in a primal arena. Fear pushes aside the high-level functions of the mind and leaves, in its place, the primal. Blindfolds can play an important part in this.

While blindfolds sometimes help those submissives who would otherwise try to watch what's going on rather than surrender to their experience, they can also let a dominant create both a heightened apprehension and the sense of not being in control in their partner.

For example, a dominant might tie up their submissive, blindfold them, attach them to a winch, and lift them off the ground. Because of the blindfold, the submissive can't tell how high off the ground they are. So, with the appropriate words and suggestions their dominant can cause them to believe that they're a metre or two off the ground when they might only be a few centimetres up. The dominant might then slowly cut the rope holding them up. The submissive feels the knife sawing through the rope and might be terrified of the fall. Their dominant might, in the meanwhile, also have placed soft cushions underneath them. This whole experience is sometimes called a *mindfuck*—where the dominant creates a false reality for their submissive—and, in an example like this, can lead to very strong fear (and an intense focus).

Similarly, a dominant might have their partner tied to a frame and display to them a fearsome-looking and very sharp knife. Then, while the submissive can't see (perhaps due to a blindfold), the dominant turns the knife over and uses the dull back of the blade on their skin. The submissive may be in fear of being cut if they move—even though there's no risk of that—and may stand petrified.

As a final example of the use of apprehension, when doing *waxing* (see previous chapter), the rate of dripping and the temperature of the wax on contact with the skin are under the control of the top. They can use this to create tension or fear in their partner in many ways, such as by gradually bringing the candle closer and closer to their partner—and therefore making each drop hotter and hotter—until it becomes unbearable.

Ritualised, symbolic, or service behaviour

In all of BDSM there's an aspect of disparity. There is one person who *does* to the other. They are in a *superior* position, being able to make the decisions about what will be done and how, while their partner is in an *inferior* position, being required to accept or endure what their partner decides. We can see this disparity clearly represented in the use of terms like, "master", "slave", "owner", "property", "dominant", "submissive", top", and "bottom".

One way for the disparity to manifest is for two people to enter into a type of *service relationship*, where one person serves or attends the other in a manner vaguely reminiscent of a butler or maid.

This sort of relationship or engagement can continue 24/7 for extensive periods. But while a butler or maid maintain their personal autonomy, the way it's done in the BDSM world is biased towards the abandonment of personal autonomy. We can this in the ways in which the types of service performed differ from what a mainstream butler or maid would perform.

For example, in mainstream service, we can find things like:

- Cleaning the house,
- Cooking,
- Polishing the cutlery,
- Cleaning the floors, and
- Acting as a chauffeur.

On the other hand, in BDSM the following will more likely be the sorts of behaviour we'll see:

- Being available for sex at any time,
- Using particular modes of speech. This might include referring to their partner as "master" or "mistress", never interrupting, always allowing themselves to be interrupted, referring to themselves in the third person— e.g., "May this girl bring Sir a drink?"

- Being given a slave name. Instead of using their own given name, their master/mistress/owner gives them a new and invented name which, through frequent and consistent use, is associated with their condition of being in service. E.g., "zela" instead of "Natasha", or "taleo" instead of "Robert",

- Beyond just being available for sex at any time, other aspects of the person's sexuality—such as when and if they can masturbate, or how they sexually identify via clothing, makeup and jewellery—may be dictated by their partner,

- Always walking on their partner's left, standing or sitting in particular postures, entering or leaving rooms in particular ways (e.g., backing out of rooms so that they never have their back turned towards their partner), have their head lowered, never beginning eating a meal until their partner has started, and finishing eating once their partner finishes, etc.,

- Sleeping on the floor or on a mat, and

- A focus on personally attending to their partner rather than, say, the house or garden.

The big difference we see in all of the BDSM service behaviours, compared to the mainstream service behaviour of a butler or maid, is that BDSM service strongly tends towards being personally or intimately invasive of the person *in service*. With a butler or maid, there is a clear boundary between their person and the service they perform. In BDSM, it is often deliberate (and important) that this boundary be breached, even if just symbolically.

That's not to say that a person engaged in some BDSM service relationship with their partner won't do things that a butler or maid would do, but that their service is likely to be tinged with something personally invasive or penetrative, such as serving a meal while naked.

This idea of penetration is something we'll see much more in detail in upcoming chapter 7, *Penetration*.

4. Conscious and unconscious

It's possible to consider the mind as having three major levels (or parts):

1. The conscious,
2. The personal unconscious, and
3. The collective unconscious.

These divisions derive from the work of Carl Jung (1875 - 1961), a famous Swiss psychiatrist, and the man considered by many to be the founder of modern analytical psychology.

Jung was not known for writing concisely, or even terribly clearly. His Collected Works consist of 19 volumes, and can be difficult to wade through. If you are interested in learning more about Jung, and about his ideas of the conscious, the personal unconscious, and the collective unconscious, I would refer you instead to shorter introductions, such as [FORDHAM1991] and [STEVENS1994]. You might also want to have a quick look at my own earlier writings on the subject [MASTERS2006] (pp. 11 - 21).

The conscious

The conscious part of the mind is where we live. It's the bit of ourselves that we are aware of. It's where we think. Generally speaking, we directly control what goes on in the conscious. If we want to think about something in particular, we can do that just by deciding to do so. The conscious is also where we make rational or logical decisions, do planning, and solve technical problems. To a significant extent it doesn't have much to do directly with the rewarding and satisfying parts of BDSM.

Scrabble™, Cluedo™, Monopoly™, chess, astrophysics, cross-stitch, baking cakes, and accountancy, for example, are purely rational, logical, or intellectual pursuits. These are in the domain of the conscious. But you won't find BDSM toy bags with travel chess sets nestled in amongst the ropes and cuffs, nor do you find Scrabble™ games in even the best equipped dungeons.

Likewise, a brisk game of Monopoly™ is never on any BDSM menu simply because the satisfying and profoundly rewarding aspects of BDSM are visceral. They have to do with animalistic drives, passions, and lusts which involve the unconscious mind, not the conscious. Indeed, trying to engage your partner—who is deeply involved in, say, being flogged—in an intellectual conversation about, say, livestock futures, is a sure way to get them out of the mood you have worked so long to get them into.

This doesn't mean that the conscious part of the mind has no place in BDSM. The conscious plays a vital part to do with the technical details of BDSM, such as tying knots safely, looking ahead or planning a scene, care and maintenance of gear, etc.

The language of the conscious

When we're interacting with other people, such as BDSM play partners, for example, we communicate with them. How we communicate with them depends on which level or levels of the mind are involved in the communication. Each level has its own way of communicating, its own language, and it tends to "talk" to the same corresponding level in our partner.

The conscious understands and operates in the realm of the rational and the logical. The conscious of one person can communicate usefully with the conscious of another person and discuss such things as Scrabble™, or accountancy, or what to do that evening, or any limits which should apply in the current play session, and so on. On the other hand, trying to talk rationally or logically (conscious activity) to someone in the throes of lust (primal activity) is doomed to frustration because the rational part of their mind, the conscious, is simply not there to talk to.

The conscious tends to communicate with spoken or written language—such as English, German, Spanish, Russian, etc. This can, of course, create problems when two people don't have a common spoken language. But supplementing the verbal language, we can also consciously use gestures (such as pointing) and facial expressions (such as frowning or smiling) to get our message across.

I noted above that the conscious mind doesn't really get involved in the profoundly satisfying, grunty, or visceral aspects of BDSM. We can see this in cases were two people, who don't share a common spoken language, can still have a deeply rewarding or intense BDSM session with each other once the initial agreement to actually engage has been reached. The lack of a common spoken or verbal language is only a barrier to the initial negotiations and planning (which are conscious activities), but is not a barrier to the visceral or primal experiences which follow.

The unconscious

The unconscious is where the things of which we aren't consciously aware happen. We might like to think we're in control of everything that we do, but there's a lot going on underneath the bonnet all the time which mostly escapes our notice.

The unconscious is the realm of habits, automatic behaviours, automatic mannerisms, and many biases.

There are two parts to the unconscious:

- The personal unconscious—stuff which is learned during our lifetimes, and
- The collective unconscious—stuff which is built in from birth.

If you delve into psychiatric texts (such as Jung's) and look to understand the unconscious, it's often referred to as the source of many of the ailments which psychiatrists, counsellors, and psychologists are called upon to fix. This is true, but don't let this deter or discourage you from learning more about it. The focus of these health professionals is, of course, what's wrong, rather than on what's right. The "what's wrong" is why people come to them, and is how they earn their bread and butter. We, on the other hand, are interested in the the good stuff in the unconscious. Keep this in mind as you read on.

The personal unconscious

The personal unconscious is where past experience goes once we have forgotten about it. It's the home of habits, of social and other conditioning, and of learned fears.

The personal unconscious is a very useful part of the mind. A lot of the things we do every day are supervised and controlled by the personal unconscious. Driving a car, and typing on a computer are two good examples. Think of how hard it was to learn to drive or type when you first started, but now you barely have to think when you want to get in your car and drive off, or when you want to turn a corner, or when you want to type a particular word on the computer. You just form the intent to do so, and then your personal unconscious takes over and does most of the work for you. Your conscious mind just makes the choice, and then your personal unconscious does the hard work of co-ordinating your muscles to make it happen.

This is tres cool, and it's happening all the time.

On the other hand, your personal unconscious can be a less-than-helpful influence at times, such as when you want to go somewhere new, but get distracted and then find that your personal unconscious has piloted you automatically to some other familiar destination.

Your personal unconscious also learns from bad experiences, and from things which have hurt you, and then tries to steer you away from those things in future—even without you being aware of it doing so. For example, if you have a bad reaction to a certain type of food, your personal unconscious will tend to steer your choices away from that type of food in future. Likewise, if a certain person was consistently mean to you at school, then later in life your personal unconscious might tend to push you away from people with similar characteristics to that mean person from school.

Your personal unconscious is heavily influenced by what goes on around you. Your personal unconscious learns throughout your life what sorts of clothes to wear at different times, how to behave towards others, how to speak, what social values to have, and so on.

Going beyond this, your personal unconscious learns the meaning of different symbols in different contexts. They become part of the language which you use every day. Traffic signals don't say, "stop." They flash red instead, and we have all learned that red means stop. There's nothing in nature to support this, but we learn this convention, and even respond automatically to it.

In the world of BDSM, we learn and then unconsciously react to collars, floggers, and ropes in ways which are personal to us, and which are particular to the context—such as in a dungeon, or at a play party. These reactions, for example, can be going into sub-space, becoming sexually aroused, becoming ready to handle another person or to be handled ourselves, etc.

On top of this, our personal unconscious helps us learn the right and wrong things to *automatically* do or not do in particular contexts—such as what's appropriate at a child's birthday party compared to what's appropriate at a BDSM play party.

There are a few of important points about the personal unconscious:

- Part of what is in the personal unconscious started out as something of which you were consciously aware, such as the bad reaction to some food, or a good initial experience while wearing a collar.

- But it all sank, over time, into the personal unconscious. Maybe the different experiences got into the personal unconscious because they were repeated so often that the personal unconscious learned them, or because they were experiences which were so intense that they embedded themselves there.

- They are influences, sometimes very strong influences, on your behaviour and choices. If you're aware of how they work, you can often override them, or compensate for them. For instance, if you always drive to work, then trying to drive to somewhere near work can be hard because, unless you're really paying attention, your personal unconscious will just automatically pilot you to work instead. These influences, and others such as a unconscious fear, are difficult to turn off, for example, but you can compensate for them if you know that they're there.

- You might have consciously forgotten about the things that got into the personal unconscious. That doesn't mean that the personal unconscious has forgotten, or that it isn't strongly influenced by them.

- A very large part of what's in your personal unconscious is going to be similar to what's in the personal unconscious of the people around you. This isn't because it's built in (for that, see the upcoming section on the Collective unconscious), but is because the people around you are subject to many of the same social influences as you. This happens through living in the same types of culture, through watching the same T.V. shows, through going to the same schools and using the same sorts of shops, to being surrounded by the same social attitudes, to shared styles of clothing, to using the same language, to talking to the same groups of people most of the time, to being subject to the same laws and moral standards, etc., etc.

The language of the personal unconscious

A lot of the language of the personal unconscious is learned and understood simply on the basis that the symbols and gestures to which we react have been experienced by us so many times that we respond to them automatically. The red stop sign I mentioned above is a good example of this. If we take a primitive tribesman from somewhere and show him a set of traffic signals, he's not going to think anything other than that they're lights on poles. They won't have the same stop/go meaning to him that they have to us.

The extent to which this happens often only becomes really apparent when we compare aspects of communication which we use in our western culture, with other cultures. Nigel Barley, an anthropologist, gives an example in his *The Innocent Anthropologist*, where he talks about trying to use photographs in discussions with primitive african tribespeople. Do you know the saying, "A picture is worth a thousand words?" These tribespeople had never learned how to *see* photographs and couldn't make sense of this aspect of what is, to us, routine communication:

> ... I tried using photographs of lions and leopards. Old men would stare at the cards, which were perfectly clear, turn them in all manner of directions, and then say something like, 'I do not know this man.'
> [BARLEY 1986] (p. 97)

In the world of BDSM, just the sight of a collar, flogger, rope, or finely-tooled piece of leather is often enough to trigger a response, and this response is something we've learned through experience. This is a bit Pavlovian, in the sense that when we start out in the world as babies, we don't have any particular reaction to these bits of hardware, but over time, and after many good experiences involving them, we start to react to the collars, and so on, directly. I'm referring here to the famous Pavlov's dogs experiments, where at the same time that some dogs were fed, a bell was rung. In response to the food, the dogs would naturally salivate. After a number of times being exposed to the bell at the same time as feeding, the dogs would salivate in response to the sound of the bell itself, even when there was no food offered.

In the same way that the abovementioned tribespeople couldn't make sense of a photograph, many—if not most—people can't "make sense" of or respond to, say a collar or flogger, the way experienced BDSM people do, because it's something that's learned.

In particular, a lot of the communication which goes on at the personal unconscious level is stuff we've learned from the people who we hang about with. It comes from these societies or micro-societies in which we spend our time, such as around particular groups of friends or professional colleagues, or from spending time in a particular BDSM subculture.

Manwatching, A Field Guide To Human Behaviour by Desmond Morris, a zoologist and researcher on human behaviour, is an excellent and copiously-illustrated book which shows the diversity of behaviour which we humans learn in our own particular social groups, and which we then use to communicate unconsciously. Morris calls the ones related to the personal unconscious "absorbed actions" [MORRIS1978] (p. 18) as they are actions, gestures, and behaviours, which we absorb from the people and the culture which surrounds us.

Importantly, *Manwatching* shows the range of different responses for the same messages which can and do occur across different cultures. For example, a fine pair of exposed female breasts can be cause for much trouser excitement in our western society, while exactly the same sight is available day in, day out, in many primitive societies without the same sexual response. This sexual response, or the extent of it (pun intended), is something we largely learn, not something that's built in to us.

Note that different cultures don't necessarily mean another country. It can simply mean just a different group of people. For example, handkerchief codes (showing differently-coloured handkerchiefs in the back pockets of a pair of pants) signalling sexual preferences are common in the gay leather community, but don't really make an appearance anywhere else, such as in the heterosexual BDSM community. Yet these codes are common, important, and often unconscious signals between the people who recognise them.

Similarly, a collar can create a much different response (or no response at all) from someone who is not involved or interested in BDSM. But, for someone profoundly submissive, a collar can trigger rapture. Again, it's learned, not built in; and it happens unconsciously—i.e., we can't choose for it to happen or not happen.

In some BDSM subcultures, or even some relationships, clothing can be a symbol or trigger. Leathers, lace, corsets, chaps, etc., or accessories, such as whips, handcuffs, etc., can signal preferences, and then over time, just the sight of someone wearing these particular items becomes a trigger in itself.

The language of the personal unconscious is not verbal or intellectual. Once we reach the level of the personal unconscious, we're moving away from languages like English, Spanish, or Russian. The personal unconscious instead communicates via, and responds to, gestures, images, and symbols encountered and experienced by the individual.

While I've been talking so far about actual instances of particular signals which are handled by the personal unconscious, whole exchanges can be heavily influenced or even scripted by the personal unconscious. Here's another example from *The Innocent Anthropologist* where Barley talks about trying to interview the local natives:

> *To begin with I was distressed to find that I couldn't extract more than ten words from Dowayos at a stretch. When I asked them to describe something to me, a ceremony, or an animal, they would produce one or two sentences and then stop. I would have to ask further questions to get more information. This was unsatisfactory as I was directing their answers rather more than sound field method would have prescribed. One day, after about two months of fairly fruitless endeavour, the reason struck me. Quite simply, Dowayos have totally different rules about how to divide up the parts of a conversation. Whereas in the West we learn not to interrupt when somebody else is talking, this does not hold in much of Africa. One must talk to people physically present as if on the telephone, where frequent interjections and verbal response must be given if only to assure the other party that one is still there and paying attention. When listening to someone talking, a Dowayo stares gravely at the floor, rocks backwards and forwards and murmurs, 'Yes', 'It is so', 'Good', every five seconds or so. Failure to do so leads to the speaker rapidly drying up. As soon as I adopted this expedient, my interviews were quite transformed.* [BARLEY1986] (p. 67)

Finally, note that more than one message can be in transit between two people at a time. For example, while the tone of voice used when speaking can be an unconscious trigger or symbol, it can be different to the conscious meaning of the words used themselves. Likewise, how someone is standing or gesturing might be being driven by their unconscious, while at the same time they're actually trying to consciously convey something completely different—for example, they may be with someone who is trying to tell them something and out of politeness they're staying to listen, but their body may be saying, "let's get out of here."

The collective unconscious

Everything in the *personal unconscious* is learned or acquired by each person individually, and is based on their own experiences. It is thus unique to that individual. Everything in the *collective unconscious*, on the other hand, is built in. What they both have in common is that the conscious part of your mind doesn't have any direct control over either of them and, often, isn't even aware of what's going on in them.

There are some feelings and reactions which we are born with, or which develop throughout our lives without any outside influences. They aren't learned. They are either there from the outset, or they appear automatically as we mature—such as the sexual hunger and the sexual responses which appear around the time of puberty.

Being touched or stroked is a good example of something pleasurable which is built in from day one. Fear of falling, and our automatic responses to pain—such as pulling our hands away from something hot—are also built in.

Certain complex behaviours and emotions are built in as well. For example, mothers automatically respond to young children, including their own, in particular ways and with particular feelings, without any special training or conditioning.

Some behaviours develop over the life of each person. Changes around puberty are particularly noticeable, such as interest in others as partners (as opposed to the "Ugh! Yuck!" attitude of many young boys and girls to the idea of spending time with someone of the opposite sex), becoming sexually active, increasing levels of aggression (typically in males), etc.

And, as I said, you consciously have little or no control over any of these responses. For example, getting horny is usually not a conscious choice—though you can control whether or not you get in to a situation which makes you horny or not.

The personal unconscious is powerful in its own right, and can play a part in how a lot of these unconscious fears, responses and behaviours appear. For example, a child who is badly abused by one or both parents, is likely to learn to respond to physical caresses and touching with fear, instead of with pleasure. This is the personal unconscious in play, overriding the reaction which the collective unconscious would normally trigger, and replacing it with something more likely to help the child avoid further abuse in their particular context.

Primal

The collective unconscious is also the home of our primal feelings. These are the most animalistic parts of us and can be overwhelmingly intense.

Our sexual energy and sexual drive comes from the unconscious. How we actually express this, or satisfy it, is going to be heavily shaped by the conscious and by the personal unconscious through what we've learned in terms of preferences and acceptability throughout our lives. The origin of the energy is mostly, though, the collective unconscious.

Many fears start out in the collective unconscious, but they also get modified by choice and conditioning. For example, people who clean the windows of skyscrapers for a living, manage their natural fear of heights to be able to do their job.

The big player for much of BDSM is the collective unconscious, and particularly the primal hungers and desires. We manipulate pain, fear, sex, rough handling, physical freedom (e.g., through bondage), both to excite and satisfy primal parts of our minds, and to drive the conscious mind out of the picture so that it doesn't interfere with all its rationalising.

One of the things that you might notice about practically all BDSM activities, is that they're all very primal.

BDSM isn't about being rational or logical. It's not about intelligence or exercising one's intellect. If it were, then we'd see BDSM versions of chess, Rubik's Cube™ or Monopoly™ meant for the dungeon. And we don't.

BDSM is instead very animalistic. It's about:

- Sex,
- Fear,
- Pain,
- Surrender,
- Restraint, and
- Hunger.

And these are all very basic, very primal things.

In fact, if we look closely at what happens in a dungeon scene, we can actually see the rational and intellectual bits of a submissive's or bottom's brain turning off, leaving just the primal bits behind.

The process can go something like this:

1. An initial struggle (against the restraint of the rope, or against the flogger, or against the grip of the master),

2. A relaxation and acceptance (surrender),

3. Along the way there's a loss of verbal skills; or, at least, a situation where using verbal skills interferes with, or destroys, the mental state they've been working to achieve. This loss of speech is a very important indicator.

Not many of our animal kin can speak, so when speech goes away it can be a sign that we're either focussing on or returning to an animalistic or primal state.

The language of the collective unconscious

Gentle caresses, sexual handling, and physically manhandling someone, all have to do with the collective unconscious. There are primal reactions to all of these. This is the visceral or primal nature of unconscious communication which is often gut-to-gut.

Indicative of the built-in nature of the collective unconscious, many of the actions or signals with which the collective unconscious communicates are what Morris called *inborn actions* [MORRIS1978] (p. 12). Here are some types of action heavily or completely influenced by the collective unconscious:

- Increase or decrease of heart rate,
- Change of breathing—faster, slower, shallower, deeper,
- Sweating,
- Change in muscle or body tension,
- Fidgeting or restlessness—possibly indicating a desire to flee from the present, or possibly upcoming, situation,
- Unconscious pelvic movements,
- Other subtle body movements—particularly unconscious gestures with the arms and hands, and changes of body posture (such as presenting),
- Pheromones,
- Facial expression,
- Change in voice—grunts, groans, moans, sighs, etc.,
- Change in ability to focus, difficulty in paying attention, and
- Change in reactions or reaction times.

Oftentimes, we don't consciously register that these signals are being sent. But the unconscious is much more sensitive to these. It is paying attention all the time, and it reacts to them. Back where I was talking about the language of the conscious, I mentioned that two people without a common tongue can still have a profound BDSM experience together. This is because they tune into the changes and signals in the list above. These form the communications between the two instead of words.

It is important to note that the unconscious isn't necessarily unified. For example, part of it could be displaying nervousness or restlessness, possibly indicating a desire to escape, while another part could be displaying signs of intense arousal, and a third could be displaying a desire to fight. Such conflicts can have the unfortunate result, if unresolved, of unprofitably wasting away the primal energy available to meet primal needs. That is, before any needs can be met, most of the available energy has been exhausted getting to the psychological point where they can be met.

Back in the section on the conscious, I mentioned that talking rationally and logically is not going to have much effect on someone in the throes of lust or passion. In fact, if you're looking for primal responses, then saying or doing things which require conscious responses is not the way to go. Trying to discuss plans for the weekend, or chat about the latest discoveries in astronomy, or ask your partner to solve a Rubik's Cube™, are all pretty much guaranteed to stir up your partner's conscious mind, while at the same time pushing aside their primal side. In other words, any BDSM-ish feelings tend to go out the window when rational or intellectual thoughts come in.

Likewise, physically handling your partner is not going to help in an intellectual discussion, but is instead going to stir the primal side of them. Take away their Rubik's Cube™, don't let them talk about nuclear physics, and instead focus them on pain, restraint, and sex, and you have the makings of a useful, and possibly spectacular BDSM scene.

It's worth noting that for some people, their specific interest in BDSM is its ability to push their conscious mind away, and let them simply be primal. For such people, who may tend to over-intellectualise, BDSM is more than just satisfying primal needs, it's also an escape from their conscious mind. I'll talk more about this later.

A wind-up on communication

Communication between a dominant and his submissive, a top and his bottom, and a master and his slave, is generally going to be occurring at the conscious, personal unconscious, and collective unconscious levels, all at the same time. While there's a tendency for each level to talk exclusively to that same corresponding level in the other person there is often significant bleed-through between the levels in each person.

That is, for example, the conscious of one person will tend to talk exclusively to the conscious mind of their partner, and not to their partner's personal unconscious or collective unconscious. But while the personal unconscious might receive a message from their partner's personal unconscious—such as the sight of the leather vest their partner always wears when they're about to do some particular BDSM activity—the personal unconscious then tickles either the conscious or collective unconscious into activity in response. This response might be a turning on of sexual juices, a feeling of apprehension or anticipation, increased alertness, descent into sub-space, etc.

There is room for deliberate manipulation here because you can learn what triggers your partner—such as the use of certain words, symbols (e.g., leather chaps), or actions (e.g., stroking their throat)—and then consciously choose to do it. This doesn't necessarily stop you responding as well, though. That is, it doesn't mean that you don't end up triggering yourself as well as your partner. Indeed, you might choose to caress your partner in some way, but while the choice to do so originates from a considered (and conscious) plan of your own, both you and your partner will respond to the touch viscerally (i.e., unconsciously) anyway.

The way the different levels "talk" to each other is often without words. If you're having an intellectual discussion with someone then, sure, you might use words, but you can just as easily use signals—such as pointing or gesturing—to get a conscious message across.

On the other hand, the personal and collective unconscious don't use words. Their language is one of actions, tone of voice (as opposed to the actual words), touch, proximity, smell, etc. You might only speak poorly the same verbal language (e.g., English) as your partner, but this isn't going to stop you having a profound and intense primal experience with them. This is because the primal language you use with them is without words.

In BDSM particularly, the role of the conscious mind diminishes as a scene develops. The need for words and for intellectualisation (the conscious) fades—but doesn't disappear completely—as the physical and primal needs (the primal and, to a lesser extent, the collective unconscious) come into play.

If you read back through my descriptions of the nature of the conscious, personal unconscious, and collective unconscious levels, you'll see that they are distinctly different. For example, the conscious mind is involved with rationalisation and the intellect. Neither the personal, nor the collective, unconscious minds actually "care" diddly-squat for things like chess or a discussion about Archimedes. The conscious has just too little in common with them. An amazing insight into the nature of Man has a chance of triggering only the conscious mind into action, while the sight of some particularly well-framed part of the anatomy of a juicy-looking person, or physical handling is going to be just the thing that makes the unconscious or primal mind start to stir.

Likewise, something related to your mutually-shared experiences is what's likely to get a reaction out of the personal unconscious of your partner, even though it may not have a direct effect on their conscious or collective unconscious. Indeed, something might trigger your personal unconscious, and then—inside you—bleed through to your conscious or unconscious. Collars in BDSM, as I've mentioned, are a good example of this.

Your collective unconscious mind sees a collar and goes, "So what?" Reacting to collars is not built in to us. If it were, priests would lead far more fascinating lives than they currently do. But after circulating a bit in a real or fantasy world of BDSM, your personal unconscious mind learns that when collars enter the scene, some very interesting and profound experiences are likely to occur. The collar and its use form the *message* which your personal unconscious receives, and then it starts to tickle your unconscious/primal mind into action.

Compare this example of learned personal unconscious responses—i.e., with a collar—to the built in primal responses to pain, physical aggression or handing, and sex, which trigger the collective unconscious directly.

It's important to remember the role of the word "unconscious" here. It means that a lot of what is going on is not something we're aware of. Indeed, Morris writes under *Incidental Gestures - Mechanical Actions With Secondary Messages* [MORRIS1978] (pp. 24 - 25) about gestures and signals that we send without realising it, that:

> *Sometimes the mood-signal transmitted unwittingly in this way is one that we would rather conceal, if we stopped to think about it.*
>
> ...
>
> *Many of our Incidental Gestures provide mood information of a kind that neither we nor our companions become consciously alerted to.*
>
> ...
>
> *But frequently this type of link operates below the conscious level, or is missed altogether.*
>
> *When the links are clearer, we can, of course, manipulate the situation and use our Incidental Gestures in a contrived way.*

Knowing the difference

It's important to know that the conscious mind is where we make decisions about our BDSM, but that it's our collective unconscious which is primally served, fed, and satisfied by the results of these decisions.

Recognising the different levels, and the messages we send and receive, allows us to get the best out of what we do with our partner. For example, a submissive from another BDSM culture is likely to get more-or-less the right message if we firmly grasp them on the back of the neck and press them to their knees—which is unconscious communication—while the same submissive might not have a clue about handkerchief codes—which are conscious or personal unconscious communications.

5. *Identity maintenance, management, and role-play*

What it is

When I talk about the *identity* of someone, I'm talking about the collection of habits, behaviours, needs, values, attitudes, and ways of thinking which defines them. There's only one such collection per person. But, importantly, there are different views of each person's identity depending on who you ask. Rarely does any one person see the whole picture on another's identity.

In this chapter I'd like to consider:

- What the person consciously thinks of themselves,
- What's going on in their unconscious, and
- What other people see.

For example, a person might think of themselves in terms of being an avid football fan, a caring parent, an occasionally impatient driver, hot in bed, adequate at their job but preferring to focus their energies on their weekend hobby of hang-gliding, a snappy dresser, passionate about cryptic crosswords, mostly honest but pleased to get away with not parking legally from time to time when in a hurry, a moderate drinker who prefers scotch, quick to anger but equally quick to calm down, a connoisseur of cheese, etc.

This is a good start, but it's what the person thinks of themselves *consciously*. As we've seen, there may be more going on in the person's unconscious which they don't know about.

For example, our hero's interest in cheese might really be due to an unconscious urge to get into the pants of a particular acquaintance who is, in fact, a cheese aficionado.

Our hero's desperate desire to be great with cheese, and thus more attractive to his cheesy acquaintance, can make him think that his cheese expertise is better than it actually is, or even that he's the bee's knees of cheese.

A person's identity is usually highly valuable to them, and they'll put in a lot of effort trying to maintain it. But what is it they try to maintain? It'd make sense if the identity they try to maintain was an accurate reflection of their real thoughts, needs, and desires, but sometimes this isn't the case. Sometimes there's a conflict between what they are, and what they think they need to be. Our cheesy pretender from above is an example of this.

He may be able to think of himself as a connoisseur of cheese while in his own home (a controlled environment), but he might baulk at being confronted by a cheese buffet attended by people who are professional cheese tasters. The inevitable comparison to these professionals may not be what his ego would like to experience, and the difference in standing may not be what he wants to make apparent to others or himself —i.e., it might turn out to be a big dent in his identity and end his dreams of entering the pants territory of his attractive acquaintance—this latter possibility perhaps being quite valuable to his unconscious.

Selective vision

Enter *selective vision* (as well as some other strategies).

This idea of selective vision is an important one, and has to do with someone seeing what they want to see, and interpreting what happens around them in the way most favourable to the needs of their identity. This might be choosing to look at what reinforces their view of the world, and deliberately <u>not</u> looking at anything that goes against it.

Our cheesy conspirator, for example, may invest a lot of time coming up with excuses not to attend cheese buffets, and finding ways of limiting situations where he's called upon to pass judgement on cheese to only those involving cheddar. In these ways he can build up and maintain his own illusory identity to himself, and may even be able to maintain the illusion in others.

Closer to home, selective vision can help a BDSM top think that they're God's gift to submissives when, in fact, their skills are merely adequate. This can work well in small groups, where there isn't much challenge, or with obscure or seldom-practised activities, such as fire-play. Such a top may be reluctant to play outside of his small group, or to pursue more challenging activities for fear of his identity being cut down a size or two by reality.

Conflict

Beyond loin-driven imaginings or ego, a person may have identity problems due to a conflict of beliefs or morals. From our society-as-a-whole we learn that it's not a good idea to hit other people or to cause them pain. Similarly, we learn from this same society that it's a good idea to treat others as our equals. Clearly though, neither of these are going to fly very well in the world of BDSM, but years of exposure to these ideas throughout our upbringing can create some fairly strong conditioning.

Even when we consciously come to terms with the idea that hitting our partner so hard that they wince and cry out in agony can be a good thing, scrubbing the original conditioning from the unconscious can be difficult.

Active subsets of the whole identity

A person only ever gets to see a subset of any other person's identity. For example, their partner just gets to see the subset that's suitable for home, but doesn't get to see the aspects which appear at work, or which appear while the person's got their pants down at the doctor's office. Likewise, the doctor doesn't get to see what the person's like in bed, and the person's work colleagues likely don't see what he's like when he's out with friends. Only the person themselves has any hope of seeing the entirety of their identity.

So, we enter the realm of *identity management and maintenance*—the range of strategies which someone uses to select and activate different subsets of their whole identity to suit whatever situations they find themselves in.

Identity management isn't always about protecting some false image of one's self as I may have suggested in some of my examples above. Often it's about putting together the right ways of thinking and behaving to suit a particular situation without any suggestion of falsity. Putting it another way, everything that is a person can't fit into what they're doing at any one time. There are just too many behaviours, attitudes, and ways of thinking—all of which are adapted to particular circumstances—to comfortably be active in just one situation. Identity management is about making sure that the right selection of behaviours and other characteristics are available for each situation.

Roy F. Baumeister and Joseph M. Boden wrote, in their *Shrinking the Self* chapter of the book *Changing the self*, about it in this way:

> The self-concept is a large and complex entity - much too large and complex to fit into consciousness at any given time. As a result, self-awareness is inevitably a mere partial self-awareness. When people think about themselves or turn attention to their self-conceptions,

only a limited part of the self-concept can be encompassed. To put it another way, the same person may have a different self-awareness from one occasion to the next, not only because the self changes, but because different parts of the self become the focus of self-awareness. [BAUMEISTER1994] (p. 143)

For example, the way someone behaves in the boardroom clearly must be different to how they behave in the boudoir... though both may have to do with screwing someone (Ha ha!). The behaviours, values, and attitudes, in each situation are adapted to suit. Likewise, how someone behaves in the supermarket, or when watching their child play sport, or while they're having their annual physical check-up, will be different in each case. It's not that the person is pretending to be something that they're not each time. It is instead that certain aspects of their identity are more suited to one situation, while different aspects are more suited in others, and they bring out the ones which are the best fit at the time.

BDSM is simply another type of situation in which the right mix of characteristics needs to be rolled out to suit. The behaviours and attitudes a person will need to successfully engage in their BDSM activities will be different to what they need in other circumstances. For instance, grabbing someone by the hair and pushing them to the floor is much more appropriate in a dungeon than it is, say, during a parent-teacher meeting about your child.

Identity management includes being able to activate the behaviours, feelings, and attitudes appropriate to each particular circumstance and set of needs—and being able to suppress those which aren't appropriate. Sometimes this switching is just a matter of making a choice. Sometimes it is helped by entering or creating a new context (e.g., by entering into a dungeon, by putting on your leathers, or by picking up a flogger). Sometimes it is activated by the behaviour of your partner—such as when they adopt a certain tone of voice, or when they do some particular action, such as kneeling and kissing your feet.

Regardless of how this switching is triggered, it is an important part of making sure that needs are met—namely, by ensuring that the behaviours and feelings are present which will allow the correct and productive state of mind to be achieved. Thus, it would be unproductive, for example, to be involved in any BDSM scene or activity while being in a state of mind more suitable for standing in a queue at the post office.

Now. Moving on a little, I'd like to look more at identity in terms of BDSM. It makes important appearances in many different places and forms, and I'd like to look at a number of these, and how different BDSM activities work to manipulate, manage, or maintain identities.

Primary identities

The sum total of everything that a person is what we can call their *core identity*. In a sense, this is the foundation on which everything else is built.

But, as Baumeister and Boden noted, this core identity never makes a complete appearance. Instead, in each situation, a subset of this identity appears.

For example, while someone might behave differently whether they're in the boardroom or the boudoir, the person underlying the behaviour in both situations is still the same. When they're in the boardroom, we see one subset or aspect of their core identity, and when they're in the bedroom we see another aspect. These are the subsets appropriate to the boardroom and boudoir, respectively. It's necessary that these subsets be different because something like boudoir behaviour is unlikely to go down well in the boardroom. Indeed, we can often see the negative impact when behaviour and thoughts appropriate to one context leak into another—such as when work-related worries make their way into the bedroom or dungeon.

A person will select one or more of these subsets and promote them to *primary* status. If you talk to them and ask them about themselves, a primary identity is usually what they'll describe, and the particular primary they use may be chosen by the context of the question—such as if asked while at the office, on the golf course, at home with their family, etc., and will usually be one of the few which they see as being the most influence in the direction of their lives.

To clarify this: if we're well-adapted to the world, we automatically pull out the right combination of attitudes and behaviours to suit each situation in which we find ourselves. Sometimes the situations occur so frequently and are so important to us, that we'll actually identify with this aspect of ourselves. For example, we develop certain attitudes, habits, and ways of thinking, which work well for us in a work environment. If someone asks us about ourselves there we can talk about this aspect of ourselves. Thus we might say we're a good decision maker, reliable, and a team player.

For us BDSMers though, we might have a set of behaviours, habits, and preferences, which bear little relation to our work persona. When asked in a BDSM context about ourselves, we might talk instead about our liking for particular floggers, curvature preferences in our partners, and how good we are at knowing what a play partner needs.

In both these cases—at work and in BDSM—we're still the same person, but different parts of us are more appropriate and useful, and we identify ourselves with these parts.

There are other situations in which we switch on particular attitudes and behaviours, but with which we don't actually identify. In fact, we might be in these situations an awful lot of the time, but not identify with them in any way. For example, most of us stand regularly in a queue at the supermarket, and we also often fill our cars with petrol ("gas" for you North American readers), but if someone asks us about ourselves we never tell them, "Oh. I'm a guy who fills his car with petrol," or boast, "I can stand in a supermarket checkout queue with the best of them!" Such situations do call for particular behaviours and attitudes which exist somewhere in us, but we usually assign these subsets to irrelevancy and never consider them as "us".

Now, ideally a person's primary identities are based on their core identity, but it may be that these are influenced, moulded, or extended, by conscious or unconscious desires.

As an example, someone whose ego drives them to be the best at whatever they do, may enter into realms of behaviour and attitudes which might satisfy their ego—e.g., to be the greatest bondage master the world has ever known—but which aren't really representative of what they are, i.e., they don't meet the needs of their core identity. Their behaviours become forced and unsatisfying. For example, our super-dooper bondage master may actually be happier tying up his partner with simple knots in some quiet corner, but his ego or drive to be the greatest may push him to spectacular exhibitions which get him lots of applause, and which satisfy his ego, but actually leave him feeling like something's missing.

On the other hand, someone might enter into the world of BDSM simply exploring one or two small parts of it. As long as they explore using behaviours which are part of their core identity—i.e., which actually satisfy what they need at a core level, then this exploration may well be fantastically rewarding. As they grow and learn, their explorations may cover more and more ground, and while this still fits in the bounds of their core identity then all is well.

Once either internal pressure—e.g., from their ego, drives, or from their fears—causes them to overstep the boundaries of their core identity, or if external pressure—e.g., from a needy partner—causes them to overstep these same boundaries, then it's time to consider what's really going on and why, and whether there really are the right benefits and satisfactions coming from it all. See also chapter 12, *Surrender and anchors*.

Identity protection

When someone has a primary identity which they've carefully built up over time, it's a valuable commodity to them. If circumstances change a little, then the identity can be updated a little to cope—such as a parent going from helping organise their child's sports club, to being a member of their child's school's parents and teachers association. Or such as a bondage dude adapting his scenes to include a little flogging or caning. This sort of thing isn't a big stretch.

On the other hand, changing activities from conventional/vanilla sex to BDSM might require completely putting aside the bedroom identity and creating a brand new— and separate—dungeon identity. For example, while someone might see themselves as having the stamina of an Olympic marathon runner during conventional sex, this doesn't necessarily have any great value in the world of BDSM. There are different skills, attitudes, and behaviours required. Stretching the original bedroom identity when, at most, only fluffy handcuffs were involved with it, to an identity that can cope with a fully-equipped dungeon, is a big, and usually unsuccessful, ask.

So, we build and use one or more separate identities for BDSM situations.

These BDSM identities serve the double purpose of letting us get the most out of our BDSM, while still allowing us to keep safe our other identities (e.g., The Tender Stallion In Bed, The Loving Father, The Respectable Church-goer, The Skilled Technician, The Efficient Manager, etc.).

For some people too, this separation between their BDSM identity and their other identities, is an effective way of managing or isolating any conflicts they may have due to a conservative catholic upbringing. E.g., a *good* man isn't going to beat his wife, and no woman should let her husband beat her; however once I've got my leathers on I can really go to town because when the leathers come off again later, I'll be back to *good* me.

Role-play

Role-play in BDSM involves adopting behaviours and attitudes well beyond the bounds of someone's normal range of identities. Often these are, to an extent, stereotypical or well-known roles—such as doctor or dentist and patient, policeman and criminal, interrogator and prisoner, etc. Commonly, as in much of BDSM, they also include some element of power difference. The roles of doctor and patient, and interrogator and prisoner, are clear examples of these. This difference of power can serve to create BDSM activities or scenes beyond what would be available to a couple using their "normal" range of identities.

For example, by adopting the roles of a Nazi SS officer and an Allied prisoner, a couple automatically has the outline of a ready-made script telling them what to say and do to play out an interrogation scene, with one being the mean, cruel, and dominating interrogator, and the other maybe being tied up, yelled at, whipped, and possibly humiliated.

People who are unfamiliar or unsure about how to express or satisfy their needs, or who have needs which require behaviour or attitudes well outside of their normal or comfortable range, may thus find role-play useful.

Protecting identities

Role-play can also have a function of *identity protection*. By using roles that are completely separate from a person's ordinary life, they can adopt these roles and engage in behaviours well beyond what they might normally do, while not impinging on any of their other identities. For example, "I can be a loving and gentle parent, while still being able to tie up and be cruel to my partner because this latter is only a role I play."

Thus, role-play can have a permissive component. We can also see this in *animal play*, where one person might play the role of a kitten or puppy, and the other might have the role of their owner. Again, there's a power difference in the two roles—with the owner being able, and probably expected, to discipline or be firm with a possibly mischievous pet.

It is worth noting that where an animal is enacted in role play, it's usually a kitten or puppy (cute and mischievous) or a pony (can be dressed up and paraded or utilised). Other animals—such as bears, lions, elephants, lice, snakes, insects, birds, and fish— are rarely used. Kittens, puppies, and ponies perhaps serve well as the prototypes because of the familiar and inherent power disparity in these animals' relationships with humans.

Ready-to-wear behaviour

Role-play of well-known or standardised roles can provide a ready-to-wear set of behaviours and attitudes. Without having to create anything new, these can be enough to create the necessary circumstances, feelings, and emotions to allow needs to be met. For example, the previously mentioned interrogator-and-prisoner roles are probably well-known enough from movies to allow a couple to recreate something useful based directly on what they've seen on the big screen.

One interesting phenomena in the BDSM world in this regard is Gor. Gor is the setting for a series of 26 science-fiction novels by the author John Norman. It is a planet on which a portion of the culture has men as the masters and women as property. For many this is an ideal representation of what they're seeking within their own BDSM. The novels discuss this aspect of the culture at length in amongst other storylines, and provide copious examples which some sections of the BDSM community use as models for their own behaviour. This even extends to adopting the vocabulary used in the novels and adapting them for "Earthly" use, such as using the word "klar" for "coffee".

Ready-to-wear feelings and responses

Ready-to-wear roles don't just provide behaviours. They also prepare the user with expected feelings and responses to associate with the roles.

Many roles, due to exposure through media or real-life, already have feelings and responses associated with them. E.g., the feeling of fear, perhaps, and no expectation of mercy, if being subject to an interrogation by a Nazi SS officer. Likewise, animal play, such as playing a puppy or a pony, also provides a role where feelings are already pre-defined or expected (e.g., friskiness, playfulness, shame or humiliation for peeing on the floor, etc.).

Baggage

Maybe also the acquisition of a new identity can be an escape from the burdens imposed by the obligations, commitments, or ways of thinking of the person's primary identities. In fact, we'll be looking at exactly this in chapter 10, *Motivations*. However, the keyword for the moment is *baggage*.

There are risks that identity manipulation is simply an opportunity for escape when a better solution might be resolving whatever issues the person has.

On the other hand, a new BDSM identity might be sufficient to allow a person to engage in some physical or psychological activity which serves as recreation, and which is not otherwise available to them due to identity constraints (such as a strict moral upbringing). This new identity might only be required for a short time before returning to "ordinary life".

Communities

One of the less obvious benefits of having clear-cut identities is that it makes socialising with others who have similar or complementary identities a real possibility. And, indeed, this is something quite common in BDSM.

There are many social groups across the world, both Internet-based and real-life, where people with similar BDSM interests and proclivities can gather, swap tales, and generally fulfil the social needs that us humans seem to have.

Sometimes it's even the case that role-play requires that the people who engage in these roles to socialise with others. The previously-mentioned Gor is a great example of this.

Gor provides a ready-made set of roles based on a fictional community on the planet Gor. The keyword here is *community*. Gor is a world where masters and slaves are part of the natural social order. This means that there are rules and behaviours already existent within the Gor context to allow and encourage social groupings (tribes) and communities to form, thus satisfying social needs beyond the needs being met by the master/slave behaviours.

By transposing Gor to Earth, *Goreans* (the people who pursue the ideals and behaviours of Gor) often need to socialise with each other to complete their roles, thus killing a plurality of avians with a single aggregation of solid mineral.

Alternate names

In some BDSM communities, the names people use for themselves are part of an identity management strategy. Also, there are BDSM communities which exist partially or completely on the Internet (via message or bulletin boards, Internet Relay Chat (IRC), web logs, etc.) and the actual form of names (i.e., how they are written) can add significance beyond what might be useful in face-to-face situations.

- These BDSM names are rarely based on commonly-used usual or civic names. This helps in the names' roles to establish a separate BDSM identity,
- Names may be based on existing words, or may be complete inventions,
- Names based on existing words are often suggestive of some characteristic which the adoptee would like to present or emphasise to others. E.g., "intrigue", "Inquisitor", "kitten", etc.,
- When written, names may be all lower-case to signify the person is of a slave, submissive, or bottom disposition, or written with the first letter in upper-case to represent a dominant, master, or top disposition,
- Using one of these alternate names is an identity management tool. This use calls forth, or triggers, the set of behaviours and attitudes (i.e., the identity) required for the person to operate well and productively in a BDSM context, and
- Names may be used to provide some measure of anonymity.

BDSM names are rarely other people names

It's unlikely that a BDSM practitioner who does adopt a new name would call themselves "John" instead of "Paul", or "Debbie" instead of "Melanie".

The BDSM name is usually chosen with the specific intent of having some extra value or meaning in a BDSM context, or to serve as a signal that the person is *wearing* one of their BDSM identities, as opposed to some other identity when they're using their usual name.

Names may be based on existing words

Names which are based on existing words can be suggestive of the role a person wishes to adopt or emphasise in a BDSM context. For example, someone calling themselves "kitten" is likely to see themselves as a bottom or submissive; someone calling themselves "Inquisitor" or "YourMaster" is likely to see themselves as a dominant, top, or master; and someone who calls themselves "debauch" may well be seeing or presenting themselves in primarily submissive sexual terms.

Here are some other BDSM names plucked from a few public mailing-lists and bulletin boards: "Sir WizDom" ("Dom" being a short form of "Dominant"), "inspire", "tinkerbell", "NotExcessive", "Domin8r" (i.e., "Dominator"), "Punished", "evilsubgirl", "EssentialNeed".

Names may be complete inventions

Rather than use a suggestive name, some BDSM practitioners will use an invented name, possibly one which sounds exotic. Again, this can serve as a trigger to switch a person from a *street*, or vanilla, identity into a BDSM one.

Use of upper- and lower-case

In communities partly or completely based on written communication between members, it's common to find people who see themselves in a submissive, slave or bottom role using names which are completely lower-case. I.e., instead of capitalising at least the first letter of their name when writing it, they write their whole name in lower-case.

Contrariwise, those who see themselves in a top, dominant or master role will capitalise at least the first letter of their name. See above for examples.

This use lower- and upper-case serves as a signal to others in the same community. This aspect is important as the name, beyond being a context-switch trigger, can be significant in the dealings the person has with others in their community. Outside of that particular community, the name may have no use or significance at all.

Identity management and triggers

BDSM names can be useful where someone maintains a BDSM identity completely separate to their other day-to-day identities. They can use their BDSM name as a signal to others that they're ready to engage in BDSM activities or conversation, and stop using it and return to their usual or civic name when they want to engage in other activities.

A dominant partner can also use their submissive partner's BDSM name to trigger them into their submissive identity. In other words, a dominant partner in a BDSM relationship, may use their partner's BDSM name (e.g. "kitten" or "slavegirl"), such as calling them into the room using that BDSM name, to begin triggering BDSM responses from their partner. When a relationship is based on the use of power by one partner (the dominant) over the other (the submissive), this sort of triggering action can be rewarding for both of them. It is an example of power being asserted, and its effects can be often easily be felt.

While it's usually the case that someone might adopt a name for their own BDSM use, a name can be given to someone as they enter into a relationship, as a sign of ownership or the fact of being property. For example, a master acquiring a slave may give him or her a new name to indicate ownership, and to signal that the master has rights over the slave, even to the extent of their name. This can also be used to represent the start of a new identity for the slave, i.e., as that particular master's property.

This is highly symbolic as a slave choosing a name for themselves is a controlling act over themselves, whereas a master choosing their slave's name takes that control away from the slave.

6. The Other

Being able to point to something and definitively say, "That is BDSM", and to something else and say, "That isn't BDSM", is one of the great challenges that this subculture has to offer.

Part of it is that BDSM encompasses such a wide range of behaviours, activities, and relationships. Participants could use canes and floggers on each other. They might be gay, lesbian, straight, bisexual, or polyamorous. Their play might involve physical pain. They could dress in black leather or jeans, or they could dress in business suits or evening gowns. They could use ropes and chains. They could do BDSM casually, or it could be their lifestyle. It might involve some sex, only sex, or no sex. It might involve blood. It might include some or all of the above, or it might include none of the above.

But there are some things we can observe:

1. Caning, spanking, flogging, and whipping are quite common BDSM activities. But autonomous machines to do caning, spanking, flogging, or whipping are never ever found, even in the best equipped dungeons.

   Therefore it's not just feeling the impact on one's butt which is important. If it were, there'd be parlours lined with corporal punishment machines and many, many endlessly happy bottoms.

   Likewise, if it were merely the act of caning which excited a dominant, there'd be similar parlours lined with cushions and pillows (which are common practice targets for the beginner top).

2. BDSM is never about equality of power or control. Even in scene-based BDSM, such as a flogging, you'll never see two people alternately taking turns to hit each other. It's always about one person having control or power over the other for a time.

Another thing which we can see is that there's always an element of *submission* or *surrender* in BDSM. But many things involve submission or surrender, such as fetishes, but this doesn't make them BDSM. The feelings inspired, for example, by a fetish object, such as a shoe or stockings, might involve profound surrender, but we can generally recognise that this is not BDSM.

What's the difference then?

We can find three characteristics which, if present, tell us that something is BDSM. If all three are not present, then it's not BDSM.

1. Surrender,

2. Inequality of power, even if just for a short while, and

3. An *Other*.

Point 3 is interesting. In many cases, the *Other* is a person. In fact, it's most obvious when the *Other* is a person because this is what we see in parties, in master/slave relationships, and in D&s relationships. But the *Other* isn't always a person.

We can see examples of a non-person *Other* playing an important role in such activities as self-bondage. Someone might tie, chain, or restrain themselves using a padlock or combination lock and then either have the key to the padlock in a block of ice so they have to wait for the ice to melt before they can free themselves, or close the combination lock in a darkened room in the evening so they have to wait until morning before they can see the combination lock well enough to be able to enter the correct combination and free themselves. In both these examples we can see the *Other* is *time*. We can also see that there is a power imbalance in both examples—in particular, the person concerned doesn't have the power to free themselves. Only *time* will allow that.

This idea of an *Other* is very important to the understanding of BDSM relationships, particularly for dominants and submissives, and for masters and slaves. The *Other* takes many forms, not just *time*. I'll be looking at this in much more detail in chapter 9, *Relationships II*.

7. Penetration

Penetration doesn't get the press it deserves. When first mentioned, it may conjure forth images of mighty cocks ramming themselves home into oh-so-snug cunts. But there's much more to it in BDSM.

If we press a few imaginative neurones into service, we might think about the following activities because they also have an element of penetration, though not the cock-in-cunt kind. Indeed, in a few of them neither cock nor cunt make an appearance.

- Cutting,
- Piercing,
- Fisting,
- Catheterization,
- Some medical activities such as vaginal and anal stretching, and dental play, and
- Gags, particularly penetrating gags.

The idea of penetration in the above is hopefully obvious. Each has to do with entering a person, with going from being outside them to being inside them. This can be otherwise thought of as passing through the boundary where the outside world ends and the "I", or self, begins.

This can be through an existing orifice, such as in fisting or with gags, or by creating an opening, such as with cutting or piercing. Some of this penetration can be sexual, such as vaginal fisting. But some of it, such as cutting and piercing, has no relationship to sex at all. And some of it, such as vaginal and anal stretching, or such as catheterization, is sexual only *incidentally* in so far that a hole was needed and, oh look!, the cunt, ass, and cock happen to be or have convenient holes.

To clarify this incidental aspect by example, vaginal stretching doesn't, *per se*, involve clitoral stimulation or rubbing other nerve-endings up the right way, but does involve opening and entering deep into the vagina. Clitoral stimulation may be added in to what's done, but it's an extra, not fundamental. However, because it's the vagina where the stretching happens, it's often experienced as a sexual activity. Ditto for the cock and ass.

It's common to think of penetration in terms of one thing physically entering the body of another. But the word *penetration* is also associated with other ideas [OED]:

- To get into or through, gain entrance or access to, especially with force, effort, or difficulty,
- To bring light into or to see through,
- To pierce,
- To have or get intellectual or spiritual access, insight or knowledge,
- To find out, discover, discern,
- To affect or influence deeply,
- To touch the heart or feelings of,
- To cause to hear or take notice, and
- To be fully understood or appreciated.

We can see that beyond the idea of physically entering someone or something, penetration also has to do with understanding or knowing. For example, when someone has a *penetrating gaze* it seems they can see into us and know what we're thinking, or when a spy *penetrates* another organisation it isn't that he actually gets in the front door, but is instead that he finds out about the hidden inner workings of the organisation and its secrets.

This idea of penetrating meaning both piercing or entering, and knowing or understanding, is apparent in the Bible (King James version):

> Genesis, 4:1 - *And Adam knew Eve his wife; and she conceived, and bare Cain...*

> Genesis, 4:17 - *And Cain knew his wife; and she conceived, and bare Enoch...*

> Genesis, 4:25 - *And Adam knew his wife again; and she bare a son, and called his name Seth...*

The point really is that these two ideas are not so different from each other. Sexual penetration is to enter and feel the sexual nature of someone. It is knowing them, being aware of what they feel like, and knowing their responses. This isn't just a matter of the male feeling what it's like to penetrate the female. While there are certainly very powerful sensations unleashed from the guy's point of view as the cunt envelops his cock, the girl also feels the guy's cock stimulating, pressing and rubbing against the nerve endings in her cunt. So even though it is the guy's cock which enters the girl's cunt, *they both know and feel each other*. In reality both the *feeling* and the *being felt* are mutual. It isn't the case that he drives his cock home and feels nothing, nor that she is penetrated and feels nothing. They both feel each other. They both feel the texture, tightness, and rhythm of the other. Generally, neither plays the dead fish, and so each also feels the *participation* of the other in terms of what they say to each other, how they move, how they respond, how various muscles expand and contract, how excited each becomes, and so on.

When we consider all the activities normally associated with BDSM—and not just the physical ones—we will see (if we haven't already) that most, if not all, have some aspect of *penetration* to them. It might not be an obvious physical or sexual type of penetration, but it can still be one person entering into and stimulating the other, while at the same time experiencing the response of their partner.

Flogging is a good example of this.

A common flogging scenario is where the submissive or bottom is stripped, at least to the waist, and then tied standing up and spread-eagled to a frame. The top or dominant then uses a leather-tailed flogger to flog the submissive. There is a strong creative component to this because the top needs to provide the right intensity, rate, and location for the strokes to allow the submissive to descend into her experience.

This experience is often one where she uses the heavy thudding or pain to displace much of her identity and awareness, and find a form of ecstasy (which we will look at more closely when we talk about motivations in, appropriately, chapter 10, *Motivations*). The thudding and pain from her partner is one of the tools she uses to do this, but at the same time her partner needs to recognise the stages she is going through and modulate or change the type of flogging he applies to assist her, even to the extent of changing between different styles of floggers, whips, or canes, as she navigates obstacles to her descent, or to pause from time to time to reassure her.

Obstacles to descent might include:

- Thoughts and pressures from her day-to-day life,
- Memories of previous sessions which may not have worked well, and
- The need for her to provide some sort of non-verbal feedback to her partner (such as making ooh, aah noises, wriggling, or flexing muscles) so he can follow where she is and continue to do his part well.

Later, once she has descended as far as she is going to go, and has "soaked" at that level for long enough, her partner then can assist her return and recovery with different types of stimulation which she can then use to come back. For example, it's not unusual for descent to use pain or stimulation which is more like a thud, and for the return or recovery phases to use pain which is more sharp or stingy, or to use hot wax or ice.

As we can see from this short description, even without any cock-in-cunt component, there is still a very strong element of penetration with the submissive allowing the pain and thudding from her partner's ministrations to enter into her and allow her to travel the path of descent and then recovery. For the partner there is also a strong penetration aspect as he responds to her actions and reactions. He is certainly part of the experience—feeling and being felt—rather than being an aloof bystander.

The parallels between this process, and sexual penetration leading to orgasm are striking (no pun intended). In both there is the mutual stimulation, the feedback and responses, a descent towards primal feelings, and then some sort of resolution. These parallels helps us to understand why BDSM and sex can go very well together.

Looking at other forms of penetration in BDSM we can see, for example, that *humiliation* is an exercise in penetrating the ego of the submissive. For the dominant it is *knowing* the submissive well enough to be able to say the right words, or to do the right things, so that they can see and feel the submissive's ego being affected.

The satisfaction comes not only from seeing the submissive in tear-filled catharsis, but from taking them there in the first place, *and* from then bringing them back. In other words, it comes from being able to the enter them to that extent, to feel them and guide them, and then recover them at the end.

When a dominant grabs a submissive by the hair on the back of their neck, or takes them by the shoulder and presses them to the ground, they are penetrating the submissive's *personal space*. This is that area[1] around us which we tend to keep clear, and which, when violated, causes us to feel that someone is uncomfortably close. Thus they are also penetrating and claiming control of that part of the submissive, entering into the submissive's boundaries, which is normally under their own control.

When a dominant or master takes charge of a submissive or slave, directs them in their daily life, or takes steps to change or modify such things as the way the submissive dresses, eats, or behaves towards the dominant, they are penetrating the submissive's *intimate autonomy*. The boundary where authority over personal choice would, in the vanilla world, only contain the person themselves, now also includes their dominant. The word "intimate" is important here because we can again see the *knowing-and-being-known* aspect of this form of penetration—the master enters into intimate control of his slave, and at the same time the slave experiences the nature (the shape and form) of his penetration of her.

---

1 Not just physical!

Similarly, tying, or restraining someone in a cage, is penetrating their *physical autonomy*. Where the Joe Average would have the choice and freedom to move physically as they desire, this freedom has been taken away from them by their top. Their top has stepped up close, and claimed that authority or power away from the bottom. The bottom feels the imposition of the limits their top has chosen, and the top sees and feels the response of their bottom to this.

Sometimes the penetrative aspect takes a well-being or health-related form. Activities such as piercing and cutting, fireplay, breathplay, and others, include risks which we allow our tops or dominants to take for us. Thus, something like cutting is a sort of doubly whammy—there's the physical penetration aspect of it, there's the entering of our partner into ourselves via the blade and, simultaneously, the taking control of our well-being.

In some cultures being stripped to the waist in public is no big BDSM deal—and, in fact, could be the norm, such as in some parts of Africa and Asia. And in some situations, even in our own culture, extreme forms of penetration are accepted without the same exciting reactions we might see in a BDSM context. Consider surgery or a visit to the dentist, for example, or a visit to a tattoo parlour. But there are also other examples of penetration which are extremely exciting without the connotations of BDSM—such as going on a scary ride at a carnival. We can see then, that the effect of penetration is going to depend on expectations as well as on the nature of the penetration.

Many of these penetrative BDSM activities are done in such a way as to plainly expose this state of affairs, namely that the dominant, top, or master has entered their partner. A submissive obeying her dominant might perform her duties or her personal service with a flourish, or excel at performing in front of others, thus highlighting and making undeniable the penetration of her by her dominant. To clarify this latter, in the vanilla world without a dominant she might be off somewhere having a chocolate smoothie, but being instead in the world of BDSM with a dominant her behaviour is now directed or controlled by her dominant's wishes. Thus, he is inside her and has changed what she does.

Going further, a dominant or master might compel their submissive partner to perform in front of others, thus deepening the penetration. That is, the *knowing* might have initially simply been shared by the dominant and the submissive themselves, but by exposing it this extends the *knowing* to the people who observe the submissive and dominant interacting.

Whipping, caning, and other forms of pain play can penetrate in two other ways:

1. Firstly, the boundary the submissive or bottom would normally have around them to prevent, deflect, or even choose their pain, is pierced by their top or dominant, and

2. Secondly, the pain itself serves to push aside or penetrate the mask of civility, politeness, and self-control which the submissive normally wears in company, even in the company of their dominant, and exposes a primal, sexual, or animal aspect of the submissive. In other words, here is more uncovering, revealing, or *knowing*. We'll see more about this in chapter 10, *Motivations*.

We can see in all of this that BDSM penetration need not be the purely physical and obvious sexual type penetration of the cunt in women, or further back "where the Sun don't shine" for both genders. It can also include psychological and spiritual penetration.

Fear is another tool used to penetrate or to expose. *Mind fucks* are a case in point. These are when circumstances are manipulated by the dominant, often to create a feeling of fear, apprehension, or uncertainty in a submissive. For example:

1. Tying them so they can't move, then

2. Laying them down horizontal and blindfolding them, then

3. Using a winch to lift them off the ground, and doing it in such a way that they think that they are much higher than the couple of inches off the ground which they really are, then

4. Slowly cutting the rope holding them so they hear and feel it being cut, and then

5. Letting them fall just those couple of inches onto soft pillows.

This sort of fear serves to expose (and, thus, make *known*) a different type of primal aspect of the submissive; and also is a case of the dominant penetrating the control of the submissive which they normally have, and which prevents them getting into this sort of fear situation. Note that the control I'm talking about here is not about letting themselves get tied up in the first place, but about letting their dominant influence and manipulate their perceptions. The blindfold is a big player here because it helps create the imagined danger, and this is something the dominant manipulates (i.e., uses to enter their submissive).

I'd like to repeat that what occurs is shared and felt by both people involved, even in the example above. While the dominant may, for example, create a fantastic mindfuck, it is not only his partner who feels this experience crafted by him. He also feels her response, and responds in turn. It would be a hollow experience for him if all he did was watch from an emotional distance and not experience the rush caused by her reactions. Just as much as she is penetrated by the scene he creates, he is also penetrated by the consequences as manifested in and by her.

In a lot of BDSM, as I have said, there is the idea of exposing the submissive to scrutiny. In some physical activities, such as vaginal or anal spreading, there is something happening which you can see with your eyes. But anything which exposes a primal side of the submissive also exposes them to view, just not in a physical way.

I was at a BDSM play party not too long ago, and at one point while we were all sitting and standing around talking, the conversation turned to oral sex. One of the female dominants then instructed her female submissive to perform oral sex on one of the male dominants, which she did. There were a few aspects of penetration in this:

- The obvious oral penetration of the female submissive by the male dominant,
- Penetration of the female submissive by her female dominant [with the act of] directing her to perform oral sex, and
- Importantly, the penetration of the female submissive by us witnesses who saw her exposed as she perform the act. Had we all turned away then this particular penetration would not have occurred, but we did watch and by doing so penetrated her.

However, just as the submissive may be opened or exposed by their dominant, the dominant needs to open or expose themselves to their submissive so that they, too, have a profound experience. As I have said, without this penetration by their submissive partner, the dominant would feel little or nothing. In this regard, see *Custodians of penetration* a little further down in this chapter.

Once we do see that some form of penetration is occurring, we immediately have another tool at our disposition to make things better and more satisfying for ourselves and for our partners. We can start to classify different activities in terms of the extent and type of penetration they involve—such as cutting and piercing being similar in that they both involve penetration of the skin—and then explore other similar types of penetration to help us find better fits to our needs.

The hunt for penetration

Some people, both inside and outside of BDSM, look almost explicitly for penetration. Consider the following extract from a short personal ad. It doesn't talk about *any* specific BDSM activities, but it does talk about three different types of penetration in just two simple lines:

> *I have been involved in BDSM for over 8 years now and delight in stretching boundaries, exploring limits and breaking taboos.*

This hunt for more penetration and more intensity can be a driving, and even overwhelming, need. Here's an interesting—if sad—news item which highlights this:

'Bizarre' sex kills woman

... Taylor told police that he had clipped an electrical cord to his wife and plugged it into a power strip, which he then turned on and off.

He told authorities the couple had used the technique before.

...

Sydney Morning Herald, January 26, 2008

If the couple had been looking for something simply thrilling they could have had sex on a cliff, in a plane, or have tried a bungee-jumping bonking double. Instead, their preferred option was using electric shocks. The shocks and the sensations are intense, irresistible, and overwhelming—and were clearly being used to penetrate the wife overwhelmingly.

Had this couple been aware of BDSM (something not mentioned in the news report) then they might have found a well-known BDSM activity which would have satisfied their need for penetration in relative safely.

An analogy

When we try to view BDSM activities in terms of penetration, some are more obvious candidates than others. Here, I'd like to talk about a useful analogy which can help us understand the penetrative side of service and control, two things in which the penetration aspect is often not very apparent.

If we have a slave in a service-based relationship with a master, such as one where she prepares his meals, organises his appointments, brings him drinks in the evening, runs errands for him, and so forth, we might not ever see any physical discipline or use of pain to penetrate her. We might also never see any particular penetrative effect on her ego or sense of self. Indeed, we may well see more empowerment for her as she takes on more and more responsibility in her service.

For this master and slave we might never see anything like the more familiar use of pain, restraint, imprisonment, or humiliation, which is so easy to recognise in other forms of BDSM. So, what's going on?

Imagine a horse and rider. At first glance the rider is directing the horse by simply pulling left or right on the reins. The horse is taking the rider where the rider wants to go, and is performing a service for the rider. This sounds very mechanical and impersonal.

But there's much more going on than this. The horse is taking direction from its rider through the reins, through the movement of the rider in the saddle, through the rider's use of his heels to press against the side of the horse, and perhaps also through the occasional use of a riding crop on the horse's rump.

But exactly as this is happening—as the horse is, in a sense, being penetrated by the rider—the horse is also feeling and knowing the rider through how the rider uses the reins—from gentle guidance to strong tugging or pulling, how the rider uses their heels and crop, and so on. The *knowing* part of penetration goes both ways here, with the rider feeling and dominating the wilfulness of the horse, while the rider is also being known and experienced by the horse at the same time.

Separate to the riding itself, the horse is aware of the how it is treated by the rider, how the rider takes care of it, feeds it, talks to it, and makes it part of the experience they mutually share. The enthusiasm of the horse for this dynamic and this relationship can be apparent when a rider arrives at the stable and their horse trots up, and when the horse responds readily and enthusiastically as the rider prepares and saddles it. There's no doubt, though, that it is the rider directing the horse, rather the horse deciding where to take the rider.

So, the horse, the servant here, feels the rider through the reins, through the use of the crop, through the vocal urgings of the rider, and so on. The fact that the rider needs to use the reins, their heels, or the crop to control the horse is not an indication of any unwillingness or lack of enthusiasm on the part of the horse. They are merely methods by which the rider communicates using their already established dominance to the animal.

It can be much the same for a master and slave. Because the slave is so enthusiastic about serving and being useful, often just the merest indications from the master are enough to set the direction of the slave. While this skill of interpreting the master's wishes without needing explicit or obvious direction can be developed, it needs to be paired with an equally adept master who is skilled at directing a slave in this manner.

This analogy is particularly useful because there is a subset of the BDSM community which engages in pony-play. This is where the master's slave behaves as a pony in the hands of the master. This is a lot more complex and profound than it initially sounds because the horse may be trained in the equivalent of *dressage*, i.e., a style of training focussed on obedience, balance, and comportment. The pony may be taught particular moves and actions performed under the direction of their master. The pony may be dressed in fashions suitable for a formal parade, and may have specially-made bridles, bits, and saddles[2].

This style of doing BDSM, namely by using physical reins, bits, and harnesses to impose control, can be seen as just a variation on the theme of feeling and being felt—i.e., penetration. And, in particular, we might see pony play as a style of D&s, but with physical reins taking the place of exercised authority, and with bits, harnesses, and saddles taking the place of structure, i.e., taking the place of fixed rules and commands.

Custodians of penetration

I once watched some activity at a BDSM party. She wanted to be tied up. He was happy to oblige. He sat her down, fully-dressed, in a straight-backed chair, and then carefully bound her in place with soft rope. Once she was firmly restrained, had begun to drift off, and once he had tested that the ropes weren't interfering with her blood flow, he left her to herself while he circulated amongst other guests in the room, always keeping an eye on her. About fifteen minutes later, once it was clear that she had "soaked" enough and was beginning to return, he went back, spoke to her, untied her, and made sure she was OK.

In terms of penetration, this is an interesting scene. She was clearly *penetrated* by the rope bondage, by the experience of the rope firmly pressing against her and holding her in place. In contrast, he was minimally involved in the penetration, per se. He was simply being the *custodian* of the experience she had. The *other* was present, but it wasn't him.

This raises the point that a BDSM scene may not be mutually penetrative. In other words, each participant may not experience the same degree of penetration. One of them may not even experience any penetration at all.

The types of penetration experienced usually differ between two people involved in the same scene. A submissive tied to an A-frame might, for example, surrender to the intense pain being administered by their partner and be mostly responding to that sensation, while his partner, at the other end of the whip, is instead responding to the physical, physiological and vocal responses of their submissive.

---

2 Note that being the rider of a human horse generally requires the rider to have a smaller frame, such as being a female or small man, to avoid breaking or straining the back of the pony. Some human ponies and their masters may solve the problem of a larger master wanting to ride their horse by using a trap or small carriage, in which the master sits while being pulled by their pony. This works well outdoors, of course, and this mode of operation also usefully allows reins and longer riding crops or whips to be used by the master to direct his pony.

Male / female differences

The journal article, *Unlawful entry: Male fears of psychic penetration*, by Dianne Elise [ELISE2001], explores the idea that males, being typically seen as the sexual penetrator, can fear being penetrated themselves as a violation of their masculine self—even if this penetration is purely symbolic, rather than physical or sexual.

With females, penetration can be experienced very differently to males because sexual penetration is *the norm* for females rather than the exception as with males.

While this is mostly speculative, being able to view BDSM in terms of penetration may be a launching point for ideas about the different ways in which males and females experience and explore BDSM. Each gender has its own socially-installed expectations regarding sexual penetration, and these may overflow into the other types of penetration used and explored in BDSM, particularly with the common perception that BDSM *is* sex. I will leave more consideration of this to the reader.

Trying to see BDSM without penetration

When we do see BDSM in terms of penetration, we can begin to understand the difficulty experienced, and the conclusions reached, by those researchers and writers who see BDSM solely in terms of pain, torture, humiliation, degradation, and so on.

The quote below, and which I repeat in upcoming chapter 10, *Motivations*, helps highlight this. It is from Baumeister and Butler's *Sexual Masochism - Deviance without Pathology*.

> *If someone who desired masochistic sex could be transformed through therapy techniques into someone who would not derive any enjoyment or pleasure from masochism, this should not be regarded as a positive mental health outcome.* [BAUMEISTER1997] (p. 227)

Completely absent from this is any mention of the person on the other end of the flogger or whip—namely the top, dominant, or master. They, at least in terms of this particular research paper, apparently remain consigned to the ranks of those in need of therapy. It's a little weird in terms of balance—namely that the people on one end of the whip can be seen as healthy, but those on the other end cannot.

Indeed, many authors can find a lot to say about BDSM masochists, but are oddly silent about BDSM sadists. And if we were to consider BDSM activities solely in terms of pain, torture, humiliation, degradation, etc., it'd be easy to hypothesise that masochists get their jollies due to some hidden desire to be debased, or because they're perpetuating some perhaps-forgotten abuse suffered in the past, or because of some weirdness of the brain which lets them internally transmute pain into pleasure.

It's a much harder reach in this case to hypothesise anything about the masochists' partners, i.e., the ones who inflict these things. Trying to suggest that there are so many actual sadists who get their rocks off by knowingly inflicting suffering on another is simply not going to fly, especially when we consider the number of people in the soft-and-cuddly BDSM ranks, such as those whose antics end at fluffy-handcuffs. And while we might like to think that humans are truly kind, generous, and unselfish, it's also not going to fly if we suggest that these "sadists" do what they do, so often and with so much effort, solely to make their partner feel good. No. There's much, much more to it than this.

But because many researchers and writers don't see the penetrative aspect, and strive to at least make some progress in explaining "this curious human phenomenon" [GHENT1990] (p. 109), we see a lot of words written about the submissive experience, but little about the experience of dominants. And, of course, many BDSM practitioners themselves don't even see this penetrative side.

When we throw penetration into the mix, however, we can see that it's not such a one-sided exercise after all. We can see that the authority, control, pain, torture, degradation, and so on, are tools which we use to effect penetration, rather than being an end in themselves. And it is this experience of penetrating, or being penetrated, which is frequently so powerful.

8. Relationships I

On my cynical days I wonder what some people mean by the labels they use to describe themselves. In, say, the days of ancient Rome, a captured slave didn't wait eagerly at the door for their master to return from a hard day at the Senate thinking, "Oooh! Oooh! Orgasms!!" This old and classical definition of "slave" is worlds apart from what some people consider to be a BDSM "slave".

Nailing down some roles and dynamics

So far I have talked about masters, slaves, tops, bottoms and so on, without actually being precise about what I mean by these terms. It's time to remedy that.

A big problem with these terms is that they're in common use with an enormous range of meanings; so much so that they're often not useful in understanding what someone really does—mostly they only tell you that someone is into BDSM and that's all.

I'm going to be spending a lot of time talking about different relationships and dynamics in the rest of this book, so for the rest of this chapter I'm going to bless you with my definitions of some roles and dynamics.

There are, according to one Peter Masters (i.e., me), five useful pairings:

Top	↔	Bottom
Dominant	↔	Submissive
Master	↔	Slave
Trainer	↔	Trainee
Owner	↔	Property

What follows in this chapter is just a quick sketch of each. Later on I'll be using these definitions, and further expanding on them.

And, before anyone jumps on me, I'd like to add that I'm not suggesting that anyone or everyone who practises BDSM matches one of these definitions. These are all for purposes of discussion. Any resemblance to any person, alive or dead, is purely coincidental.

You might have your own understanding of these pairings, and you might even strongly disagree with my definitions. This'd be a bit of a bummer, especially if you paid full price for this book. There are no refunds though, and I encourage you to just bear with me and my wacky definitions to see if you end up getting your money's worth.

Tops and bottoms

During a BDSM activity of some sort—such as a bondage scene, a piercing or a flogging—the *top* is the person in charge. He is the one tying the ropes and making sure that they're snug, but not too tight. He's also the one with the antiseptic, and is the one who is pushing the needles in. And he's the one holding and wielding the flogger.

The *bottom* is the person who is being done to. He is the one being tied up, or the one who is having needles stuck in him, or is the one on the receiving end of the flogging.

With tops and bottoms, what you see is what you get. Their BDSM activities are limited to scenes. At BDSM parties they might meet up with someone new, find a convenient dungeon or play-room, and then do a little something together. Outside of the bedroom or dungeon they are Joe and Jane More-Or-Less-Normal, though perhaps with an interest which they only share and discuss with other like-minded souls. They may or may not be in a long-term relationship with each other.

The most important characteristic here is that the BDSM part of their lives is something that is well-defined, and which is kept separate from the rest of their lives. While they might talk about it with their partner outside of the dungeon, or tease each other playfully about it, it is something which they only do during their scenes.

Because there is no ongoing BDSM dynamic between the people involved, it means that *switching* is possible, easy, and sometimes quite common. Switching is where one person adopts one role (top or bottom) for a while, then they switch and the other person takes over that role. For example, a night's BDSM fun might consist of partner A tying up partner B for a while, a brief pause to catch their breath, and end up with partner B giving partner A a nice, relaxing flogging.

Some people like to commit to being top or bottom for all of a scene, while others might switch in the middle of a scene if the mood takes them. Some might also prefer to be the top each time they play with particular partners, and the bottom with others.

Dominant and submissive

Tops and bottoms do things by mutual agreement. If one wants to do something, the other has to agree on each occasion. The key words are: *on each occasion.*

With *dominants* and *submissives* however, the dominant already has the authority to decide what's going to be done. This has been pre-agreed in some manner by the dominant and the submissive.

Where a top and bottom get together and agree on, say, a bondage session and how it's going to be done, a dominant will instead simply decide that he's going to do a bondage session with his submissive partner, and then go ahead with it.

While a dominant and a submissive might do things that look like top-and-bottom activities—like bondage and flogging—there's the important, and often critical, element of the dominant taking charge and giving direction. This means that dominance and submission can and do extend out of the bedroom or dungeon, and into other activities. The dominant can actually exercise authority in many more situations than where there's rope or an A-frame. It can flavour almost anything that the dominant and submissive do together, even just walking along the street, with the dominant, say, directing his submissive to always walk on his left and one pace behind him—or eating a meal together, with the dominant requiring his submissive to not start eating and drinking before he has done so, and that she must finish eating and drinking when he does.

Because there is this ongoing agreement that the dominant can and will take charge, switching roles—in terms of one being dominant and the other submissive—is far less likely to occur. This doesn't mean that they both might enjoy a good flogging from time to time, and that they each take turns at giving or receiving it. Instead it means that the dominant will be the one who decides what, when, and how, and the submissive will be the one who submits to that decision.

Master and slave

A bottom and a submissive can always say no safely. I very quickly add here that I'm not talking about "safely" in terms of possible consequences from their top or dominant. Instead I mean that they can say no without there being any negative consequences coming from within themselves. Their identity is not tied up in obeying or serving their top or dominant. If one day he's being a bit of a dick for the last time, and they tell him to fuck off, then all there might be is a sense of disappointment, sadness, or frustration followed by a bit of a break, and then a hunt for a new top or dominant.

Likewise, a top or dominant who splits from their bottom or submissive will move on, possibly just with a sense of regret marking the passing of something that worked for a while.

There's always an aspect of agreement or ongoing consent with tops, bottoms, dominants, and submissives—and at any time this consent can be withdrawn. It is not like this with masters and slaves.

Instead we're talking about something much deeper. A master doesn't choose to be a master. It's not something he agrees to. Likewise, a slave doesn't choose to be a slave. They simply are. A slave needs to be commanded and handled. A master needs to command and to handle. I will talk more about wants and needs in chapter 11, *Need*, but for the moment I'd like it to suffice that masters and slaves don't just do what they do to make their sex that much hotter.

They do it because it is as much part of them as are eating and breathing. Indeed, to continue with food analogies, we might say that dominance and submission can be the icing on the cake of a satisfying life. Mastery and slavery is, instead, the nutritious meal which fuels the lives of the master and the slave.

Because of this, saying no is not something done lightly. Saying no to a part of themselves is not brushed off as easily as a bottom turning down a bondage session because he's not in the mood. Saying no can be genuinely harmful to the slave's identity.

In common with dominance and submission, mastery and slavery isn't tied to a dungeon or bedroom. The master and slave could express themselves at times by sessions in a dungeon, but just as easily might never enter a dungeon at all.

Trainer and trainee

I will be talking more at depth about authority in a later chapter (chapter 19, *Types of authority*), but here it's important to quickly explain two types of authority:

1. The first is being an authority in some domain of learning—presumably in what the trainee wants to learn. Without knowing a subject well, or at least better than their student, a trainer can't hope to train.

2. The second is the authority to command. Being shy, or introverted, or lacking in self-confidence, or being embarrassed to talk to others, is not a good basis from which to teach or train. To train someone it is necessary to take charge of their learning, to command them in that context.

So. A trainee submits to at least the two sorts of authority I listed above. Without accepting both of these, they aren't likely to learn anything at all. The trainee is there, of course, to learn something. It might be that they're getting training in how to kneel, or how to present themselves, or how to perform oral sex, or how to do any number of other things. If the trainee is a master, top, or dominant, they might be there to learn how to command, how to tie someone up, how to recognise and handle misbehaviour, etc.

The trainer is there to teach them. This isn't just explaining or giving exercises, otherwise books and videotapes would be sufficient. It's instead usually about the trainer presenting material, observing and directing the trainee, keeping the trainee focussed, and recognising the trainee's unique abilities or problems and dealing with them in the best way possible.

Trainers and trainees have an interesting form of dominant/submissive relationship where the trainer nominally leads and the trainee nominally follows. It is limited in two interesting ways:

1. Firstly, the trainer has extensive authority—and one to which the submissive or student is probably well habituated after years of school—to command the student in areas relating to the study-at-hand. In fact, this is probably a requirement.

2. Secondly, how long the trainer and trainee are involved with each other is limited by the time it takes for the trainee to learn. In other dynamics, time is usually not a factor in the same way.

Note that if the trainee is a submissive, they might already have a dominant, and the limited nature of the engagement between the submissive and the trainer doesn't or shouldn't interfere with the submissive's primary dynamic.

Dominants and masters can have trainers too, of course. They can be a bit of a problem to train because of their natural inclination to lead and, therefore, their natural inclination to stuff up the training dynamic.

Owner and property

I was talking above about the exercise of command or authority, and about handling someone.

An owner/property dynamic is not like this. Ownership is instead about use. For example, while you can command a slave, or a butler, or a maid, you can't command a table. A table is property. A chariot is property. They aren't commanded. They are simply there to be taken and used. It's about attitude. Similarly, telling someone to bend over, and then fucking them from behind can be not so much about commanding them, and instead be about simply using one of their orifices.

A common thread

You might be able to see a different thread, but the common thread I see in all of the above is surrender[3]. A couple of quick observations now are probably apropos.

If you're a bondage bunny or a flogging fanatic you'll know that you get the most out of a scene when you relax into it, when you simply open up and let it happen to you. Instead of fighting it, you accept it and embrace it. You surrender to the embrace of the rope, or the pain of the whip knowing that you can't and don't want to escape.

Likewise, dominance and submission afficionados don't fight the authority or the power—they welcome it. Indeed, they go looking for it and immerse themselves in it. The flow of power is not something they push aside. They surrender to it, and to its effect on them. It's what they are looking for.

And property, of course, surrenders to being just an object, to being used, to not being in control. It is surrender, complete and abject.

There is surrender in all the above roles and dynamics. Even masters and trainers must surrender, though the nature of their particular surrenders might not be immediately apparent. A master must surrender to his own nature and needs, and the trainer must surrender to the needs and nature of his student.

Hunter and prey

> So crucial is the interaction of wills between dominant and submissive that pain itself, supposedly of cardinal importance, usually becomes a secondary affair; a consequence, not a prime mover. [ANTHONY1995] (p.117)

It's easy for me, as I write, to reduce the different relationships which I've been talking about in this chapter, into clinical definitions. While this might give you a good academic view of what's going on, it doesn't convey to you that there is a passion and intensity involved with all of these relationships. It doesn't convey that there can be a hunter-and-prey aspect to these, nor does it convey that tactics and creating strategies are also often vital components.

How so?

---

3 See also chapter 12, *Surrender and anchors.*

Let's look at the example of a dominant and a submissive. Simplistically speaking, we can say that the dominant is in charge, and that the submissive surrenders within that authority context. This is all well and good, but for both the dominant and the submissive to *feel* the rewards of this, the authority needs to be exercised by the dominant, and experienced by them both.

If the authority isn't exercised, then neither have any experience of it, and therefore don't have any benefit of it.

But going further, it isn't very rewarding to tell someone to do something and they do it automatically. You might just as well be directing a passionless robot, or driving a car where all four wheels are jacked off the ground—yes, you're pushing the pedals and turning the steering wheel, but you're not going anywhere, nor are you feeling the acceleration, the cornering, or the braking; nor are you having the experience of going anywhere.

Similarly, commands issued mechanically are not satisfying or rewarding for a submissive. They need to feel the challenges and demands of the dominant who is attempting to control and direct them.

The satisfaction then doesn't come from just issuing orders, or in blindly obeying them, but in the exercise and utilisation of the submissive by the dominant to achieve a particular goal. It is the complexity and challenge of directing someone, not because they're resisting, per se, but because of the richness of their own personality and skills, and the expertise required to drive them to the full range or level of their ability.

We have to keep in mind that the goal of the submissive is not always to just obey. Instead, what the submissive often seeks is to experience the authority and power of their dominant over them. This doesn't happen if they simply and unresistingly obey or submit. It is in the interests of the submissive, therefore, to create a context, or to provide a challenge to the dominant so that they (the submissive) can feel their dominant pursuing them (hunting them) and their dominant can likewise feel the reward and satisfaction of pursuing and catching (hunting) the submissive.

It follows, therefore, that the submissive will often be planning and strategizing, even if unconsciously, to challenge the dominant, to maintain the satisfaction for both of them. The purpose of this is not necessarily to defeat the dominant, because this would instantly render them valueless, but to maintain the *edge*. Indeed, providing this edge and making sure that the dominant can feel their domly muscles being exercised is an important part of how a submissive can serve their dominant.

Challenge

I think that it's important here to talk more about the word *challenge*. It might seem that this can be adversarial, where the submissive tries to defeat the dominant, or where the dominant tries to defeat the submissive. But this is only part of the picture. If I were a civil engineer given the task of designing and building backyard garden sheds, then there's no doubt that I could do an excellent job. They would the finest and most robust garden sheds around. Would I be satisfied doing this? Certainly not. For me to feel satisfied doing my civil engineering I would need to feel that my skills were being pushed, that I was learning new things, and that I was achieving new things. Perhaps, ultimately, once I have developed the skills, I would be able to design and build a replacement for the Golden Gate Bridge. But that will only happen, I will only get that level of skill and consequent satisfaction, if I am challenged, meet those challenges, and grow.

The same can apply to both dominants and submissives. A submissive may need to feel themselves being pushed, may need to feel they are growing and learning. Part of achieving this is due to the opportunities or demands placed on the submissive by their dominant. Likewise, the opportunities a dominant has for development and growth are going to be dependent on the challenges their submissive provides. Thus challenge may not be something which holds the person back, but can be something which lets them move forwards with their own development. Without challenge they may merely coast along, not getting better at all, and not getting a whole lot of satisfaction.

Challenge also has the purpose of assuring the submissive that the dominant is still able to provide the level of engagement necessary to be satisfying and rewarding to the submissive, just as the dominant also tests the submissive to make sure that they, too, are able to engage the dominant in a way that is rewarding and satisfying to him. It's not enough to be conquered once and then stay conquered for the rest of your life. It needs to be ongoing.

Being challenging is not, and probably should not, be the whole point of a D&s relationship. There are other things that can and should be satisfied within a full relationship, such as sexual needs, need for feeling valued, companionship, etc. A casual (occasional) or professional (BDSM) relationship may, though, just provide for one or two needs..

This hunter-and-prey aspect is also apparent in top-and-bottom relationships. There is often planning and strategy involved in any moderately complex flogging scene, for example. It's a rare top who will use only one implement (such as a crop) during a scene. More often, they choose and wield different implements, including their hands, to achieve a desired series of responses from their submissive partner, leading perhaps to some orgasmic outcome. The point is, that they don't mechanically apply the same implements, but instead have their own plan based on experience and what they want to achieve, and execute this plan, dynamically adapting as their submissive partner's responses ebb and flow. The fact that most tops have a large collection of implements—ranging from numerous floggers, crops, canes, paddles, and clamps—is testimony to the fact that strategy is a vital part of a good top/bottom scene. Looking at it like this, we can see the top as the hunter, while the prey here is something like the submissive's sub-space or orgasm.

Likewise, for a trainer, it's not satisfying to merely repeat lessons, or to explain exercises, and see these mechanically adopted. The challenge and reward comes from studying the trainee, finding their strengths and weaknesses, adapting the lessons and the material taught, to draw out the most from the trainee. Similarly, it is in the trainee's interest to present their complexity, not to make it difficult for the trainer, but to give the trainer a rich experience, to give them as much as possible to work on, and to allow the trainer to fully see and mould what they become.

Finally, although it is tempting to see the top, master, dominant, or trainer, in the role of the hunter, the strategizing and planning required to be a good submissive, bottom, or trainee, also has a hunter aspect. They, too, have prey—something they are trying to achieve from and through their counterpart, and this also requires planning.

9. Relationships II

The aim of science is not things themselves, as the dogmatists in their simplicity imagine, but the relations among things; outside these relations there is no reality knowable. Henri Poincaré, Science and Hypothesis, 1905.

When we look at two people and try to understand their relationship it's very easy and very tempting to just consider what they're like when they're together. The story doesn't stop there though. A slave, for example, doesn't stop obeying her orders just because her master has left the room. A husband still tends to feel like he's a husband even when his wife's not there, and perhaps more so a wife tends to feel like a wife even when her husband's not there. A dominant doesn't loose his feeling of empowerment over his submissive just because they're not together in the same room right now. And a fuck-buddy doesn't stop getting horny about his partner when his partner isn't there. What is it that persists when the partner is not there?

Roles and relationships don't stop just because the other person isn't in the room to practice them with. This is because there are actually other elements involved. In the world of BDSM we can highlight this by means of some questions:

1. Why do some submissives obey readily when with their dominant, but when on their own they have little interest in doing what they've been told?

2. When a master's slave is away doing something, does the master feel less of a master than when the slave's actually present? Or is it just different?

3. How can two people meet for the first time at a play party or social event, and have a deeply intimate and profound experience with each other right then and there?

4. Why does a slave keep obeying even when her master isn't around?

In all of the above, the unasked nub is: What's the difference between being with your BDSM partner and not being with them. For example, a slave obeying her non-present master isn't getting any sort of pat on the head or feedback from her master because he's simply not there to do it. Is she anticipating a pat on the head when they're together again? Is she toeing the line to avoid some future punishment? In reality, while possible, neither of these are the likely reasons.

In most cases, the slave is going to be feeling good about doing what she's been told *while she's doing it*. She's going to find it satisfying and rewarding in itself to do her best, to maintain the standards her master has set for her, and to do a generally good job. Maybe an extra bonus will be when she gets back to him and he smiles and tells her that she's a good girl, but this isn't why she's obeying in his absence.

The case of two people who meet at a play party for the first time and have a rollicking good time BDSM-wise presents a similar situation. If she sends him off to get her a drink, how can he get that much out of it if he's only just met her? In fact, he can be having a fantastic time, but the question is: Who is he having a good time with? After all he knows next to nothing about her. Can he be having a such a profound experience with an almost complete stranger? If he has barely known her for a few minutes or seconds then isn't this much the same as not knowing her at all? Why can't he then have the same quality of experience just on his own?

Or consider where a dominant and a submissive know each other very well, and respond to each other strongly. She's eager to please him, she'll bend over backwards while she's with him as they play, and her focus is totally on him when they're together. But once out of sight, she'll do her own thing and any standards of behaviour he might have for her, or any orders he gave her, quickly drop in priority.

In all of the above the common thread is *absence*. Plainly, one person can't be having a jolly good time reacting to someone who isn't there. A slave can't find an intensity and profundity from someone who isn't actually there. To whom or to what are they then responding?

The answer is that we need to start expanding our understanding of the role of the *Other*. When I wrote about the *Other* in an earlier chapter (chapter 6, *The Other*) I mentioned that BDSM requires an *Other*, and that this *Other* need not be a person. Specifically, I mentioned *time* as a non-person *Other*, commonly seen in how some people practice self-bondage. But the *Other* appears a lot more than that and, as we'll see shortly, provides a way of answering all of the questions I've been asking so far in this chapter.

Time is an external *Other*. It is something external to us, and is something we can't control. But we also create, and react to, our own *Others* internal to ourselves. Let's look at this more closely and I'll explain what I mean.

The work of Carl Jung (1875 - 1961), the famous Swiss psychiatrist, is useful here. He wrote extensively about *archetypes* and *complexes*. These are images of particular types of people or personalities which are either built in to each of us, or which we learn to recognise from experience. Typically we respond to these images automatically. Common among these images are The Child, The Mother, and The Hero. There are potentially hundreds more. Having these images inside us helps us to straight away recognise and respond appropriately to the type of person in front of us without having to go through the onerous job of consciously analysing each person we meet.

For example, having this built-in image of The Child helps us straight away recognise and respond to a child, or a child in distress, not just by their looks, but also by how they sound and how they behave. Because we have this built-in knowledge of what a child is like, we can immediately recognise them and easily tell the difference between a child and, say, a midget, or a person standing in a hole, or a lifelike doll.

While there's some argument about exactly which images are built in to us, there certainly are other images which we learn. In the BDSM world we learn, for example, what a dominant looks like and how they sound and behave. Likewise, we know what a submissive looks like, how they sound and how they behave. Ditto for all the other common BDSM roles. Partly we learn this from seeing them so often, but also we come to recognise the types of people who push the right buttons for us, and the types of people who don't.

I'd like to stress here that although I'm often referring to *images*, I'm not just referring to a static picture such as a photograph, but instead to the whole person—their looks, their facial expressions, how they move, how they talk, the sorts of gestures they make, how they think, and how they behave. This is important because it's the whole package to which we respond most strongly, not just to the right pose or to the leather chaps.

Having these images serves a couple of purposes. One of the most important is that it lets us quickly recognise the types of people to whom we want to, and should, be attracted. This doesn't need to be something we do consciously. We have our own needs and desires, and the quicker we find the sort of person who can *do it* for us, the faster we'll get those wants or needs met. Consciously sorting through people who might be eminently wonderful but who aren't the type we need is wasteful, and our unconscious mind does a lot of the sorting for us by automatically classifying each person according to the images we have in our minds.

If we consider my earlier question about two people meeting at a play party for the very first time and almost straight away having a jolly good time, then we can start to answer, "How do they do it?" by thinking in terms of images, archetypes, complexes, and psychological reactions.

Joe Submissive might arrive at this party and be introduced to Jane Dominant. Consciously or unconsciously he might notice that on the outside she looks and behaves a lot like what he imagines an ideal dominant female should be. But what he sees is incomplete. He hasn't yet experienced anything like a full range of behaviour from her, hasn't explored her opinions and attitudes, and certainly doesn't know how skilled she is in the dominant arts. None of this stops him beginning to respond, be it with a stirring in his pants, with some desire to abase himself in front of her, or with some other feeling. Clearly he can't see the whole package in the real person in front of him, at least not straight away. He might start responding to her just from an initial glance, so what is it that's triggering him?

The answer is that he is engaging in the time-honoured and well-known psychological phenomena known as *projection*. He is taking the image of a Dominant Female from his own mind, and projecting it onto Jane Dominant to fill in the gaps. That is, his *hunger* and his imagination help him to create the missing parts, the things about her which he doesn't know, so that what he is responding to is a complete Dominant Female, composed of the real Jane plus stuff from his own mind.

Mostly, this process isn't something which Joe does consciously.

It may be that the bulk of what he is seeing and responding to is coming from his own mind. As long as Jane doesn't have any obvious features or behaviours which make it impossible for him to project onto her—such as if she's wearing a loud Hawaiian T-shirt or is speaking in a high-pitched squeaky voice—Joe will be able to see her as someone to whom he can respond.

We can see this same process in the words of Frieda Fordham, in her *Introduction to Jung's Psychology*, where she talks about our built-in images of Man and Woman:

> *Later the image is projected on to the various women who attract a man in his lifetime. Naturally this leads to endless misunderstanding, for most men are unaware that they are projecting their own inner picture of woman on to someone very different; most inexplicable love affairs and disastrous marriages arise in this way. Unfortunately the projection is not something that can be controlled in a rational manner;* [FORDHAM1991] (p. 53)

What we are talking about here, and what Fordham is talking about, is a form of the *Other*. The actual genuine real Jane is simply there to bring Joe's constructed *Other* into existence, providing the skeleton on which the idealised female dominant *Other* will be fleshed out in the mind of Joe. Like a movie, there must be a screen onto which the moving images must be projected. Without the screen there is nothing. And without Jane there to project onto, Joe would have nothing to respond to.

When we look at this example more closely we can also see that there are actually at least two relationships going on:

1. There's a relationship between Joe and real Jane, and

2. There's a relationship between Joe and the idealised image of the Dominant Female which he has projected on to Jane.

How much of each of these he is responding to at any particular time will vary, often depending on what Joe is needing at the time. For example, during a quick chat about the weather Joe might be mostly engaging real Jane, but while kissing her boot Joe may be mostly engaging the idealised dominant image he is projecting onto Jane.

It might be difficult to imagine that Joe is responding, not to Jane, but to something in his mind which he is projecting on to Jane. How can it be that Joe is reacting to something that isn't really a person? Fordham comes to rescue here when she writes:

> *A complex may be conscious, that is to say we know about it; or it may be partly conscious, in which case we know something of it, but are not fully aware of its nature; or it may be unconscious, in which case we are not aware of its existence at all. In both the latter cases, and especially when the complex is unconscious, it seems to behave like an independent person, and the ideas and affects centred round it will pass in and out of consciousness in an uncontrolled manner.*
> [FORDHAM1991] (p. 23)

We see that this image can indeed function "like an independent person" and, thus, meets our criteria for an *Other*.

If Joe and Jane are to have any longevity together, then Jane is going to have to demonstrate the attributes Joe needs and these will have to replace what Joe is projecting. Although what Joe is projecting could be quite exciting, it's not reality and lacks the substance to be satisfying in the long-term. It's a bit like comparing masturbation to real nookie. If Jane has the goods, then the relationship may flourish. If not, Joe will tire of projecting to fill in the gaps, and the relationship will fade just as quickly as Joe's projection fades.

Note that although I've been talking about this in terms of Joe projecting onto Jane, the same could be happening with Jane projecting on to Joe to fill in what she needs.

In a relationship which is well-established there is more which we can see, and this can help us understand why a slave might obey in the absence of her master, why a master might feel "masterly" even in the absence of his slave, why a submissive might feel "subby" when her dominant is away, etc. The key word, again, is *absence* and now we can start to look at what remains when a longer-term partner is absent.

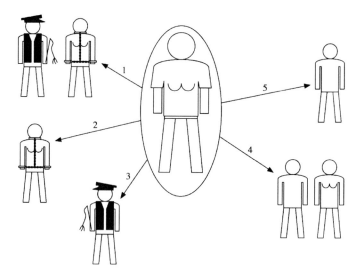

Figure R2-1. Submissive Relationships

Figure R2-1 shows just some of the relationships involved when a submissive is involved long-term with a dominant. The figures not in uniform represent the real people—the submissive and the dominant themselves—while the figures in uniform or chains represent their ideal forms or images in the mind of the submissive herself. Each arrow represents a separate relationship.

This submissive has an image in her mind of her ideal dominant (3). This is what she measures her dominant against when he's doing "dommy" things. In fact, when she sees anyone at all, the closer they are to this image the more readily she'll recognise them as a dominant. More than this, and in a similar way to what Joe was doing with Jane earlier, our submissive here can use her image of her ideal dominant as a source of material to fill in the gaps with her real dominant, such as when he's talking to her on the telephone and she can't actually see him, when he's physically unwell, when he's lost his voice, or when he's wandering around wearing a Hawaiian T-shirt.

I'd like to remind you that, as I said earlier, this image isn't just about how the person looks. It's also how they behave, think, act, speak, and so on. In particular, it's how they do these things *to her*, i.e., in her regard.

She also has an image in her mind of an ideal submissive (2). This is, you'd imagine, herself, but is actually an idealised form of herself. It's her own internal guide to how she should look, speak, and behave as a submissive

In reality neither she nor her dominant are exactly like her ideal images. For this reason the diagram contains the figures which aren't wearing typical BDSM gear, i.e., chains or leathers. These represent the real forms of themselves (4 and 5).

So our submissive sees herself in relation to all of these things, and these serve to guide and regulate how she thinks and behaves.

Let's go through some of these relationships:

1. Her relationship to her ideal dominant (3). This is what she responds to as a submissive. If at any particular time the real person happens to be an unshaven, desperately-in-need-of-a-coffee, not-a-morning-person, T-shirt-clad being, then she's going to have to do a whole lot of projecting to get her submissive juices running.

   On the other hand, if he's dressed in his leathers, has grabbed her by the scruff of the neck, and is talking to her in that smooth and authoritative voice she knows so well, then not much projecting needs to happen at all for him to match the ideal image in her mind and to get the strongest response out of her.

2. Her relationship to him as a mere mortal (5). A lot of the time she might be responding to him simply as a companion or friend. This is the guy who may be complaining about the traffic, who might have just spilt his coffee, and who can't quite get the T.V. remote control to work right. If they have a well-founded and honest relationship then she might be happy to see him as he really is at these times because this side of him might also fill some of her needs.

3. She also has a relationship to their relationship. In other words, they have a relationship together and she sees herself in terms of that. She understands her role in that relationship and what she needs to do as part of it. When she can't directly relate to him, either in his real or idealised form, such as when he's not around, she can continue to feel that she's part of the relationship she has with him. This is one of the things that persists in his absence.

   She can see this in terms of their real relationship (4), or in terms of their idealised D&s relationship (1), or both.

4. She also sees herself in terms of what she thinks a submissive such as herself should be (2). This is strictly something between herself and herself, and so this also persists in his absence.

When she's with her partner/dominant the other relationships are there as well, such as her relationship to her idealised form of herself as a submissive, and her relationship to their relationships. These provide continuity, context, guidance, and support for her as she behaves as part of the relationship as a whole, whether her partner's there or not.

Even when they are physically together her partner may or may not be actually paying attention to her or stimulating her. But the rest of the relationships will be there at these times and these give her the sense of continuity of the relationship as a whole.

Thus, even when he's not there or is not focussed on her, she is still present with at least their relationship, her image of herself, and her images of him (both as a mere mortal and as a dominant), and she continues to function in relation to them all.

That these constructs are powerful and fully capable of triggering her and providing opportunities for stimulation and satisfaction is clear. And these constructs are indeed *Others* in the sense I wrote about earlier.

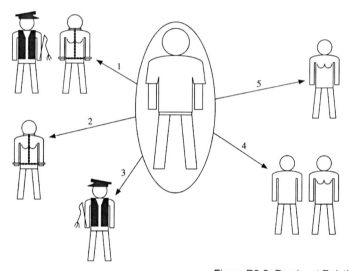

Figure R2-2. Dominant Relationships

In a similar way, her dominant is going to be involved in many relationships which bear a striking similarity to those of his submissive as we can see in figure R2-2.

Importantly, he will also have an idealised image of himself as a dominant (3), an idealised image of his girl as a submissive (2), and idealised images of themselves as a D&s couple (1).

Although I may not have made it clear so far, the images our dominant and submissive maintain of themselves and each other serve two purposes:

1. They provide a source of material to project on to the other when the other is not living up sufficiently to what is needed by them to respond. For example, if our submissive needs to feel "subby" and her partner is not doing it for her for some reason—such as he's tired and unable to focus— she can tap in to her ideal image of a dominant and project/imagine onto the real him to fill in the gaps.

2. As well as having a relationship with the real person, they have a relationship to the ideal form, i.e., to their image of a dominant or submissive, and they lean on this during absences of their real partner to provide continuity of context.

At this point we've explored enough to be able to return to the original four questions from the beginning of this chapter and start finding answers to them.

1. Why do some submissives obey readily when with their dominant, but when on their own they have little interest in doing what they've been told?

One reason for this can be that the submissive has no well-developed image of herself in a dominant/submissive relationship with her partner. This could be that she doesn't have a well-developed image of an ideal dominant/submissive relationship (arrow (1) in figure R2-1) or that she doesn't feel a particularly strong relationship with it if she does. Thus, once her partner is absent, there's little sense of continuity for her.

Another reason could be that she may want to think that she is strongly submissive, but actually has no strong image or connection to herself as a submissive, and instead relates most strongly to her partner. Again, when he's absent, the sense of continuity fades because she has no strong connection to an image of a submissive on which to lean, and through which to be guided how to behave.

2. When a master's slave is away doing something, does the master feel less of a master than when the slave's actually present? Or is it just different?

Here we can see that the answer may well be that when the slave is away the master's relationships with his image of her, or with his image of their relationship, come to the fore to give him a continuity of the master/slave context.

If there's actually little or no change for him, then it may be that he simply unconsciously uses her for his projection of the images that he needs to see to have his experience of mastery.

This latter has a something in common with the Joe/Jane example I discussed at length earlier. The real slave is not so important as the need to have any slave on to which to project his image of a slave.

3. How can two people meet for the first time at a play party or social event, and have a deeply profound and intimate experience with each other right then and there?

This is the Joe/Jane example. While each person has a strong image of their complement, namely a submissive if they are dominant, or vice versa, then this can work when each projects sufficient of their own internal image onto their transient partner.

Long-term this is not a good way to go as it's a bit like masturbation—i.e., each person is doing whatever they're doing with a projection of themselves (i.e., of their own image of their complement), rather than with the intimate involvement of another *real* person.

4. Why *does* a slave keep obeying even when their master isn't around?

Of course, we can now see that a slave keeps obeying because she has a strong relationship with her image of herself, and a strong image of the relationship she has with her master, so when he is not present she can happily continue to feel herself serving within these contexts.

Plato steps in

The idea of us humans having perfect images of things in our minds is not new. Plato (424/423 BC – 348/347 BC) wrote about *forms* and *shadows* over 2000 years ago, and these fit closely with what we've been talking about. Below is an extract from Plato's *Cratylus*, as translated by Benjamin Jowett [PLATOCRAT]. The "shuttle" being referred to here is the instrument used in weaving to pass the thread from one side of the material being woven to the other.

Socrates	And suppose the shuttle to be broken in making, will he make another, looking to the broken one? or will he look to the form according to which he made the other ?
Hermogenes	To the latter, I should imagine.
Socrates	Might not that be justly called the true or ideal shuttle?
Hermogenes	I think so.
Socrates	And whatever shuttles are wanted, for the manufacture of garments, thin or thick, of flaxen, woollen, or other material, ought all of them to have the true form of the shuttle; and whatever is the shuttle best adapted to each kind of work, that ought to be the form which the maker produces in each case.
Hermogenes	Yes.

When each of us thinks of a master or slave, or a dominant or submissive, we each have an image of what they are to us. These are the perfect images of these individuals. Plato writes above about a weaving shuttle. If it breaks, does the artisan make a new one based on the broken one, or does he have an image in his mind of the way a shuttle should be and make the new one based on that image in his mind? It is, of course, the latter. The artisan has an image in his mind of the perfect shuttle, the *ideal* shuttle, and this is what he uses as his model. Similarly, a weaver using a new shuttle is going to be doing so based on their past experiences with shuttles and what they expect them to be. They aren't going to learn it all anew with each particular shuttle.

Likewise, a submissive with a new dominant is going to initially react based on their past experience—on what they have learned a dominant should be like. It may turn out that the dominant doesn't live up to the submissive's conscious or unconscious expectations. The outside may look good, but the inside is not what's required. It could be like a poorly made or hollow shuttle: the weaver picks it up with the full expectation, readiness, and creative state of mind to weave something spectacular, but the shuttle fails or crumbles in use and the weaver is left unsatisfied.

Considering forms, archetypes, and images can also help us see how someone can participate in BDSM activities in different roles depending on the *type* of partner they have, rather than their roles being specifically based on the actual characteristics or nature of the person they are engaging. For example, a man who is submissive to women and dominant to men.

10. Motivations

She [St. Mary Magdelene dei Pazzi] would have herself tied to a post and demand to be insulted, or drop hot wax on her skin... She was canonised in 1668. [TAYLOR1953] (p. 44)

There are perhaps as many reasons for being involved in BDSM as there are people involved in it, ranging from light entertainment to profound journeys of self-exploration and discovery.

We're looking for motivation and mechanisms in this chapter. And we're actually quite fortunate because science and academic research can come to our partial aid. Up until not very long ago, things such as sexual masochism were considered to be pathologies; that is, they were thought to be psychological afflictions which should be cured so that the sufferers could go on to lead happy, healthy, and perhaps boring, lives.

Things have changed somewhat, and the border between sick and healthy has moved:

> *If someone who desired masochistic sex could be transformed through therapy techniques into someone who would not derive any enjoyment or pleasure from masochism, this should not be regarded as a positive mental health outcome.* [BAUMEISTER1997] (p. 227)

> *[S]adomasochistic sexual practices may be regarded as a sexual orientation similar to homosexuality, and should not be targeted for change in psychotherapy unless requested by the client;* [HOFF2003] (Abstract)

As a result, there is an ongoing modern clinical interest in such things as submission, surrender, non-standard sex, and masochism, and we can use the resulting research papers and books to better understand what is going on in the world of BDSM. We'll do this in this chapter.

We saw in chapter 7, *Penetration*, that the BDSM activity—such as flogging or piercing—may be the avenue through which penetration is experienced, and that penetration can be a goal in itself. On top of this, there are quite a few other satisfying or pleasurable experiences which can be achieved through BDSM, and oftentimes these experiences occur in combination during BDSM activities or scenes.

This can make it hard for the average researcher because there's usually no single button being pushed, and while engaged in the same BDSM activity different people might experience different buttons being pushed.

In this chapter, and going beyond penetration, I want to look at a handful of these other buttons, namely:

- Chemical highs,
- Sub-space,
- Transformation of pain into pleasure,
- Uncovering or releasing the True Self,
- Minimising self,
- Experiencing power,
- Ecstasy and rapture,
- "Deep play",
- Catharsis,
- Recreation, and
- Built-in physiological responses

Some of these, such as sub-space, chemical highs, the experience of power—both asserting power over someone, and feeling them assert power over us—and ecstasy and rapture, may be familiar to experienced BDSMers. Some of the others, such as the two to do with self, and "deep play", are perhaps less well known.

Chemical high

Endorphins are natural chemicals released by the brain. They can have a similar effect as morphine or other analgesics, i.e., they can create a floating, euphoric feeling, or *high*. They are non-addictive. Research indicates that endorphins and other similar chemicals are released by the brain during prolonged and difficult exercise, and during pain and stress. This is sometimes called a "runner's high" because it is commonly experienced by long-distance runners.

Thus, a prolonged workout with a cane, flogger or whip is likely to trigger the same release of chemicals, giving the same feelings of euphoria, and a possible explanation for increased tolerance of pain.

Endorphins is a good, but only partial answer for why someone does BDSM. If it was the whole answer, then why not instead just go to a scary movie, do mountain climbing, of become a marathon runner? Why seek the chemical high specifically in a BDSM context? Why isn't some other context just as good, or better, or even less painful?

The answer I propose, is that there is rarely just one button being pushed in any BDSM activity, be it a quickie flogging, or a long-term enslavement. A chemical high is often just the icing on the cake—i.e., a bonus on top of all the other pleasures and satisfactions which BDSM might be affording the individual.

Sub-space

Sub-space is a term in the BDSM world which refers to a psychological state experienced by a submissive or bottom, usually while deeply engaged with a top or dominant, either through intense physical stimulation—such as pain—or through intense personal interaction—such as handling or contact, or through being commanded or used. The experience may be euphoric.

It may be accompanied by a flood of neurochemicals—including endorphins (see above). The experience may lead to feelings of physical detachment, and even to an inability to recognise or respond appropriately to injury. It may also be accompanied by a reversion to a pre-verbal or elemental mental state [MASTERS2006] (pp. 92 - 93, 105 - 108). In this state the person affected may deal poorly with complex thoughts and ideas. The ability to speak or construct sentences may become difficult or impossible.

In her book, *Subspace - The Journey of a Submissive,* Toya writes:

> *I also find it hard trying to explain to new BDSM explorers exactly what subspace is. There is always the confusion with the 'floating' of an endorphin high achieved from pain play. Subspace to me is not so much a space as an awareness. It's where my focus is entirely on my master's voice, his commands, and his wishes. Its [sic] where I can still function, albeit vaguely and it feels like all my senses are tuned into my Master's presence. Speech is something that happens only when required by Master; otherwise it's just too hard to do. Coherent thought is gone, his words become my thoughts, and his touch becomes my reason for being.* [TOYA2001] (p. 54)

And, in private correspondence with the author, Karen wrote:

> *Sir, when I go way out in subspace, I get to a point when the only things I can say are "more", "harder" and "yes" and when I go out even further, I can't say anything, nor am I able to respond to any kind of question. The first few times it happened, it scared both Master and me, but then we realized it was just a good thing and accepted it.* Karen, private correspondence, 2008

Sub-space is a very vulnerable state, and one in which the submissive or bottom is very dependent on their partner for their well-being. In some, but not all, submissives, such as Toya, sub-space can create feelings of closeness and intimacy with their dominants.

In their *Shrinking the Self*, Baumeister and Boden talk in terms of mental narrowing, and we can see the similarity with sub-space and what they're saying:

> *The hallmarks of mental narrowing include an altered sense of time which focuses narrowly on the here and now; attention to rigid, concrete matters rather than abstract or complex thought; and when thinking is necessary, it follows simple, standard, familiar patterns and formulas rather than examining anything new. Movement and sensation replace action and experience.* [BAUMEISTER1994] (p. 151)

It's clear from both Karen and Toya, that sub-space is a worthy goal in itself.

Bad sub-space

While sub-space is generally referred to as a positive experience, it's also possible to get into the wrong head-space instead of the right one, and to come out of the experience traumatised to a greater or lesser degree. This could be due to something completely internal to the submissive—such as bad memories being innocently awoken, or could be due to unexpected, unsafe, or non-consensual behaviour of the dominant or top, or could be due to other factors.

It's important to remember that sub-space (good or bad) is characterised by decreased ability to make decisions and mental narrowing, and this leaves the person often unable to get themselves out of a situation which they would normally be able to defend themselves against. Thus, something which appears initially minor can lead them into a very bad state of mind while in sub-space. This magnification effect can make the experience one from which it is difficult to recover.

Transformation of pain into pleasure

One of the things that can be hard for an outsider, i.e., someone not involved in BDSM, to understand is how pain can be transformed into pleasure. Nicola Abel-Hirsch writes in *The perversion of pain, pleasure and thought* [ABELHIRSCH2006] about the difference between how pain can be, by one person, simply felt, compared to another person who uses it to construct an experience. That is, in the latter case it's not an end in itself as it would be in a truly masochistic experience. In BDSM pain is used to construct an often very profound experience. The pain is a doorway used to reach somewhere else, to some state of mind which is difficult, impractical, or impossible to reach any other way.

But Abel-Hirsch also makes it clear that the sort of pain she is talking about is not just the physical pain you might get from sticking a pin into your finger. It is also about psychological or psychic pain. I referred to this in my earlier work *Understanding Submission* [MASTERS1998] where I talked about "pain, discomfort and restraint" as being factors in the BDSM experience. One example of this sort of pain or discomfort is humiliation and, again, where it is used in BDSM it is as a doorway to a greater experience, not just to inflict suffering on the person being humiliated.

One of the reasons why many BDSM practitioners who explore pain or impact play have such a variety of implements in their toy bags is to allow them to create a variety of sensations to help their partner to navigate to a particular state of mind. For example, a submissive may initially need frequent and heavy thudding to help them detach from the here-and-now and turn inwards to their own feelings, followed by lighter and less frequent thudding as they approach the state of mind they're seeking. After this, they may need something which stings instead of thuds to help recover them from the detached and intense inward focus they were experiencing.

The *art* of some aspects of BDSM can be in the dominant being aware of the internal state of mind in which their submissive finds themselves, and being able to choose the right actions, words, and intensities needed to help them along in that particular experience.

One of the things that some BDSM practitioners find through this doorway is their True Selves.

True Self / False Self

Donald W. Winnicott was a pediatrician and influential psychoanalyst, active through the middle part of the 1900s, who wrote about, and developed, the idea of the *False Self* and the *True Self*.

The False Self is that part of us which forms to interact with society and those around us in acceptable ways, even though these might be ways of thinking and behaving contrary to what we'd really like to do. The False Self is compliant, and looks to help us, or make us, fit in so that we can continue to have useful and productive relationships with those around us. It can include being polite, avoiding some topics of conversation, allowing others to go first, not thumping assholes who clearly deserve it, keeping sex [mostly] out of the office, etc.

But, as Winnicott notes, the False Self is not really us. It is not an expression of what we really want or need. It is instead what people around us and society need from us, or is what we think we want from ourselves.

> *Only The True Self can be Creative and only the True Self can feel real. Whereas a True Self can feel real, the existence of a False Self results in a feeling unreal or a sense of futility.* [WINNICOTT1960] (p. 148)

As a consequence, we can only find real satisfaction of our needs through the True Self because the False Self is exactly what it says it is: false. It can never be the path to deep and true satisfaction. That said, however, the False Self still has an important part to play in most day-to-day life.

BDSM provides an opportunity to allow the False Self to fall away, or to be pushed away, for a time, to allow the True Self to surface and be engaged—and sated—directly.

In the normal course of events the True Self clamours for opportunities to get out from behind the False Self. There's even a common term to describe this: *letting one's hair down*. We create these opportunities if none occur naturally such as by our choice of hobbies (such as skydiving). There are at least two of these opportunities specific to BDSM:

1. The use of pain to generate such an intense True Self, often primal, reaction that the False Self is driven aside, its politeness and socially-conforming behaviour suppressed, at least for a time.

2. Role play, particularly when involving power roles, serves to create a context for which we have no False Self available. In other words, the False Self develops in response to some of the situations we routinely encounter. In a new or novel situation, we may find that there is no effective or developed False Self prepared, and so the True Self lies naked and exposed.

   This will work best, and probably only, when we are in a safe environment— i.e., with a partner familiar to us and trusted enough for the True Self to come out *and stay out* for the duration of the activity.

We can see this latter occurring in the words of John Warren, author of *The Loving Dominant*:

> *Some submissives say they can really let go only when they have intentionally adopted a role. In effect, they create an internal psychodrama in which they are captured secret agents, molested peasant maids, or blackmailed debutantes.* [WARREN1994] (p. 20)

It definitely wouldn't be the case that a real secret agent would get as much of a thrill out of this sort of role play, and almost certainly a woman who is molested without consent isn't going to get much of a buzz either. But, somewhat paradoxically, creating a role with the idea that it's a situation where the True or primal self can more easily come out to play is a useful tool to some.

When pain is used, it doesn't need to be physical pain, such as that caused by a whip or cane. It can also be, as we've already seen, psychological pain or discomfort, such as that caused through humiliation or fear. It's important to distinguish though, between the sort of pain which simply hurts, and the sort of pain which is transforming. In *The perversion of pain, pleasure and thought*, Nicola Abel-Hirsch writes about this difference, in particular about how pain can become something used instead of something merely felt:

> *Bion wrote little directly on perversion. However, his work introduces the possibility of distinguishing between what he describes as pain 'suffered' and pain 'felt'. This difference is not to do whether the experience comes from inside or outside, but with how it is received by the person... Bion suggests that a difference between 'suffering' pain and 'feeling' pain is that the former is a discovery made in contact with reality (internal and external reality). By 'discover' he conveys a sense of finding the pain within oneself, as an experience of what it is to be oneself.* [ABELHIRSCH2006] (pp. 99 - 100)

We can see that Abel-Hirsch is talking here about using pain to uncover the True Self.

The internal psychological mechanism which allows this uncovering to occur—i.e., welcoming and using the pain, instead of trying to reject and pull away from the pain—is one that depends on both the internal and external context of the person, namely:

1. What sort of pain they need or want to experience, and how strongly,

2. The level of confidence they have in their partner (who will be inflicting the pain) and,

3. The level of trust they have in their partner to handle their uncovered True Self appropriately.

This last point is particularly important. As we've seen, the False Self develops to allow us to fit in with society and with the people around us. In a sense it is defensive—it presents us to the world in such a way that we are accepted, and not rejected; so that we are praised, and not condemned. By engaging in activities designed to push aside the False Self and uncover the True Self, we are pushing aside that very part of us which ensures we are liked and accepted. By exposing the True Self, we can risk being rejected (which can hurt), and this is why some people don't engage in BDSM activities publicly, and engage only with people who they can deeply trust to support and accept their exposed True Self.

Finally, a little more from Winnicott, this time from his *Clinical Varieties of Transference*:

> *In the cases on which my work is based there has been what I call a true self hidden, protected by a false self. This false self is no doubt an aspect of the true self. It hides and protects it, and it reacts to the adaptation failures and develops a pattern corresponding to the pattern of environmental failure. In this way the true self is not involved in the reacting, and so preserves a continuity of being. However, this hidden true self suffers an impoverishment that derives from lack of experience.* [WINNICOTT1955] (pp. 296 - 297)

Minimising self

In the chapter 5, *Identity maintenance, management, and role-play*, I wrote about how our entire self can't be present and active all at the same time, and that we use various management strategies to ensure that only those attributes and behaviours are active which we actually need at the time.

This is an ideal. In reality, sometimes some attributes which would be useful—such as a razor sharp wit to give you a clever response to what someone just said—just won't turn on, and sometimes other attributes, which are a distraction, just won't turn off. BDSM can't help too much with turning on required attributes, but it can turn other attributes off.

We see this with people, such as the classic high-power executive who visits a dominatrix for a flogging, and who uses the flogging to minimise his self. I.e., instead of looking for something to expand his mind, he looks for something to contract it, to turn off things like worries and preoccupation, to push aside conscious thought. In other words, if he can't find an off switch just on his own, then maybe a dominatrix can provide the intensity of experience to drive out the mental behaviours which are preventing him from unwinding.

A highly intelligent friend of mine, for example, uses bondage to find a time of quiet when her brain stops its otherwise relentless thinking. As the experience of bondage reduces her self down to the simple feeling of the ropes tightly restraining her, she finds the peace from her own thoughts which allows her to recreate.

This is a short-term minimisation of self, and similar effects can be found in activities such as skydiving, thrill rides, and even through immersing one's self in certain movies at a cinema with a loud sound-system.

While this minimisation of self can be healthy in small doses, there is the possibility that this can be abused and become pathological. It's unlikely to occur in the short-term scenes which I've mentioned so far, but a significant retreat from, and minimisation of, self can be a possibility where, for example, a slave's focus turns well away from themselves and focusses towards the requirements of their master for a longer period of time. Where intense service is a goal, it can be necessary to implement strategies to require the slave to focus on themselves regularly to ensure that the retreat doesn't become unhealthy or irretrievable (such as a mandatory day every week with her friends away from her master).

Experiencing power

It's interesting to note that in one piece of research [HILL1996], where 586 people were asked what their motivation for sex was and were given 8 selections to rate, two of these had to do directly with power, namely experiencing the power of their partner or experiencing power over their partner. About 20% of men and 20% of women responded that each of these selections were important to them.

I talk about this much more in the upcoming chapter 14, *Comments on some research into BDSM and sex*. However the most important point to make is that if these motivations exist and that sex can be used to satisfy them, why can't something else— for example, BDSM—be used to satisfy them as well, or possibly even better?

Indeed, this is exactly what happens. As we've seen, BDSM is fundamentally, explicitly, and overtly about an inequity of power, and this is very different from what we see in many other activities, vanilla sex included.

Ecstasy and rapture

Many people experience episodes of rapture or ecstasy doing whatever they do BDSM-wise. This may be during a flogging, while serving their master, while being handled by their dominant, and even during BDSM-flavoured nookie.

I'd like to argue that this ecstasy comes from penetration. We've seen that many aspects of BDSM are about either penetrating—in one form or another—or about creating situations and circumstances of openness and vulnerability, which thus enhance any penetration.

I suspect that while, say, skydiving or vanilla sex may be fantastic, they are really just about one type of penetration. Combining multiple forms of penetration into the one activity—as we can do in BDSM— stacks experience on top of experience on top of experience, and raises what we do subjectively beyond merely fantastic and into ecstasy. See also *Hotter sex* coming up in a few paragraphs.

Intimacy and bonding

Increasing the intimacy and bonding between a couple can also be a meaningful motivation in BDSM. At perhaps its most mundane, this can occur when an intense experience is shared, and this is common in many forms of BDSM.

Going beyond this, and pursuing the *penetration* idea, we also expose ourselves to our partners in BDSM with a depth that is difficult to replicate in other experiences. Even during cock-in-cunt sex, considered by many to be quite intimate, it's easy to pretend involvement, or to hide ourselves (behind faked orgasms, for example). In BDSM, this sort of pretence is harder to achieve because BDSM is that much more engaging and demanding than many other activities. In vanilla sex, though, it can be enough to hide behind automatic physiological responses to put on a good show. Not so with BDSM most of the time.

Thus, the mandatory openness of BDSM tends to lead to more intimacy and, often, directly into greater bonding.

Hotter sex

Maybe the sex is hotter...

> *Q: But how does the sex become hotter?*

> *A. By combining multiple acts of penetrating or being penetrated.*

The sex part, at base, is physical penetration with the corresponding stimulation of some very sensitive nerve endings. In BDSM this can be combined with any of a range of other forms of penetration before, during, or after the cock-in-the-cunt phase. For example, placing someone in a collar, exposing them naked in front of others, confining them, or even actual physical piercing with, say, hypodermic needles, all add to the sense and experience of penetration.

Likewise, for the person doing the penetrating, the experience of the physical/ genital penetration can be added to by the additional types of penetration BDSM has to offer, such as the list in the previous paragraph. Baumeister and Butler, in their *Sexual Masochism - Deviance without Pathology*, also give an example of a "triple whammy":

> *A spanking, for example, is a means of administering pain, but is probably also a humiliating and embarrassing experience, and it may also contain some element of being under the control of someone else.* [BAUMEISTER1997] (p. 231)

This contains a number of elements which we've seen so far:

- Physical pain—displaces the false self,
- Psychological discomfort (humiliation), and
- Feeling the power of the partner.

Do take this opportunity to note that, as Baumeister and Butler indicate above, it doesn't always have to be about sex.

Play versus "deep play" versus work

It's useful to reflect on what BDSM practitioners call "play". As we'll see it turns out that there are at least three sides to this.

Play for fun

> Play: *Exercise or action for enjoyment or recreation, ... [OED]*

> Recreation: *The action of recreating (oneself or another), or fact of being recreated, by some pleasant occupation, pastime or amusement [OED]*

Some types of play are simply for fun. Typically there's not a lot at stake should the play not work out, or should it be interrupted or end early. This type of play is sometimes a diversion or a distraction from what's going on elsewhere in life—a chance to recharge one's batteries away from whatever has been consuming one's time and/or energy.

Alternatively, this sort of play can be simply a change of pace, or a novel or different way of doing things to add spice or variety.

"Deep play"

Clifford Geertz wrote about an interesting phenomena in his *Deep Play: Notes on the Balinese Cockfight* [GEERTZ1973]. He called this [no surprise!] *deep play*, and while Geertz was an anthropologist writing about Balinese cockfights (i.e., fightin' chooks, not duelin' dicks!), it's something we can see in BDSM as well. It's where some form of what superficially might appear to be simple recreation actually contains some deeper and more important purpose. Sometimes the purpose is even hidden from the participants themselves. As Geertz writes:

> *For it is only apparently cocks that are fighting there. Actually, it is men.*

In BDSM it might be apparently about sex when actually something more profound is involved.

For example, we might consider a submissive who looks for profound surrender, and who finds it with her partner by totally immersing herself and giving herself up to the pain in a heavy flogging session. Even though the session might wrap up with an aggressive fucking by her partner, and that it might seem from the outside to be that the sex at the end is the culmination, from the submissive's point of view the culmination was the surrender, with the sex act at the end being perhaps just irrelevant icing on the cake.

It might even be the case that this submissive is unaware of the relevance of the surrender and only gains some glimmer on those occasions when her partner rushes through the flogging without her having the chance to submerge herself and re-create herself within it, before he moves on to the shagging part of the scene. At these times she is left unsatisfied or incomplete. Possibly she's even frustrated because she might have been able to partially make the journey to the surrender she needed before being plucked back prematurely by her partner's cock in her cunt.

Like much in BDSM, this isn't solely the realm of the person who is done to. As we've seen earlier, penetration is one of the constants of BDSM, and a man who is surrendering to his penetration of his partner—whether this be sexual penetration, or whether it's spiritual or psychological surrender through teasing, fear-play, humiliation, or any other activity—is going to experience the same sort of frustration should his penetration be brought to an abrupt and unexpected end by either circumstances (e.g., doorbell, telephone, or unexpected orgasm), or by his partner who suddenly urges him to do something else.

As I've suggested, it can be the case that a person doesn't actually recognise what's being satisfied by the activity or relationship they have with their partner. The pink fluffy handcuffs and the always-ending-with-sex parts might help them justify in their own minds that what they're doing is not as heavy or profound as it really is, or that it's really just kinky sex. But deeper motivations may be involved and the false self may get in the way of this being acknowledged.

Play versus "deep play"

There is a relationship between the identity of the person and the type of play. Fun or recreational play can be distant from the self, perhaps being superficial, or merely entertaining. It may apply to the false self, possibly using the false self as a way of getting some limited satisfaction for the true self, but in a cloaked manner. There's not a lot at stake in this level of play.

On the other hand, "deep play" is typically addressed directly to the true self, exposing the underlying and vulnerable self. A scene addressing the false self has few consequences should it go awry, be interrupted, or otherwise fail to complete. But if a scene addressing needs of the true self fails to complete, this can lead to negative psychological consequences, or cause issues, tensions, or stresses. When tied to expectations, or built-up in anticipation of the scene, the unconsumed energy can find an outlet or manifest itself as anger or frustration.

This has some similarity with the what's at stake in Geertz's balinese cockfights. They can be just cockfights—simple vehicles for recreational gambling—but the stakes can be much higher with the identity and status of individuals, or even families, actually being in play, projected through the fighting cocks. Likewise, a BDSM play scene can just be a play scene with maybe a bit of hot sex or perhaps pleasant relaxation, or it can be addressed at something far more profound and less obvious than a simple flogging or bondage scene. Outwardly, it might not be obvious what is actually going on, but inwardly a whole personality can be being addressed, and/or reconstructed and/or re-created.

The people involved in play and "deep play" may not even be consciously aware of the differences between the two when they're engaging in "deep play", or may not be aware what internal goals or needs it satisfies. This can sometimes be apparent when a scene fails to come off and one person is irritated or frustrated more than you'd expect.

Thus, we can have a situation where the apparent goal is simply (for example) extra-hot sex but, in fact, some deeper need, or needs, is being addressed and satisfied, possibly without either participant being aware of the fact.

Work

The ideas of work and play can begin to blur when we start talking about deeper needs being met by BDSM "play". This might be particularly obvious when one of the participants is sought out by the other especially for some activity, such as may be the case with someone seeking out a professional dominatrix.

But this is less obvious when one of the participant is meeting their needs through what looks like light-and-fluffy BDSM or sex play. Their partner needs to be aware of this so that they do go through the required actions to ensure the surrender, descent, or whatever reaction is needed. This can be part of normal "play", as long as the partner is aware that there's a more serious purpose beyond the light-and-fluffy part which they themselves may be exploring. At times, for the partner, this may make it work.

Catharsis

Catharsis means "[T]he purification of the emotions by vicarious experience" [OED]. Commonly, this is the cleaning out of stress, tension, irritation, or other feelings, by working them out in some other context than the one which caused them (hence the "vicarious"). We see this with people who go for a good run along the beach at the end of a stressful day, and who might run a bit longer than usual if the day has been more stressful than usual; and amongst those who look for a good massage (or a good fuck, for that matter) to achieve the same purpose.

In BDSM we could see this catharsis being performed by a good flogging, or even by the Deep Pressure Therapy effect of some forms of bondage[4]. Indeed, we might even call this use of BDSM therapeutic. Here's a quote from Edward Anthony in his *Thy Rod and Staff - New Light on the Flagellatory Impulse*:

> *Only the actual nature of flagellation itself prevents it from being classified as a bona fide form of therapy, since so far as I can see this is as accurate a definition as any.* [ANTHONY 1995] (p. 309)

We can also see this relationship between BDSM activities and stress in DSM-IV-TR, under *Sexual Masochism* (302.83) where it says:

> *Others, however, increase the severity of the masochistic acts over time or during periods of stress...* [DSMIVTR] (p. 573)

---

4 Also called Deep Touch Pressure—see *Physiological* up ahead.

We can further see BDSM creating a context in which catharsis can occur in the words of John Warren in his *The Loving Dominant*:

> *Some submissives say they can really let go only when they have intentionally adopted a role. In effect, they create an internal psychodrama in which they are captured secret agents, molested peasant maids, or blackmailed debutantes.* [WARREN1994] (p.20)

Catharsis can be experienced in different ways. It can a quiet internal experience, or it can be a loud and emotional release accompanied by howling or sobbing. The point is: it's a release.

Recreation

The quietness, intense focus, or sub-space, experienced and sought by many BDSM practitioners is another way in which a sort of cathartic recreation can be achieved. These experiences, in a way, force the mind to take a holiday. It becomes reduced to something minimal and it is forced away from thoughts, feelings, worries, or persistent thoughts which might be preventing stress and tension from being relieved.

This is related to, and is perhaps an end result of, what I was writing about under *Minimising self* earlier. And, indeed, the friend I mentioned there is an excellent case in point. She is very bright. She is constantly reading, studying, and will endlessly debate and discuss with anyone who has a point of view they're prepared to air. In other words, she's got an overactive mind. One of the ways she can escape from the constant cerebral restlessness is through bondage. This takes her into a mental space where her mind largely shuts down and she, like many other submissives, just floats. It is her *recreation*.

Physiological

There's evidence that some BDSM activities lead to an actual productive physiological outcome, such as physical manhandling leading to relaxation. In regard to this, I'd like to look at two pieces of research which are applicable to rope bondage.

Temple Grandin is a high-functioning autistic woman. She is an expert in livestock handling facilities, and is a Professor of Animal Science at Colorado State University. In learning to deal with the problems raised by her own autism, she observed that *deep touch pressure* worked to effectively relax her.

> Deep touch pressure *is the type of surface pressure that is exerted in most types of firm touching, holding, stroking, petting of animals, or swaddling.* [GRANDIN1992]

What she is describing includes the same sort of pressure applied by snug, full-body rope bondage.

In Grandin's case she developed a machine which she called the "squeeze machine", a pneumatically-actuated device which would uniformly apply a steady pressure over her whole body. It was adjustable, and the pressure was something which she could control herself while she was in the machine. Note that because this was something which she could fully control herself, it falls outside of our definition of BDSM. But, as we'll see, we can observe the same positive results in common bondage activities.

In a bondage session where the submissive or bottom is firmly tied and "left to soak" it's common for them enter a phase of stillness which lasts 10 minutes or so, after which they become restless and it's time to do something else (like caress them, poke them, tease them, move them, or untie them). Grandin writes:

> *I learned that if pressure from the squeeze machine is applied at a steady pressure, habituation would occur and discomfort would begin within 10 to 15 minutes.* [GRANDIN1992]

Grandin appears to be describing the same sort of reaction in herself as we see in some forms of bondage.

Indeed, she goes on to write:

> *Instead, if the pressure is increased and decreased slowly, the soothing effect could be maintained for up to one and a half hours.*

And, again, this is something we can see in full-body bondage scenes: with extra input from the person doing the tying—such as changing the submissive's or bottom's position, or changing or adding to the ropes—the scene can go on much longer than in a simple "soak".

While I've been talking just about Temple Grandin and her own reactions so far, the paper from which I've been quoting is called *Calming Effects of Deep Touch Pressure in Patients with Autistic Disorder, College Students, and Animals* [GRANDIN1992]. It's a clinical paper based on research using, amongst other types of creatures, healthy college students to try out the squeeze machine. One section, called *Effects of the squeeze machine*, notes that after 5 - 10 minutes 45% of the participants described their reaction as "relaxing" or "sleep" while 10% used the words "floating," "weightless," or "flight" to describe the sensation. These are the same words which many submissives and bottoms use to describe their BDSM experiences.

In a separate study, *The Effects of Deep Pressure Touch on Anxiety*, Kirsten E. Krauss did similar work using a machine she called the "Hug'm" [KRAUSS1987]. While the design of the machine was entirely different, using levers and pulleys manipulated by the participant to control the pressure experienced rather than the pneumatics in Grandin's "squeeze machine", the results are notably similar.

In particular, as we read through the reactions of Klauss's participants, we see descriptions such as: "feeling of floating on a cloud", "floating", "floating on a raft", and "I would have liked to experience even more pressure".

From these two studies we can see that it's likely that there are physiological reactions involved in at least some forms of BDSM play.

Pretenders

There are some people who are into the symbols of BDSM rather than what they represent. That is, they want to look like they're into BDSM, either to themselves or to others, without actually being into BDSM, or while only being into BDSM in a minor way.

This can be because they're using BDSM symbols—such as black leather, shiny chains, collars, etc.—to make some sort of fashion statement; or because they're using BDSM as a symbol of rebellion—instead of wearing a conventional uniform of, say, jeans and a T-shirt, or a business suit, they choose to wear a BDSM uniform of black leather instead.

This is not to suggest that these people don't have a legitimate interest in BDSM, just that their BDSM can be a statement (fashion, political, or otherwise) as much or more than anything else.

Aligned with this, BDSM can be a symbol of liberation. Because BDSM is often associated with sex, some people think that joining the ranks of BDSM practitioners allows them to express themselves more freely in the bedroom or, at least, without feeling bound by the restraints of sexual conventionality.

Subtle

While BDSM can be "in your face", many people practice aspects of BDSM even without realising that they're doing so.

For example, as we've seen, the search for the experience of power with a partner—either being powerful or being subject to their power—is a drive in some people. They can explore this in the context of a normal, vanilla-looking relationship without the need for chains, whips, rope, needles, fire, or black leathers. It simply requires that each person express their inclinations in that direction. It doesn't need to be done in the bedroom or without clothes, and can be simply a matter of one person yielding to, and encouraging, the choices of their partner.

Failing to recognise

There appears to be little study or deeper understanding of what needs BDSM actually satisfies. This can, I think, lead to people trying to satisfy themselves with what they know, even though it might not be the best fit. For example, vanilla people who may have a need for pain, but who either don't consciously recognise it or who don't realise that there are avenues for exploring it, may end up playing with rough sex. This may partially satisfy them, but not go the whole way and so they keep looking for more and more rough sex hoping to meet their needs with it. If, instead, they had explored some variety of pain play in a BDSM context, they might have found that they could get complete satisfaction.

Likewise, the couple I mentioned in chapter 7, *Penetration*, which used electricity straight from a wall outlet to stimulate and, ultimately and unintentionally, kill the wife, would have perhaps been better served if they had discovered what BDSM can provide.

Consequences

While BDSM, or some aspects of it, remains socially and legally unacceptable, it will always be difficult to engage in it for one reason or another—be it due to the need for secrecy, or because it conflicts with religious or moral beliefs. This isn't to suggest that BDSM is a bad thing, but does indicate that there are more psychological obstacles to being able to completely enjoy it than, say, enjoying a lie down on the beach or a game of tennis.

There are, thus, consequences to pursuing BDSM. Here is how the *Diagnostic and Statistical Manual of Mental Disorders (IV)* puts it:

> *Many individuals... assert that the behavior causes them no distress and that the their only problem is social dysfunction as a result of the reaction of others to their behavior. Others report extreme guilt, shame, and depression at having to engage in an unusual sexual activity that is socially unacceptable or that they regard as immoral.*
> [DSMIVTR] (p. 567)

For the moment, this is simply how it is.

A role for self-harm

Self-harm deserves a mention here. Self-harm is where a person deliberately injures themselves or causes themselves pain. This is more common in women than men, and often takes the form of cutting one's self with a knife or razor blade. Common places to cut are the forearms, thighs, and belly.

As BDSM often involves physical pain, some questions arise about where and how self-harm might enter the BDSM picture.

For some people who would otherwise engage in self-harm, BDSM can be an alternative. I would quickly add that I think the ideal situation would be to treat the underlying cause so that the person didn't need to seek out pain at all. But where they do look for pain, and will hurt themselves if no one else will do it for them, BDSM can be a safer and more healthy alternative than self-harm. There are a couple of reasons I say this:

- Firstly, the options available to someone pathologically seeking pain, are very limited. Cutting is about the best option at causing significant pain, and when done cleanly will likely heal well.

  This is not the case with one of the other common the alternatives, namely burning, done perhaps with a cigarette lighter, matches, or a cigarette. All of these, in any case, risk infection because the skin is broken.

  When someone else is inflicting the pain, tools like whips and crops become practical, and these tend only to leave bruises—if used well—which will certainly heal, do not have the same risk of infection, and which do not involve breaking the skin.

- Secondly, self-harm is a solitary activity. There are no evenings where self-harmers get together and cut themselves with friends. They do it on their own. For someone whose self-harm behaviour is related to depression, this is a recipe for disaster because if things go awry they may bleed out and die alone.

  When pain is inflicted in a BDSM context, by definition it isn't done alone. Therefore, it's unlikely to go too far because a steadier head than the one needing the pain is regulating it. And should anything go wrong, there's someone there to assist both emotionally and medically, or to call for help.

Note that there are people who may also be unconsciously attracted to BDSM because of the safer alternative it provides to their predisposition towards self-harm.

The key word in all of this though, is *safer*. BDSM may be a safer alternative to self-inflicted harm, but the <u>safest</u> will always be no need to self-harm at all. Treatment to reach this point, if available or even possible, may take considerable time, and in the interim BDSM may be the best way to go.

11. Need

Back in the chapter on penetration (chapter 7) I quoted from a newspaper story about a couple who used electricity in their bedroom play. Unfortunately, it ended in death for the wife, but it's an important story to consider in terms of need.

The way they did it was that the husband wired his wife to an electrical outlet, and then quickly turned the power on and then off. They had done this before, he told police, with no ill effects.

Maybe there's more behind this than super-dooper orgasms. I mean, why didn't they get a Sybian (which is a commercial device to create super-dooper orgasms in women)? I suspect that the orgasm alone, or the sexual jollies, or perhaps his desire to see his wife jerking around uncontrollably, were not the only motivating factors for the husband to use such an extreme technique. Why use such a known-risky process to provide satisfaction if it were merely a desire for a rush or an orgasm? Why take such a big risk with a person's life, especially your own or your wife's?

Perhaps it was a need, and not just a want, that they were trying to satisfy. Perhaps, orgasm or not, without that intensity she couldn't feel fulfilled. And, perhaps, if they'd been better educated about the opportunities which BDSM affords, they could have met this need some other way without her dying.

So. What's a need?

I like to define *need* as something required for the well-functioning of the person. While food and drink are obvious biological needs, what about other things? If a person is being distracted by a persistent itch, and therefore unable to function at their usual high level, then scratching that itch could be defined as a need. And if that "itch" was actually a profound hunger for surrender, penetration, or pain, and the person wasn't able to think clearly for the distraction the hunger caused them, then wouldn't that be a need?

A need may be a one off, such as when you get your back out by lifting something you shouldn't have, and having to go to a chiropractor to your spine manipulated back into its usual place. Or it may be a recurring, or cyclic need, that keeps coming back, such as a hunger for food or sex.

How can you recognise something as a need?

As we've seen in the last chapter, there are many possible reasons for someone to do BDSM. And, many of the activities in which we BDSMers engage can actually provide multiple opportunities to satisfy various urges.

For example, a scene at a play party might provide an opportunity for light fun with friends, and that's the end of it. Or it might also allow something deeper where the people involved can let their primal selves out for a bit of grunting and heavy breathing in a safe environment. Or it might provide both.

Likewise, a humiliation scene might provide a simple recreational escape from self, or may provide a deep catharsis which isn't otherwise available to the person anywhere else. Or it might provide both.

We often can't tell just by looking what wants or needs are being met by particular activities. Indeed, the person concerned may not even be aware themselves which wants or needs are stirring. On top of that, the same activities may scratch different wants and needs on different occasions depending on the same person's mind set.

We can, though, get some clues about a person's BDSM wants and needs by observing the person before and after opportunities to engage in BDSM.

Two clues which we might observe prior to any BDSM engagement are:

1. Distraction. Similar to a hunger for food, a hunger for some sort of BDSM can make it hard to focus, or hard to stay focussed. Or, at least, to stay focussed on things unrelated to the BDSM want or need. For example, someone itching for a flogging may find a discussion about flogging or a display case filled with floggers to be endlessly fascinating because these brings them closer to getting their itch scratched. But the same person, in the same needy state, may have immense difficulty in talking about anything else, like what movie to go and see, what to have for dinner, or what to do during their upcoming holidays.

2. Irritation. Once the need becomes strong enough, and it's requiring significant mental effort not to let the need seriously affect other things which need to be done, the person may become irritated. This irritation might occur, for example, when the person has been devoting significant

internal effort to controlling the need, and something comes along to upset this internal balance.

Note that we might not be talking about conscious awareness of what's going on. It's entirely possible for someone to be under the influence of BDSM-satisfiable wants or needs without realising it. For example, someone with a lot of nervous energy, or who has a strong aggressive streak, may unconsciously learn through some unrelated involvement in BDSM that BDSM can provide a safe and healthy outlet for these. In this case, they may internally reorganise themselves so that BDSM becomes the primary outlet for these energies. They may become completely habituated to satisfying these needs through BDSM without even realising that it's happening.

Pre-BDSM they may have used an energetic sport, or even sex, as imperfect outlets, but after their introduction to BDSM they unconsciously discover that BDSM is better. It may even become the case that these previously effective outlets will stop working leaving BDSM as the only effective way to satisfy themselves.

As a result of all of this, someone who engages in regular BDSM play may, at times, use the play merely as something light and fun; or they may use that same play—though possibly in a more intense form—to satisfy internal needs which have arisen. We may even observe this in ourselves when we play, when sometimes we're happy with something light and easy, and at other times we really want to get into it.

One of the useful ways we can observe how profound a need is in someone, is when an opportunity to satisfy that need is missed. For example, we might consider a submissive who goes to a play party regularly with her partner who, typically, will give her a thoroughly good flogging each time they go. It becomes interesting when circumstances prevent this from happening. This might be that her dominant gets distracted by some visitor to the party, or if someone is using the dungeon all night, or if the submissive's parents unexpectedly show up and they can't go to the party at all.

We may see that the submissive has been working herself up in preparation for a longed-for engagement with her partner, and then it doesn't happen. This mental preparation may not be solely conscious. If there are drives and needs active which the unconscious usually deals with, then the frustration of this expected satisfaction can make its appearance in a number of ways. The submissive may become intensely disappointed, angry, snappy, irritated, or act out, without fully being aware of why.

Where a lot was at stake in the expected BDSM play, then there will be observable reactions—usually of the pissed-off variety. Where there are no needs at stake, just wants and pleasures instead, then the missed opportunity for play can be easily brushed off and, while there might be mild disappointment, anger and irritation don't make an appearance.

Importantly, when there are unconscious needs stirring, and these don't get met during some expected BDSM scene, then it's likely the unconscious will then start to take matters into its own hands in some way, especially if no other BDSM play is on the horizon. This *sublimation* may take some safe outlet, such as an urge to go for a long run. But for someone who has an inclination towards self-harm—which they normally dissipate or satisfy through safe BDSM means—it could mean a self-cutting exercise results.

Satisfying need

As I said above, many BDSM activities may at one time simply be fun, while at another time exactly the same activities may be a means to satisfy a deep need. Often, unless it's you we're talking about (and, sometimes, not even then), you can't easily tell.

When your partner isn't fully aware of when their own needs stir, then experience with your partner using the observations I've made above can give you some good clues about what's happening.

When it's not you whose needs we're talking about, then there's often not a whole lot you need to do specially. Play more-or-less as normal, but keep in mind that something important is at stake. It does pay to ensure that distractions (and visits from parents) don't occur, so that the need can properly, completely, and safely, be satisfied. The important thing is to provide your partner with the opportunity to experience profoundly whatever it is that you do with them. They need to begin and work through the process that satisfies their particular needs.

Five phases

As it may play out just the same as any other scene, albeit with perhaps more focus and intensity, I'd like to briefly mention the five phases that this needs-meeting process can go through:

1. Preparation: creating the context, creating expectation. It's worth noting, as I've mentioned, that this phase can be days or weeks long, such as where a person is looking forward to a play party where they expect their needs to be met.

2. Descent: when the actual scene activities begin. There can be two sub-phases here:

   a) resistance,

   b) surrender.

3. Resolution: this is where the need is resolved or satisfied. It often requires a soaking period, however short, where the person—having descended—

stays down for a time. At this point whatever was done to get them through the descent may need to be stopped, or be dramatically slowed. They may also need to feel that they're not alone—such as through physical contact, e.g., a hand kept on their shoulder, or through noises that reassure them that someone's nearby—without necessarily being distracted by needing to interact with their partner (such as needing to answer questions, follow instructions, etc.)

4. Recovery, reclamation: this is where they come out of the state of mind where they found resolution. They may do this on their own, or they may require some different form of stimulation to what took them through the descent to reverse the process.

5. Post-process physical, mental, and spiritual rebuilding: this can be a time where they re-orient themselves to a world where a major need, which was intense and distracting perhaps only fifteen minutes beforehand, is now suddenly gone. This can involve a major change in perception.

At the same time, psychological or spiritual doors which were opened to let the process occur, may need to be closed again. This phase can also stretch to days or weeks.

None of the above phases should be cut short or rushed, as this can lead to the need only partially being satisfied, or may lead to the person not being fully recovered/reclaimed. This can be worse than not going through the process at all because while the person may have strategies and techniques for managing themselves when they're waiting for their need to be met, they may not have any such strategies for when it has been only partially met, or when an attempt to meet it has failed or been frustrated.

While it might look like the three middle phases— descent (2), resolution (3), and recovery (4)—are the important ones, the first and last phases can be equally, or even more important than the other three. In particular, the preparation (1) phase, where expectation is created, often sets things up in the person's mind so that the rest can smoothly and easily fall into place. Without this initial set up the rest of the process may have no useful effect.

In other words, if your partner is in need of, say, a flogging, and is anticipating and expecting one at an upcoming a play party a week or so hence, and you decide to suddenly give them their flogging early without warning them, then it might not have any useful effect because they didn't have the time to build up the mindset for the flogging to work at a deep level. They still might enjoy it, but it may not scratch the deeper itch.

It's worth noting that during the descent (2), resolution (3), and recovery (4) phases, the person may experience a limited ability to interact with their partner. It can be, and often is, worthwhile to come up with a system of signals, akin to what can be used as safewords, but which instead help the partner provide what's needed to reach any of the phases I mentioned above. Such signals might indicate, for example:

- Faster,
- Harder,
- Change implement,
- Leave me to soak for the moment,
- I am ready for recovery, and
- I have recovered. Now I just need to be quiet for a bit.

Health concerns

In the early part of their lives—in childhood, adolescence, and even early adulthood—people who later use BDSM activities as tools for catharsis or resolution find alternate ways of satisfying their needs. They may engage in heavy sporting activities such as marathons or martial arts; self-harming activities like cutting or substance abuse; meditation, long walks, sublimation through sex or chocolate, etc.

Later, when they do discover BDSM, they may find that instead of being merely adequate—like their earlier solutions—that BDSM is a better or safer fit than what they were doing before, and that their needs can be addressed and satisfied neatly and efficiently through BDSM.

Up to this point, this can be a very healthy outcome. But it can have a down-side.

For example, over a longer period, the person may find that they associate the satisfaction of their need, or their catharsis, or their resolution, with the BDSM context, such as being *in collar*, and/or with the BDSM activities they use. Indeed, this association may become so strong that the person is unable to achieve satisfaction without the BDSM component.

Put another way, the person may become so used to being satisfied in one BDSM context that it becomes unimaginable, difficult, or impossible to satisfy in any other.

This *may* be OK, particularly if the BDSM context which works for them is one which is readily available—such as a heavy flogging.

However, this may become not OK when the context is tied to one person—e.g., one particular dominant, or to one obscure BDSM activity in which few are expert. When this person is no longer available, or the BDSM activity is not available, the person may end up:

1. Being compelled by their need to play with whoever is available—i.e., non-ideal partners—in a desperate attempt to get the need met, or

2. Being compelled to find an alternate, and possibly unhealthy, solution, such self-harm, drugs, etc.

It's worth remembering is that if the person has completely adapted to being satisfied in one BDSM situation or through one particular partner, then strategies which worked previous to BDSM may not work any more. For example, a long run—no matter how hard—may not dispel the need any more; or cutting—no matter how deep or how much blood is released—may no longer work.

It's not just subbies

Throughout this chapter I have been careful <u>not</u> to say that it's only submissives, slaves or bottoms, who may experience needs which can be satisfied through BDSM. Dominants, masters and tops, can have their own needs which are best met through BDSM activities with their partners.

Flogging is a good example where we might be tempted to focus on the submissive who is being flogged as the one who goes through a process of need satisfaction. We must not forget that their partner, their dominant, is also possibly going through an intense psychological and physical experience with their partner. If they, the dominant, seek out partners into heavy pain, then it may be that the intensity and physical exertion is part of what they themselves need. They may also experience the same symptoms I've listed above when their needs aren't met if, for example, their partner has an injury which prevents play.

Flogging isn't the only example of where the dominant or top may get needs resolved. Less tangible needs—such as to dominate or control—may, from time to time, be met within the activities they engage in with their partners.

12. Surrender and anchors

Before BDSM can "work" for someone, they have to be in a receptive state of mind. As I reported in chapter 10, *Motivations*, Nicola Abel-Hirsch wrote in her *The perversion of pain, pleasure and thought* [ABELHIRSCH2006] about how some people can just feel pain—and grin and bear it, compared to how some people take the pain into themselves and construct a useful experience out of it—such as catharsis, or sub-space.

This difference is important in all areas of BDSM. The nature of BDSM activities is that they are, at base, difficult, confronting, painful, or uncomfortable. This may not be obvious to the experienced BDSMer because many BDSM practitioners have long-since learned how to automatically make those experiences pleasurable or satisfying. For example, being ordered around by her dominant may be a submissive's greatest joy, but that same ordering around by anyone else is going to be offensive, and when required by, say, a policeman, is going to be uncomfortable and an intrusion. Likewise, few schoolchildren relish the idea of a cane being taken to their rear ends, but once involved in BDSM, and having learned how to make the appropriate mental switch, a good caning can be something to genuinely look forward to.

The difference between the pleasure and the discomfort has to do with state of mind, and to get into a state of mind where BDSM is a pleasure or satisfaction, rather than pain or a burden, requires *surrender*. It's like a metaphorical sphincter where if you tense your muscles the penetration really is going to be unpleasant and hurty-hurty-type painful, whereas if you relax those sphincter muscles and let it happen, it'll be much more of a pleasure for all concerned.

There's that word "penetration" again. Be it a flogging or caning, a humiliation, a master/slave engagement, or a bondage scene, the conversion of the external physical activities into internal satisfaction and pleasure happens when there's a surrender allowing the penetration to occur. Without the surrender—i.e., when the sphincter remains firmly and irresistibly shut—then the pleasure, satisfaction, or the mental processes required to satisfy need, will remain shut out and simply won't happen.

Masochism is always a topic near at hand when talking about BDSM. As we've seen, the fact that pain or discomfort are sought as part of BDSM doesn't mean that they are the end-of-the-line, as they would be for a true masochist, but are instead a way-point, or doorway, past which something much greater, and possibly self-transforming is found. It's interesting to note that for someone who doesn't go through the process of surrender, then the pain and discomfort *do* become the end-of-the-line without the other jolly bits. Surprisingly, many BDSM people choose this latter.

Emmanuel Ghent, in his *Masochism, Surrender, Submission - Masochism as a Perversion of Surrender* [GHENT1990], wrote exactly about this. A little unfortunately he uses the word "submission" in the sense of abandoning attempts to succeed or giving up which tends to conflict with the common BDSM usage of "submission", which is more like surrender. Or, to put it another way, he writes of submission as involving endurance of pain, whereas surrender is the embracing and transforming of it, this latter being closer to what happens ideally in BDSM. (See also my discussion about *Transformation of pain into pleasure* back in chapter 10, *Motivations*)

In regards to surrender Ghent he writes that:

> It may be accompanied by... clarity, relief, even ecstasy. [GHENT1990] (p. 111)

As a whole, Ghent writes in psychoanalytical terms about surrender, and thus writes about what happens to an individual in isolation. We BDSMers now know that the BDSM-flavour of surrender occurs in the context of an *Other*, be this *Other* our partner or just circumstance (such as time, as mentioned in chapter 6, *The Other*). In John Warren's book, *The Loving Dominant*, we can find something similar to Ghent's idea extended to where it applies to couples. Warren includes in his book the "levels of submission" of Libby, a submissive woman [WARREN1994] (pp. 53 - 54). She writes in the context of exploring BDSM with a dominant, and talks about about three levels of submission, which are:

- Fantasy,
- Clarity, and
- Transparency.

It's noteworthy that both Ghent and Libby use the word "clarity" in regards to surrender, and it's clear from Libby's writing that both her *clarity* and *transparency* involve internal surrender—i.e., surrender within herself to her own feelings and nature, though externally this surrender is qualified by the level of trust the submissive has in her dominant.

Libby's *fantasy* is the equivalent of Ghent's *submission*. This is where the ideas are there, the desire is there, and perhaps the person is even going through the motions, but without the surrender which makes the experience complete.

Ghent notes that *submission*—i.e., doing BDSM with the metaphorical sphincter closed:

> *is the ever available lookalike to surrender. It holds out the promise, seduces, excites, enslaves, and in the end, cheats the seeker-turned-victim out of his cherished goal, offering in its place only the security of bondage and an ever amplified sense of futility. By substituting the appearance and trappings of surrender for the authentic experience, an agonizing, though at times temporarily exciting, masquerade of surrender occurs...*[GHENT1990] (pp. 115 - 116)

Anchors (and masochism)

One of the things we can often see in BDSM is partial surrender. As I discussed in chapter 10, *Motivations*, any single BDSM adventure can be rewarding or satisfying in a number of ways all at the same time. For example, a cutting scene may—and often does—involve multiple rewards for the participants such as:

1. The cutting itself involves a form of physical penetration,

2. The person doing the cutting will almost certainly take on some form of authority in regards to the scene, directing how their partner should lie, deciding what designs to use, regulating the pace, etc., thus giving both the experience of power being used, and

3. The person being cut may be tied to a bench, or restrained in some way, thus giving them a physiological reward (refer to chapter 10, *Motivations* for details on this).

However, each of these, to be experienced productively and fully, requires surrender. If, for example, our submissive doesn't like the bondage side—i.e., being tied to a bench—but recognises it as a necessity to prevent unnecessary and possibly dangerous wriggling on her part, then the scene may still be satisfying and enjoyable because of the remaining two pleasures. It does mean though that she:

1. Surrenders to, and embraces, the experience of being cut (sphincter open),

2. Surrenders to, and embraces, the feelings of power being asserted over her by her partner (sphincter open),

3. But she merely submits to (in Ghent's meaning of the word), or endures, the ropes tying her to the bench (sphincter closed).

The title of this little section of the current chapter is called *Anchors*, and this is the term I use to describe those things which hold us back from surrender when the opportunity presents itself.

In the cutting example above, our submissive doesn't surrender to being restrained, but merely endures it to get the other benefits and pleasures that particular scene with her partner offers. I said that she "doesn't like bondage", but this is often too simple a phrase. Perhaps it is the case that she lacks sufficient trust in her partner (or herself) to feel completely comfortable being defenceless. This lack of trust is an anchor which prevents surrender. Surrender can be like a doorway, and once you've stepped through that doorway there may be no turning back.

The famous guy thing—i.e., fear of commitment—is a flavour of this, and while other pleasures may be explored in the general area of the doorway, the fact that the doorway is not passed creates the masochism which Ghent writes about—namely the real masochism of inflicting pain on one's self by not stepping through the doorway—such as the masochism of enduring the restraint or rope without embracing it. In the current example, the lack of trust is the anchor which prevents the girl stepping through the doorway of surrender to the ropes and restraint.

There are many anchors in common use in BDSM today. Some are obvious, some are subtle. Many times the anchors aren't even conscious. I'd like to look at a few anchors here.

Scheduled obstacles

Starting some BDSM activity, or allowing it to start, knowing that something is going to come along which will interrupt it, is an excellent anchor. For example, a submissive visiting her master's home an hour before his kids come home from school is an excellent way to allow something to happen, but to also ensure that it won't go too far. Compare this to the same submissive arriving at her master's home on a Friday evening knowing that there'll be no interruption all weekend until he has to go to work on Monday.

The fact of kids coming home is a planned obstacle. Although she might not actually think about it consciously, and may actually think that she's got an hour to get something going with her master, the fact that there's a ready-made interruption which will arrive on schedule can be a great way of creating a limited BDSM environment in which she can actually relax and surrender partially, but know that no matter how much she surrenders, that it's going to end soon anyway. This is very different to the state of mind—and extent of surrender—which may occur in an all-weekend get-together.

Likewise, play at a party can have a limit on time, e.g., the party may be scheduled to end at 3:00AM; or may a limit on what can be done, e.g., one partner might not like fucking with others present and, thus, no fucking is going to occur; or there may be people to talk to and socialise with, and thus nothing "heavy" or intense can get started.

Limited partner

A different sort of planned obstacle is picking a partner who has some form of limitation. Chatting up a top at a party who has his right arm in a sling and who can only flog with his left, can be a good choice if you're after a flogging, but not one that's too intense. You can give yourself up to the experience as much as you like, but you'll know that there's definitely a limit that your evening's chosen one can't reach.

An interesting and clever anchor is where the dominant is typically male, and where the submissive—who consciously or unconsciously realises that she is approaching a doorway that she doesn't want to enter—may suddenly get the urge to perform oral sex on her dominant. Bingo! Problem solved! He'll no longer be focussing his domly attentions on her, and she gets a chance to relax and pull back from that particular doorway, all the while perhaps still satisfying other BDSM needs or desires. She may not even be aware of why she's suddenly overwhelmed with the urge to suck cock. In all likelihood he won't complain.

In the longer term, picking a partner who has some other form of limitation, such as picking a dominant who is physically unfit or significantly overweight, is another way of ensuring that there's an anchor in place which will prevent some areas of BDSM being approached too closely. For example, a dominant who is physically quite unfit will often have to abandon some physical aspects of their relationship, or heavily depend on his partner for them. This presents the submissive with an ideal environment to ensure some things are avoided when she's not ready for them.

Similarly, a submissive who chooses a dominant who is not as clever or intelligent as she is creates the opportunities for her to consciously or unconsciously manipulate how scenes or the relationship develop, and permit her to avoid areas in which she doesn't want to go. At the same time, she may be able to consciously or unconsciously out-think him and thereby limit any control or power he may try to assert over her.

This sort of limitation goes both ways. While it might seem that picking a partner who is *more* intelligent than one's self is not a limitation, for a dominant who doesn't consciously or unconsciously want to go too close to areas of authority or control— i.e., who for some reason isn't keen on the D&s aspects of BDSM—choosing a bright submissive may be a way of ensuring that doesn't happen. In other words, when she's smarter than he is, she'll always stay one or two steps ahead of him and, thus, he can't ever be in full control.

Anchors of choice

So far I've mostly been talking about anchors which are external to the person, such as anchors which have to do with time or opportunity, or to do with limitations of one's self or one's partner. There are also internal anchors.

The not-surrendering-to-restraint in the cutting example above is a case in point. While it might not have been a conscious choice, where the submissive has the opportunity to surrender but fails to do so because of some internal choice or fear, she is using an internal anchor to prevent surrender.

There may be many reasons for such an *anchor of choice*. Fear is always at the top of the list of likely reasons and can be:

- Lack of trust in the partner. Therefore something needs to be held back in case the partner slips up or proves themselves to lack the necessary competency, or

- Lack of trust in self. This is when the person is afraid of how they themselves will react or change if they do surrender. This may even have something to do with a part of themselves that they have for a long time kept bottled up and are now afraid to release. Passion or intensity within themselves that they have no experience at controlling may be part of this.

Anchors which aren't a bad thing

Anchors aren't always a bad thing. Such as on ships that don't want to drift too far, anchors can help someone who has, for example, a deep and powerful need to surrender in some way, from surrendering too early in their relationship with their partner.

In this case it can be an entirely responsible way to manage what goes on for them. Instead of struggling to maintain self-control (which, as we've seen, can be a form of masochism in itself), they can create the anchors which both limit what can go on internally to them, and what can go on between them and their new partner. Then they gradually lengthen the chain as they become more comfortable, until the chain is cut altogether and full surrender can be safely achieved.

The above is, of course, the ideal. In real life some anchors may need to remain. This can happen when there is something external to the two people involved which needs to be protected. For example, one person may see that some particular aspect of BDSM presents a threat to some part of their lives. For example, they may see a need to function fully autonomously in some other areas of their lives and that their D&s inclinations seem to risk this. Or, they may have children and feel the need to keep their BDSM light so that it doesn't have a chance to infringe on their children's development.

13. Health concerns

Risk

BDSM is often a risky activity. In fact, the risk can be part of the attraction.

We can look at something risky as being inherently penetrative. Firstly, and by definition we must open ourselves up to the risk. Secondly, once we are open to it, we ride the thrill or fear of being penetrated by the consequences of what we engage in.

Riding the ragged edge

In terms of physical risk, many of the dangers involving BDSM are self-evident, and riding the ragged edge of accident or disaster is part of the excitement for some BDSM players.

In normal, everyday life, we naturally and automatically avoid many of the risks to which we're exposed before they even become risks. For example, if we're walking along the street and a trash bin up ahead is on fire, we don't wait until the heat becomes painful before we change our direction and steer a wide berth around the bin. Even if an unexpected gust of wind blows some burning debris in our direction, we have already automatically literally taken steps to avoid this causing us physical harm.

In BDSM instead, many of the activities deliberately put us in risky situations. With fireplay, for example (see chapter 2, *Survey of physical activities*), we deliberately set out to have fire as close to our skin as we can get it. In such a situation, it's hard to get out of the way should something go wrong—the margin for safety is very slim.

Likewise, when done well vaginal stretching can be very exciting and completely safe, but as the important thing is often pushing the limits, rather than just approaching a known-safe limit, there's the imminent risk of tearing, and once it starts the damage is done.

Not focused enough to notice

While in, say, a doctor's surgery, all attention might be paid to doing vaginal poking without taking any chances, and with an intent focus on what's happening in case things start to go wrong, in BDSM the focus of the participants is not always 100% on picking up when things start to go awry.

As we know, BDSM is sometimes characterised by emotional, psychological, physical, or spiritual reactions—such as detachment or euphoria—which can make it it difficult or impossible for someone to be able to actually recognise when physical harm is occurring. Permanent damage may occur without them even realising it.

Sub-space, for example, turns the focus of the person experiencing it strongly away from their own physical well-being and awareness of what might be genuinely harming them, and turns it inwards to their own emotional and psychological experience. Indeed, combined with the flow of neuro-chemicals and other intense experiences being thrown at them by their partner, they may not even be aware when something seriously bad is happening to them.

Similarly, and because a BDSM scene is a shared experience, the top, dominant, or master involved is likely to also be spending some of his focus on his own pleasure and satisfaction, rather than on the well-being of himself and his partner.

While manageable, this issue of focus is one which can and does add to the risk involved in BDSM.

Physical health concerns

Clamps

Clamps, like nipple and labial clamps, shouldn't be left attached for very long. Most practitioners advise that 15-20 minutes is about the maximum.

Because they squeeze the skin fairly tightly, they block the flow of blood—specifically to the the skin they squeeze, but also to the surrounding tissue—and when left in place can lead to permanent damage to nerves and flesh. As nipples and cunt lips can be sources of great pleasure, rendering them permanently numb is probably not a good outcome.

Infection

Some BDSM-related activities—like flogging, caning or whipping—may lead to skin being broken. Skin abrasion can occur during bondage. And the whole of point of some other BDSM activities—such as piercing or cutting—is to break or pierce the skin. In all these cases, infection is a real possibility.

This risk is usually managed by keeping the implements used, such as knives, well-sterilised; by using only new, factory-sealed hypodermic needle tips; by the use of latex gloves; and by the generous application of antiseptic to any affected areas of the body both before and after the fact.

Some activities, particularly those relating to something sexual, might cause the exchange of fluid involving most bodily orifices. Infection is a potential risk here too, notably between casual partners. Condoms and other safe-sex practices are used to manage these risks.

While branding is uncommon, if done poorly it can lead to third-degree burns, major infections, disfigurement, and severe nerve damage.

Nerve damage

Nerves are usually not too vulnerable, though there are circumstances in which they can be temporarily or permanently damaged. The typical outcome of this is numbness or loss of feeling. Alternatively, damage to nerves in the knee, elbow, or shoulder joints through poorly aimed floggings or badly applied bondage, can render hands or feet partially or completely kaput.

Ropes themselves are fairly innocuous most of the time, but the knots used to tie them can cause big problems, particularly when applied for a long period of time. Knots can press into joints, or against veins and arteries, or into nerve bundles located in different parts of the body, and cause damage.

Nerves can also be damaged by needles/piercing or knives/cutting. As the idea with both of these activities is to penetrate the skin, unlucky nerves might get hit and damaged.

Poorly aimed blows with a whip or flogger can also cause nerve damage, particularly if there are repeated hits on a vulnerable nerve bundle or on a joint.

Circulation

As mentioned above in regard to clamps, blood circulation can be affected by BDSM activities. This can also occur in tight rope bondage, particularly where the upper arms or thighs are tightly bound. It may not be apparent straight away that there is a blood flow problem, but this can be checked by occasionally feeling the temperature of the hands and feet to make sure they're warm, and ropes should never be tied so tight that a finger or two can't be slipped under them.

Keeping someone tied in the same position for long periods of time can also cause blood circulation problems akin to the airline traveller's problem of DVT (Deep Vein Thrombosis). DVT is the forming of blood clots in veins, and is usually due to blood flow being restricted due to pressure. Bums and upper thighs are common locations for this when sitting in the same position for extended periods of time. Regularly moving or shifting the position of someone in bondage can ameliorate this risk.

Another circulation problem is where someone who is standing, and who may have their hands tied above their head, say to a hook or to a flogging frame of some sort, can become faint or light-headed, and then pass out.

Impact in the wrong place

Using whips, floggers and canes on the human body can be jolly good fun, but impact can cause injury or permanent damage if done poorly, or if the wrong part of the body is hit.

Apart from obviously poor choices of target, such as anywhere around the head or neck, there are some soft and vulnerable bits between the bottom of the rib cage and the hips. The liver and other fairly vital organs are around here and this part of the anatomy should never be a target. Potentially there can be internal bruising or actual damage/scarring to the organs.

Breasts can be an endless source of pleasure for some, but there is evidence that deep impacts can lead to cysts or breast cancer.

The best targets for whips and floggers tend to be the upper back (avoiding the neck), the buttocks, and upper thighs.

Burns

Friction burns can be caused by pulling a rope too quickly across someone's anatomy in the process of tying or untying them.

Burns can also come from fireplay. Done well, fireplay involves setting fire to flammable vapour *above* the skin. Done poorly means flames make contact with the skin, or can mean setting chest hair on fire. Using the wrong liquid (i.e., one that burns in its liquid state) can cause flesh to burn, or practising fireplay on someone who is standing up can mean getting flames in a person's eyes, or in their face where they can inhale them.

Branding, of course, involves intentional burns. But using a brand which is too hot or too heavy, or applying the brand for too long, can lead to deep or third-degree burns. Infection enters the picture here, as does possible permanent nerve damage.

Waxing can also cause burns if the wax is dropped from too-low a height, not giving it a chance to cool sufficiently before reaching the submissive's skin, or if a candle made of the wrong sort of wax is used.

Finally, a violet wand can cause burns like sunburn on the parts of the body where the wand was used. These can take a day or to to appear to their full extent. Extreme or extended use of a violet wand can cause severe burns. Note that this can also apply to internal use of the wand, such as in a cunt.

Suffocation and overheating

Suffocation, leading to death, can occur with very tight bondage with rope, or with leather or elastic bonds, or when using cling wrap. They can be so tight so as to hinder or prevent someone breathing (i.e., stopping them expanding their lungs to draw in air) even though their mouth and nose might be clear. Also at risk is someone with a cold or flu, or someone who is asthmatic.

Note that the characteristics of some materials (such as leather) can change when they become wet. So, for example, someone who is easily able to breathe while bound at the start of a scene, may find it more and more difficult as they sweat and the ties which bind them become wet and shrink.

The risks from strangulation, from plastic bags over the head and so on, should be apparent.

Overheating can occur when someone is enclosed in bondage. Cling wrap is a particular concern here because the person so enclosed can't regulate their body temperature by sweating, and they won't experience an cooling by air blowing past them due to the insulation effect of the plastic. Thus the two main ways in which they cool themselves are rendered ineffective.

Unconsciousness and comas

Passing out, losing consciousness, and even comas, can be consequences of some forms of BDSM play. I've already mentioned that fainting can occur during some forms of bondage. Losing consciousness due to lack of air is clearly a possibility during breathplay, and a prolonged ice-water enema can lead to a coma by drastically decreasing blood temperature. Obviously, none of these are good.

Infertility

Damaging the testicles, such as by extended periods with circulation limited by tight bondage, or caused by impact play—such as with whips, floggers or canes, can lead to decreased or no fertility.

Vein or artery damage, or nerve damage, can lead to problems achieving erection.

Gags

Gags must be used cautiously, particularly if they penetrate deep into the mouth or throat. Someone with a cold, or who has an allergic reaction during the scene, might become unable to breathe. Someone who vomits (maybe because of the penetrating gag or some other reason), might inhale vomit and begin to suffocate.

Psychological health concerns

While BDSM psychological activities don't generally carry risks of infection, bruising, broken limbs, or nerve damage—which can all occur as a result of some physical BDSM activities—there are still things which can go astray.

Panic

Someone who is blindfolded, or who is involved in some new activity which they've never done before, or who is doing something which triggers unpleasant memories, or who becomes sick during the course of a scene, or who may have an unexpected bout of claustrophobia, might begin to panic. Particularly if they're bound, they need to be released and the scene ended as quickly as possible.

Enabling unproductive behaviour

One of the biggest categories of "astray-ness" is where someone who is not firing on all cylinders finds some BDSM activity or group which allows them to exercise some not-entirely-appropriate ideas under the guise of legitimate BDSM behaviour.

For example, a woman who hates men might look for men who like to be physically trampled and walked upon. While the guys might get their rocks off while she's doing this, the woman herself is reinforcing her own unhealthy way of interacting with men. She might even be able to convince herself that she's doing it for the guys and to make them feel good, but it's still unhealthy for her.

The wacky world of BDSM can provide contexts, situations, and relationships in which one person can be behaving in a psychologically unhealthy way without necessarily having any negative consequences for their partner. Through the rest of this section, and throughout the rest of this book—particularly in chapter 22, *Abuse*—I'll be looking at more of these types of behaviour.

Perpetuating abuse of self

Where someone has a poor self-image or low esteem, particularly where this sort of belief has been instilled in them by abusive partners or family, they may look for BDSM-type activities to reinforce this when their original abuser is gone. Like a woman who is abused by her husband, the abuse can be something which the person is familiar with, and to which they've adapted as part of their feelings of inferiority.

Where the original abuse was emotional, psychological, or verbal, being insulted or humiliated in a BDSM context can be a comfortable and familiar experience for them. Likewise, where someone was abused physically, BDSM activities like caning, flogging, or being caged, can be like coming home.

This is not healthy of course, because this is all causing the original abuse to be replayed and continued into and beyond the present. More than this, the abuse is being done by a usually unaware and non-consenting partner. Even the person themselves may not be aware of what they're doing to themselves.

While we commonly consider abuse in terms of the person who is on the receiving end of the abusive behaviour, the person committing the abuse is also a victim in the sense that their abusive behaviour can be reinforced by what they do, such as in the example of the "trampling woman" mentioned above. The *Diagnostic and Statistical Manual of Mental Disorders* by the American Psychiatric Association notes:

> *When Sexual Sadism is practiced with nonconsenting partners, the activity is likely to be repeated until the person with Sexual Sadism is apprehended.* [DSMIVTR] (302.84) (p. 573)

And it's important that in this regard *consent* refers not just to what physically happens, but also to the intent of what is happening. If a guy thinks that a woman is trampling him because she's turned on by it, then his experience will be entirely different than if he thinks she is doing it because she hates men and wants to really hurt him. The physical aspect of it may be the same in both cases, but he may well consent to it only because he thinks she's being turned on. He may in fact baulk if he thinks that she is genuinely a man-hater. If she does trample him while allowing him to believe that she is getting turned on, then he is actually a non-consenting partner, having agreed to the activity under her false pretences.

Depersonalisation and derealisation

As we've seen, there can be a significant aspect of identity management and even identity manipulation in BDSM. For someone predisposed towards a dissociative psychological disorder—that is, loosely defined, a disorder where they start to lose touch with themselves or the world—it's possible that the identity manipulation engaged in as part of BDSM activities may contribute to dissociative episodes.

Some BDSM activities, particular the longer-term ones where, for example, a submissive or slave enters into a service-based relationship with their partner or master, can involved elements of depersonalisation or derealisation. Depersonalisation is where the person feels detached or distant from themselves. Derealisation is where the person feels detached or distant from reality—such as where they feel that everything around them is unreal, for example.

We can see that immersive BDSM activities—such as where a slave or a submissive is given a new name, must behave or speak in rigid and unfamiliar ways, must refer to themselves in the third-person, and so on, are going to create a distance between their behaviour and what they normally think of as as themselves. This can be ideal for creating depersonalisation in particular.

As we've seen above, many activities deliberately involve an element of diminishing of self. For example, humiliation attempts to push down or suppress some aspects of someone's self, and ritualised service deliberately imposes behaviour on the submissive or slave which they wouldn't do outside of the relationship, and also disallows behaviour which is an expression of the slave's self.

All of this is a process of disabling or suppressing some aspects of the personality of the slave or submissive. I hasten to say that this isn't necessarily a bad thing because the time during which aspects of the personality are turned off can be a good time for recreation. We saw this in chapter 10, *Motivations*. But when this is engaged in long-term, the submissive or slave may start to see themselves solely in these restrictive terms.

This sort of situation can arise, for example, when the person is required to be "in role" 24/7, regardless of what she's doing. This can be the case if she is a stay-at-home slave where her partner and their friends are all into BDSM, and they all encourage or require her to be "in role" 24/7.

Derealisation is similar in that it involves a restricted or shrunken perspective. A depersonalised slave sees herself in terms of the limited personality which she is allowed (by her master or by herself) to express. Derealisation is a shrunken perspective, but this time it is of the world itself, or or what she is allowed to see of it.

This latter doesn't mean that she's locked in a box with only a tiny slit through which to look out upon the world, but instead can be where she is not allowed to make major choices (and must pass them on for her master to make), such as what to spend money on, what to wear, where to go on holidays, what to do in her career, who to socialise with, etc. Rather than see herself as small, by taking choices away from her which have to do with the larger world, she consequently comes to see it in smaller or different terms and as less real than it is. In other words, because she is allowed to interact with it less (in terms of decisions and choices) it becomes less tangible to her and she feels less connection to it.

In both these circumstances—depersonalisation and derealisation—over the long-term the person subject to these situations may lose the skill (through lack of practice) of either dealing with herself as a full and whole person, or to effectively and competently interact with the world as an independent individual.

When this happens, it may be necessary for the submissive or slave to go through a form of exit phase or exit training as she is leaving the environment. This should confront her with the fullness of herself and the world and give her opportunities to re-develop the skills to effectively deal with both.

Depersonalisation and derealisation can be valid BDSM goals, and can be useful, productive, and satisfying in the right context. But, like any other profound experiences—in BDSM or not—they can also be harmful.

I'd like to add that it's not only the submissive or slave who is prone to depersonalisation or derealisation. It may well be the case that a master or dominant who is constantly "in role" also experiences these same things. Where a submissive or slave might need to learn to be independent and assertive as they leave such a situation, a master might need to learn to not be so bossy.

Annihilation

When I was talking about humiliation in chapter 3, *Survey of psychological activities*, I also briefly discussed annihilation. Humiliation and other BDSM activities can focus on piercing or collapsing a person's own sense of self. When this is done, they can feel and be extremely vulnerable to their partner, particularly because their own sense of self—and, therefore, their own set of reference points for forming value judgements—are crippled.

This is a good thing from the point of view of *penetration*, but may not be a good thing where the person concerned is not robust enough to reclaim their sense of self at the end of the scene, or if they have a predisposition towards feeling inferior and thus use BDSM as a support to *enable* themselves to have ongoing feelings of non-existence or inferiority.

Similarly, they or their partner may not be aware enough to realise when something is going seriously astray, and might see what they are doing and experiencing together as just "really intense".

Dom's disease (also known as top's disease)

Dom's disease is something that's not exclusive to the BDSM world, but BDSM provides unique opportunities for it develop to excess.

It is a form of arrogance. It's a conviction that what you believe or invent is the absolute truth. As BDSM often occurs in private or in relatively small groups, there's little opportunity for what one person says or believes to be definitively debunked because small groups rarely include a definitive expert. Thus, if a person comes up with an idea or theory about BDSM, and if they're very assertive or outspoken about it, then it's likely to be accepted.

Also, in a small group it's possible to build a mini-empire or kingdom, and by manipulating who joins the group, a loud or strong member can be sure that their way is "the right way" because anyone who might say that it isn't is cast out. This forced biasing need not be deliberate. Someone might genuinely believe that what they think is the true and right way, and might see anyone who thinks different as harmful to their group and as someone who needs to be defended against.

It's called *dom's disease* because dominants and masters are particularly exposed to this ailment by their submissives' or slaves' inclination towards worshipping them and needing them to be right. That is, for a submissive or slave to most readily yield to the influence of their master or dominant, they need to have confidence in their master's ability and skill. As this is a *need* for many submissives and slaves, they have a consequent predisposition towards *needing* their master or dominant to be right all the time (thus ensuring confidence in them). Thus they'll readily give their master or dominant any possibly benefit of doubt. So, if master says something and there's even the remotest possibility that it's true, then for them it is true.

Example

Many years I attended a BDSM conference where a well-known and respected BDSM master presented a demonstration of fireplay as part of the planned programme. I mentioned this particular activity in chapter 2, *Survey of physical activities*. It's where a volatile liquid is poured on a submissive and then the vapour is lit. The liquid itself doesn't burn, but its vapour does, and so the submissive experiences some heat and the appearance of being on fire. The psychological effect is quite powerful.

For his demonstration, this master had his submissive sitting up. He poured the liquid on her chest and then lit it. Not surprisingly the flames reached up towards her face. This is not safe, as it can cause damage to the eyes or the flames can be inhaled. The master was quickly taken to task by more experienced masters in the audience who urged him to quickly put out the flames, and who then pointed out how unsafe his technique was.

The point here is that this master had learned about fireplay in a small community where there was no one who knew better. He had done it his way numerous times without bad consequences, had had good results with a small number of submissives, and so had come to believe that he was doing it the right way. This belief was so strong that he was quite ready to demonstrate this "skill" and teach it to others, many of whom he knew to have at least as much experience as he.

Shrinking the self

Baumeister and Boden's *Shrinking the Self* is a journal article to which I've already referred, and one part of it has particular bearing on the subject of health concerns in BDSM.

The purpose of many BDSM activities is specifically to distract the participants from the world-at-large and cause them to focus tightly on their immediate physical or psychological experiences. As a result:

> ... *initiative is largely diminished and the person becomes passive, because to act in a meaningful way is to implicate self and take responsibility, which is exactly what the person wants to avoid.* [BAUMEISTER1994] (p. 152)

For people with a predisposition towards denying responsibility or of blaming others that this would be like suddenly finding themselves in an ice-cream factory. It would provide situations and contexts in which their poorly-adapted (read: reckless) social behaviours and habits could readily come out and play.

14. Comments on some research into BDSM and sex

Hill and Preston 1996

It's common for people, including researchers, to see sex in terms of either making babies, or just having a jolly good time. It's more than that, and the motivations behind sex can actually bear heavily on our understanding of why people do BDSM.

Hill and Preston, in their *Individual Differences in the Experience of Sexual Motivation* [HILL1996], researched a larger range of motivations than those typically explored. Their list of eight motivations (p. 28) are listed below. Note the ones I have highlighted in bold:

1. Feeling valued by one's partner,
2. Showing that a person values his or her partner,
3. **Obtaining relief from stress or negative psychological states,**
4. Providing nurturance through sexual interaction to improve a partner's psychological condition,
5. **Enhancing feelings of personal power,**
6. **Experiencing the power of one's partner,**
7. Experiencing pleasure, and
8. Procreating.

It's important to note that this comes from a research paper on people's motivations for sex. It follows then, that these motivations exist *a priori* or, in other words, that these drives and feelings exist separately to sex, and that this particular paper only looks at people's use of sex to satisfy them. This doesn't mean that sex is the only way of satisfying them.

Indeed, we could argue that that (5) and (6)—to do with the experience of personal power—are only indirectly, and possibly only poorly, satisfied in a sexual context. Sex is often taking off clothes, and getting down and dirty, and that any exploration of personal power must occur in, and is limited by, that sexual context.

On the other hand, BDSM is not limited by having to occur in a sexual context, and explorations of personal power can be the primary activity, rather than a secondary or incidental one. Explorations of personal power in a BDSM context can occur without sex, can last much longer than any sexual encounter, and can be done in most social circumstances (e.g., in public).

Thus, for individuals for whom (5) or (6) are strong motivations, BDSM may be a better way of satisfying them than sex.

Indeed, this preference for BDSM over sex is well recognised by some. For example, Pat Califia writes in *Public Sex: The Culture of Radical Sex*: "if I had a choice between being shipwrecked on a desert island with a vanilla lesbian and a hot male masochist, I'd pick the boy" [CALIFIA1994] (p. 158)[5].

For those who are constrained by the conservatism or beliefs of their current partner, or who are limited by their own conservatism or beliefs, and who are highly motivated to explore personal power, sex can be their "poor man's BDSM".

Hill and Preston found in a survey of 586 participants [HILL1996] (p. 34), that as far as sexual motives were concerned:

1. Women's motivations were:

   (a) 22.25% - relief from stress,

   (b) 23.10% - enhancement of their own power, and

   (c) 24.82% - experience the power of their partner.

2. Men's motivations were:

   (a) 25.78% - relief from stress,

   (b) 24.30% - enhancement of their own power, and

   (c) 28.16% - experience the power of their partner.

The above numbers are not mutually exclusive, by the way. In other words, there can be significant overlap, with some people reporting more than one motivation. This is what we see in BDSM also—namely that there can be, and often is, more than one motivation in play at any one time.

---

5 Written while Califia was, presumably, identifying as a female.

We see in these results that these three motivations, which I deliberately selected because they are common in BDSM, are each experienced by a relatively high percentage of the general population.

We can go a little further and look at a couple more of the motivations in Hill and Preston's list. In particular, items (1) and (2) from the list have to do with feeling valued by, or valuing, one's partner, respectively. Outside of BDSM this can be done by gestures, such as buying your partner a flower, washing the dishes, making your partner a cup of coffee, going on a fun run with them, complimenting them on their hairstyle, taking an interest in their work or hobbies, fucking them regularly, telling them how highly you think of them, and so on.

In the grand scheme of things, the above are small gestures. I mean, it's not like you're going to hell and back for your partner, is it?

Enter BDSM...

Given the sometimes-focus on torture, pain, and suffering in BDSM, going to hell and back for your partner becomes more of a possibility, even if only just symbolically, and even if the end result is a good one for you anyway. What we can see is either a large amount of effort being put in to create the pain and the suffering in the first place, or the large amount of endurance and acceptance of the partner's efforts. These may directly translate both to expressions of value of, and of being valued by, your partner.

This relates well to what Edward Anthony says in his *Thy Rod and Staff*:

> The central objective of this book has been to deconstruct the flagellant experience [flogging, caning and whipping, etc.] in order to identify what I believe to be its keynotes - humanity, sensitivity and affection - thereby showing the whole in a rather better light than it has historically enjoyed." [ANTHONY1995] (p. 306)

Meston and Buss 2007

While Hill and Preston took the approach of offering a choice of eight possible reasons to have sex to their research participants, Meston and Buss, in their *Why People Have Sex* [MESTON2007], did two studies, the first of which was to get participants to suggest their motivations themselves. This led to a list of 237 different reasons why people have sex. The second Meston and Buss study then asked people to evaluate the 237 reasons from the first study in regards to how they related to themselves.

These two Meston and Buss studies about why people have sex show some useful parallels to the reasons why people do BDSM. Without going into detail, I'd just like to quote some of Meston and Buss' reasons for sex and match them up with the reasons I cited in chapter 10, *Motivations*.

Meston and Buss	**Motivations chapter**
I wanted a "spiritual" experience I wanted to feel closer to God	Ecstasy and rapture
I wanted to dominate the other person I wanted to feel powerful I wanted to make my partner feel powerful I wanted to submit to my partner I wanted to display submission	Experiencing power
I wanted to get rid of aggression I wanted to release tension I thought it would relax me I was frustrated and needed relief I wanted to relieve menstrual cramps	Catharsis
I wanted to be used or degraded	Humiliation
I wanted to communicate at a deeper level I wanted to become one with another person I desired emotional closeness (i.e., intimacy)	Intimacy and bonding

And, just as there are people who will abuse most anything, including BDSM, there are, of course, people who will abuse sex. Here are some of the less healthy reasons to engage in sex given by people in the Meston and Buss studies:

- I wanted to punish myself,
- I wanted to break up another's relationship,
- I wanted to get even with someone (i.e., get revenge),
- I wanted to manipulate him/her into doing something for me, and
- I wanted to give someone else a sexually transmitted disease (e.g., herpes, AIDS).

Even without any sort of detailed analysis, just the list of reasons uncovered by Meston and Buss gives us pause to think about how these same reasons operate in the world of BDSM. There are people who do BDSM to get feelings of power, or intimacy, or spirituality; and there are people who come into BDSM with less than healthy goals for either themselves or for others.

15. The role of groups

In the great morass of literature about BDSM, not much time is devoted to the role of groups. While it's easy to find analyses of individuals, and theories of why they do BDSM in more technical or psychological literature, and while it's easy to find lists and explanations of BDSM activities in for-practitioner books and web-sites, it's almost unheard of to find anything about the groups which BDSM people form.

This area is, I think, very important because we humans are fundamentally social creatures, and this aspect of BDSM is, as you'll see below, quite rich. Also, as I mentioned in the introduction to this book, one of my interests is looking at BDSM as a cultural and anthropological phenomenon. Thus, looking at groups is an absolute requirement.

When I'm talking about a *group* I mean a number of people who interact because of a common set of goals or interests. This is different to a group of people with no common interests or goals who are thrown together by fate, such as a group of people waiting at a bus stop.

We can split groups into two types:

1. Social groups, and
2. Structured groups (by far the most interesting of the two).

16. Social groups

Perhaps the simplest type of group to form in the BDSM world is a few people who get together for coffee after discovering that they share a mutual interest in some particular aspect of BDSM. But even this might not be as simple as it sounds.

If the people involved are only into, say, rope bondage and have their meetings in a public coffee shop, then the needs that they satisfy in their group are likely to be limited to things which are strictly social, for example:

1. Sharing experiences and war-stories,

2. Discussing techniques,

3. Comparing knowledge,

4. Measuring one's self against others in the group,

5. Exchanging details of suppliers,

6. Arranging future get-togethers, including play sessions, and

7. Meeting or sizing up potential new partners.

If these same people were to have their meetings in someone's home, and particularly if there are people present who like doing the tying and people who like to be tied, then rope's likely to come out of the closet and we'll start to also see:

1. Demonstrations of techniques and ideas,

2. Training and lessons,

3. Impromptu play sessions, and

4. Measuring of one's practical skills against those of others in the group.

In this sort of private setting, even though the major goal may be social, the possibility of impromptu sessions allows scope for some BDSM itches to be scratched, even if just a little, without having the need for a fully-fledged scene or engagement, or for a dungeon to be prepared.

We can see the beginnings of *ranking* occurring in social groups. This is the process by which one person is placed ahead of or behind others in terms of some criteria—such as technical skill, trustworthiness, leadership ability, skill at organising, prowess with a flogger, elegance of knots, etc.

In social groups we also tend to see *roles* being defined for the participants, such as the-person-who-fetches-the-biscuits, the-person-whose-home-gets-used, the-person-with-the-best-rope-skills, the-person-who-does-the-demonstrations, the-person-who-decides-when-the-next-meeting-is, etc.

In strictly social groups, such as in the above example or in a coffee klatsch, ranking is self-imposed and people tend to opportunistically fall into and out of roles, i.e., the roles are interchangeable, often depending on who is present at the time.

Boundaries

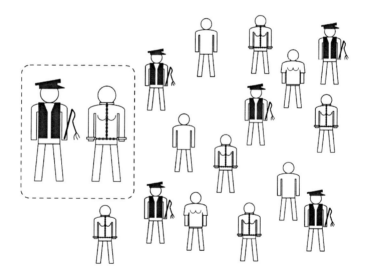

Figure B-1

The issue of boundaries is worth a mention in the context of groups. Figure B-1 shows a dominant/submissive couple on the left, and the rest-of-the-world on the right. The rest-of-the-world consists of ordinary, vanilla people, and people who are involved in BDSM in some way. The dotted line around the couple on the left represents the border or boundary between them and everyone else.

So, what does the boundary..., well,... bound?

There are four things I'd like to discuss:

1. Consent,

2. Rules and expectations,

3. Intimacy, and

4. Authority.

1. Consent

Consent is an issue which appears frequently in the world of BDSM. Because many of the activities in which BDSM people engage can be risky or even illegal in their part of the world, it's important that each participant be fully informed about what they are getting themselves in for.

The average Joe or Jane, as part of their social contract with the world—or with the society in which they live—has certain expectations and rights. These might include being able to come and go as one pleases; to not be beaten up, cut, or bruised; to not be humiliated, etc. But preventing someone coming and going as they please (via, for example, a cage); cutting, piercing, and thumping the daylights out of; and humiliation, are all common BDSM activities. What makes them productive and positive experiences for the participants is, in part, the context in which it occurs and their agreement to it in advance.

A well-experienced BDSM couple, such as the dominant and submissive represented in the diagram above, should have no problems with consent. But if their activities spill out beyond the privacy of their own bedroom or dungeon, then what of the outside-world people with whom they come into contact?

For example, the Sydney Morning Herald, on the 24th of January, 2008, under the heading, "Pet goth girl on leash thrown off bus", reported that a couple were kicked off a bus when they attempted to board while the guy had his girlfriend in a collar on a leash[6]. While this might be common, or even expected, dress and behaviour in parts of the BDSM world, it's not expected outside of BDSM, and the vanilla folk the couple encountered had difficulty with it. It was beyond their expectations and they hadn't consented to it. If, instead of seeing the girl on the leash at a bus stop, people had seen her, at, say a fashion show on the catwalk they almost certainly wouldn't have objected because the context would have been one where they implicitly consented to seeing unusual and unexpected fashion.

---

6 This same story was reported in the UK's Daily Mail on the 23rd of January, 2008, by the BBC on the 23rd of January, and by Melbourne's The Age on the 24th.

2. Rules and expectations

The boundary between our dominant/submissive couple and the outside world also delimits some of the rules which the couple apply to themselves. These could have to do with how they behave towards each other—such as the submissive always calling the dominant, "Master"—or expectations about who does what in the relationship.

Indeed, most relationships such as the one between this couple come into existence so that each can satisfy wants or needs that they can't satisfy elsewhere (i.e., in the outside world). Thus there is an expectation within the relationship that each will contribute towards satisfying the needs—BDSM or otherwise—of the other. This expectation doesn't exist with the outside world.

3. Intimacy

Of course, the level of intimacy between a committed couple—be they dominant/ submissive or vanilla—is a lot higher than either would have with the general public. This isn't just the being-naked type of intimacy, but is also the exposing of personal weaknesses or foibles (which can be exactly the point in some BDSM activities).

4. Authority

The authority which the master exerts over his submissive also does not extend beyond the boundaries of their relationship to people in the outside world. He may be free to direct *her* in all manner of ways, but the authority he has outside of the relationship is completely unrelated. That is to say that he may have some authority over others outside of his relationship with his submissive—for example ,if he were a police officer—but this is completely unrelated to the authority he has inside the relationship.

With the like-minded

Figure B-2

The picture changes when we consider a slightly different social context. In figure B-2 we just have lots of masters, slaves, dominants, and submissives thronging around, perhaps at a BDSM conference.

In this particular case, one boundary is the physical walls of the conference centre. Within those walls the social rules and expectations are different to the outside, vanilla world. For example, being addressed as "Master" by someone you've never met would not be a surprise (unless, of course, you're grovelling at someone's feet at the time). Neither would seeing a woman leading a scantily-clad man on a leash. Indeed, if anyone complained about seeing someone on a leash at such a conference, *they* would be the one seen as out of place.

Thus, the context changes expectations, and this has a flow-on effect to consent.

Likewise, standards and levels of intimacy would also change in this sort of environment. Seeing far less clothing, and much more skin would be expected. Physical intimacy— i.e., touching—might not change, but what's there to be looked at would.

In terms of authority, submissives and slaves may more readily defer to or serve masters and dominants they have never met before—some may make themselves available to serve drinks and fetch nibblies, for example. Likewise, masters and dominants in this sort of environment may more readily assert themselves over submissives and slaves who are perhaps signalling their availability.

147

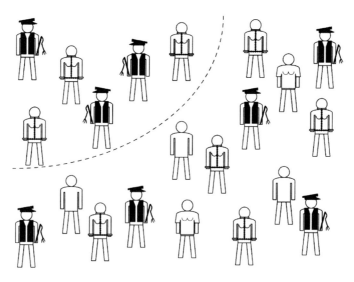

Figure B-3

The picture changes again when we have masters and slaves, or dominants and submissives who are part of their own social group, such as in figure B-3.

Here we can see a social group of masters and slaves in the top-left of the diagram. The dotted line shows the boundary between them in their group and the rest of the world (which may or may not include other masters, slaves, dominants, submissives, or vanilla folk).

This social group is significantly different from just a bunch of BDSM people who show up at a conference probably not all knowing each other.

Indeed, their group exists specifically because they do have common interests. And because they know each other, the level of intimacy between them is likely to be higher. Indeed, it could be that when they all get together, any of the masters could engage any of the submissives without asking because the fact that the submissive is present in the group indicates that they have already consented.

Because they are all part of a group, there will be expectations and rules which each will have to meet. For example, a master who never attends to any of the submissives, or a slave who never serves, may quickly fond themselves out of the group.

Thus, the boundary between the members of the group and the rest of the world is one of:

1. Consent,
2. Rules and expectations,

3. Intimacy, and

4. Authority.

It is, in practically all respects, comparable to the boundary we saw above between a couple and the rest of the world. And the same as with a couple, the boundary between this group and other people will not be a physical one.

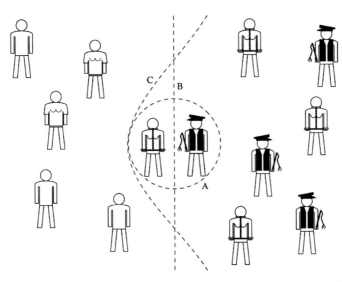

Figure B-4

No man is an island, and neither are a BDSM couple or group. In reality there are multiple boundaries between us and the people around us. Figure B-4 shows a simple example.

In the centre, inside circle A, we have a couple. They have their own levels of intimacy, their own rules and expectations of each other, and their own types of authority. But the female may well see herself as having a strong connection to vanilla colleagues and friends (e.g., through family, work, or from before she became involved in BDSM) and so the line B shows this aspect of the separation she sees between herself and people in the BDSM world. Her dominant though, is deeply immersed in a world where the people with whom he mostly interacts are BDSM folk. He is on the right-hand side of line B, firmly in the world of BDSM.

But the female also sees herself as sometimes in the world of BDSM, as shown by line C which includes her, at least sometimes, in the BDSM world.

This situation may create conflict. Her vanilla friends may not understand how she behaves towards her master, and she may feel the need to "tone it down" when she is with them. Her partner may feel conflicted because his inclination is towards a fuller

BDSM relationship with her, but must accept that sometimes when she is with her vanilla friends that his influence and authority must be suspended or superseded.

Going further in regards to authority, her master might give her certain standing orders—such as being polite to other males—which could be entirely reasonable in a BDSM context. In a vanilla work environment, or if approached by a dickhead in a vanilla social context, being polite may not always be the best strategy. Indeed, she could be dealing with a difficult customer when her vanilla boss tells her to tell the customer "to fuck off". If she were in a BDSM-aware-context when this difficulty raised its head, she could explain herself, but in white-bread land she must not say anything (per her master's orders), and thus ends up in conflict.

17. Structured groups

When we start talking about *structured groups*, ranking and roles become formalised, and rules start to make a bigger appearance. Structured groups also have goals beyond just providing social opportunities for their members.

A simple example of a structured group is a club. Members of a club might pool their resources—such as time, money, or skills—and then a committee will use those pooled resources to benefit the group. A movie club, for example, will have the members pool *themselves* so they can go to an agreed movie every month as a group and thereby get a group discount. In the case of a movie club, the committee is usually composed of the entire membership of the club who agree to be bound by the common choice each week or month.

In the BDSM world, a structured group can be created when a group of people realise that the scope for their activities is going to be increased if they pool their resources. For example, they might agree to set up a shared dungeon space and equip it using contributions from each member of the group.

Let us look at the goals, or reason for existence, of structured groups—particularly in the context of BDSM.

Resources

The big word in terms of structured groups is *resources*. Structured groups come into existence either to create resources or to collect resources for the benefit of the members of the group. The goal of the group itself becomes to encourage, develop, grow, or foster those resources.

No deadheads or voyeurs

One of the problems for serious BDSM practitioners is that if they get together to play or exercise their skills, there's a chance that "the wrong sort of people" will come along to their gathering or party and spoil things. This is commonly seen at public play parties where someone ignorant of the nature of BDSM will walk into the middle of a scene and either talk to, try to join in with, shout encouragement to, or interfere with the people participating in the play. This will often destroy the states of mind of the people involved, and these can take a long time to recover.

Similarly, because BDSM is commonly seen to be about sex, at public parties and get-togethers there'll often be people there only to look. They can be an unpleasant distraction for people who are there to hang out with friends rather than put on a show.

A BDSM structured group typically tries to exclude such people who don't contribute to the goals of the group or its members. As a consequence, the group provides an environment where its members can more comfortably interact with each other.

Technical skill or experience

The wide world of BDSM encompasses many interests and activities, and so at any BDSM gathering you might find yourself sitting next to a rank amateur, or just as easily next to someone with many years of hard-won experience. In structured groups, membership is usually made available or offered on the basis of expertise or skill. Within the groups there may also be some form of ranking to allow members to determine how good each member is. Thus, in a structured group members can be assured that any people with whom they are engaging, even if not known to them personally, are of a certain standard or level of skill. This can be invaluable, for example, with someone who is a heavy player looking to immerse themselves with a partner who won't back out when things start getting serious.

Quality members

It's not always about technical skill. There are many other factors which are usually considered for someone to be allowed to join, or remain in, a structured group. For example, in the BDSM world the fact that someone is into BDSM could be harmful to their family or to their career if it were to leak out. Therefore the ability to keep one's mouth shut can be a vital attribute for a member of a group.

Similarly, a sense of honour and trustworthiness are significant in groups. Being able to be sure that when someone says they'll do something that they won't disappoint is important.

Other qualities which might be important in members are punctuality, cleanliness, etc.

In many groups the certainty that members possess these attributes can be one of the highly valuable resources of the group.

Shared and specific interests

BDSM can attract anyone from fetishists, to those just looking for kinky sex, to swingers, to bondage artistes, to body decorators, to occasional players, to lifestylers[7], to masters and slaves. When looking to be with like-minded others, wading through an unsorted collection of other BDSMers at random gatherings can be tedious. A structured group can ensure that its membership is all like-minded, such as in a rope-bondage group. Therefore, when you meet up with other members, you're sure to have something to talk about and share.

Common standards

Structured groups often require their members to adhere to specific standards. Thus members can be sure that other people they meet in the group will have the same minimum standards as they themselves have.

Beyond standards to do with mental and physical health, safety, and cleanliness, common standards may extend to training, the way slaves address masters, other matters of protocol, and so on.

Consequently...

As a result of the above, a structured group can provide an ideal environment for someone looking for a partner.

Complaints desk

While it's unlikely that there is is an actual desk with someone sitting behind it who receives complaints, it's important in a group that there be a way for members who don't follow the rules, who don't maintain the standards of the group, or who are simply harming the group, to be handled.

This may involve a system of warnings, or an arbiter to resolve disputes. In any case, if warnings and discussions don't do the trick, some form of correction may need to be applied. Commonly the following are used:

---

7 A lifestyler is someone who tries to incorporate as much BDSM flavour into their life as possible. For example, if they have a master/slave relationship with their partner, and they live together, they may keep the dynamic active 24/7 through service, formal titles (e.g., "Sir" or "girl"), etc.

Fines

In the first instance, it may be sufficient to impose a financial penalty which corresponds to whatever the infraction is. Of course, the person being corrected may simply decide to leave the group instead of pay but, either way, the problem is likely to be solved.

Loss of privileges

This can be read as loss of access to group resources for a time. This could be not being allowed to come to meetings, not being allowed to use the shared dungeon, not being allowed to serve, not having access to group slaves, etc.

As the person concerned probably joined the group to get access to these resources in the first place, this can be an effective punishment—often more so than any financial inducement to behave.

Loss of rank or demotion

Ranks usually have to do with having a recognised level of skill, and certain privileges usually go hand-in-hand with this. I will be talking more about ranks shortly, but one of the forms of discipline which can be applied in a group is demoting a person, i.e., lowering their rank. To regain their rank they then have to go through re-training and re-evaluation. This will also have an impact on the person's access to resources, but instead of there being a waiting period involved—as there usually is with loss of privileges, they have to make a specific effort themselves to re-earn access to the resources which their rank had afforded them.

Expulsion

And, of course, the ultimate penalty for a group: being kicked out, possibly with no option of return.

Protection or safety from the eyes of the law

Fortunately, or unfortunately, depending on your point of view, there are a number of activities in the world of BDSM which might be illegal in your jurisdiction.

- Slavery, for example, is pretty much a no-no wherever you go,
- There are many jurisdictions where you can't consent to being hit. Thus, having actually agreed to be tied up and flogged may not stop the boys in blue carting your partner off to the big house if he's caught in the act, and
- In some places breaking the skin in any way, even with a knife or needle is illegal, unless you're some form of recognised practitioner—such as surgeon.

Thus, a benefit which a structured group might give its members can be safe places to exercise their interests, free from worry that the police will interfere. This can be either by providing private locales, or by ensuring that the membership is such that trouble with the police is avoided—e.g., that they're sworn to secrecy, that they're level-headed, and that they're not prone to get annoyed by someone and then do something unwise with a telephone.

Privacy and confidentiality

I've already mentioned that the ability to keep one's mouth shut can be an important, or even necessary, attribute of a group member. Beyond protecting the privacy of individual members of the group, this ability to maintain confidences can be important to the structure of the group itself.

For example, someone may enter a group at a low rank and not be fully initiated into all of the *mysteries* the group has to offer. For example, there may be activities in which senior members of the group are involved, and which are only revealed once a person has reached a certain level of skill or has demonstrated their ability to respect the goals of the group. This might have to do, for example, with highly technical aspects of the group, or sections of the group membership which are far more sensitive to public scrutiny than the rest of the group.

Roles

Because structured groups come into existence to provide something that the individual members cannot provide for themselves on their own, it follows that the structured groups contains *roles* which don't and can't exist in simple social groups, or which can't exist in a simple relationship between two people.

For a simple structured group where the individual group members pool resources for their mutual benefit, a role comes into existence which is basically the keeper or caretaker of the shared resources. In some clubs or groups this role is called the *secretary*. While not necessarily the person who decides what happens with the shared resources—such as how shared money gets spent, or who gets how much time in the shared dungeon—this is still a formal role within the group. In very small groups this might be the only formal role.

Commonly the person fulfilling the role of secretary will have volunteered, and a majority of the other members of the group will have in some way agreed for that person to have that role. In other words, even though it might be done in a very ad-hoc way, the secretary is elected.

Let's look a bit more closely at the secretary.

Taking the shared dungeon as an example again, we might see that the dungeon itself is in the home of one of the members, possibly because they are the only person with enough space. It might be that this particular member of the group effectively becomes the manager or custodian of this shared resource, i.e., the dungeon, by default, simply because they own where it is located.

On the other hand, the dungeon might be located in, say, a warehouse and each member of the group gets the key when it's their turn to use the dungeon. Who minds the key though? It could get passed from member to member, and this might happen at the beginning, but it's far more likely that for the sake of simplicity one person will be chosen, i.e., *elected*, to be the main key holder, i.e., *secretary*—possibly because they're more reliable or easier to get hold of than anyone else in the group.

In this we are seeing that one person ends up being the safe-keeper of the shared resource—be it access to the dungeon, the key to the dungeon, or the shared calendar in which each person writes down when they want to use the dungeon, etc. This is the role of the secretary.

It's important to recognise that the person filling the role of secretary, or keeper-of-the-shared-resource, doesn't get any particular rights over the dungeon. They can't spend all the time using it themselves. They can only share out the resource—e.g., dungeon—as agreed by the group. That is, the group makes the rules and the secretary enacts them.

In a small group the process of election of the secretary might be as formal as getting everyone in the group together and voting, or it might be as casual as one person ending up with the key all the time because they're closest, or because they end up using it the most.

Let's now move on to another group role.

In more complex structured groups, particularly as they grow, it may become cumbersome for all members of the group to be involved in decision making. In such cases it is common for a central *committee* or *council* to be selected. Again, this might not be as formal a process as it sounds.

This council becomes responsible for deciding how the secretary will manage or use the group's resources—e.g., money, collective expertise, shared dungeon, etc. Commonly, the committee will vote on issues which need to be decided. In many cases one person from this central committee or council is chosen to organise and run meetings of the committee. They will usually have only one vote, the same as the other members of the committee. This person is the *president*.

It's important when you're considering what I've just written that you don't spend too much time on the labels. Look at the groups in which you're involved and think about how they're structured—such as who does what for the group—and see how well it matches my descriptions. It might be, for example, that the person who I've called the *secretary* has no official name other than Sue or Malcolm or dd or houseslut, but they still perform the same secretarial role of shepherding resources for the group.

Another role which makes an appearance in structured groups is that of deciding who can become a member of the group. It's not enough that everyone likes the candidate member and enjoys being with them. Potential members must be able to contribute something which advances the goals or purpose of the group. The choice to allow in a new member may be a decision made by the group as a whole if it is small or manageable enough. But once a structured group reaches a certain size, or when it becomes difficult for all of the members to contribute to the deciding on the yea or nay for a potential new member—such as for all of them to get together in the one place at the one time, this job must be delegated by the group to an individual or sub-committee who makes the choice on behalf of the group. Perhaps we can call this role *membership secretary* or *membership committee*.

In the shared dungeon example, a potential new member might be keen to join up, and contribute a new St. Andrew's Cross and a fancy selection of new ropes and chains to the group, but maybe this isn't enough to become a member. It might be that he is a dickhead, a voyeur, or that his bondage play is far riskier than the other members of the group feel comfortable with. If it's likely that by joining the group he or she will move the group further away from its goals, rather than closer to its goals, membership will be denied either by the group itself, or by its delegate, i.e, by the membership secretary or committee. Again, this selection process might not be as formal as it sounds, particularly in small groups, but it will happen, and it will happen in line with the goals for the group.

Roles explicitly come with authority. The secretary of a group, for example, is granted the authority by the group to manage the resources of the group. This has interesting ramifications in regards to dominance & submission, and to mastery & slavery. As roles are often allocated based on the ability to perform the role, it might be that a slave or submissive ends up with this authority which they might need to use against the desires of their dominant or master from time to time, or that they need to give orders or instructions to other dominants or masters. Going back to the shared dungeon, for example, it might be that a submissive must refuse his dominant's request to use the dungeon on occasion and let someone else use it if that's what the sharing rules say.

Likewise, in larger groups, it might be that a slave or a number of slaves are on the administrative council or committee of a larger group and end up laying down the law to *all* of the members of the group, masters included.

It's very important here to differentiate between the slaves' or submissives' personal authority and its exercise, and the authority of the role and how they exercise it. While it may be that a slave is required by their role in the group to direct one or more masters, including possibly their own, both the slave and masters concerned need to be aware, for their own health and the well-being of their relationships, who has authority and who is merely delegated it. I will be looking at this more in chapter 19, *Types of authority.*

As a final note here, a *role* is sometimes called an *office*, and we hear about it in terms of, say, the Office Of The President Of The United States Of America. While the office is ongoing, the person who occupies that role will change over time. The role and duties remain the same, but the actual person doing them will change from time to time. This is the same in structured groups. The role of, say, the secretary may be constant and well known to the members of the group, but the person carrying out that role is likely to change from time to time. The responsibility of the role and its authority remain the same though, regardless of who is performing that role.

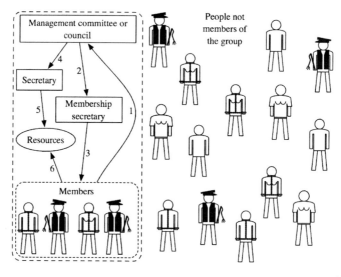

Figure H-1

Figure H-1 shows the roles I have been talking about in a BDSM context, their relationships to each other, and their relationship to people not members of the group, regardless of whether they are masters, slaves, dominants, submissives, or just plain vanilla folk.

Firstly, there is <u>no</u> relationship between the roles inside the group and the people outside of the group. They are completely separate. No group role wields any authority outside of the group. This is important as we shall see later in chapter 18, *Analyses.*

Next, on the left-hand side of the diagram is the structure of the group. I have ordered this hierarchically in terms of *operational authority*[8], with the roles with the most authority (in relation to the group) at the top, and the roles with the least authority down the bottom. Note that individual masters and slaves have the same authority[9] in terms of the group, and are down the bottom.

The value of the group comes from its resources (on the left-hand side of the structure), and these commonly come from and are the members of the group itself (6). The central committee or council of the group is also formed from members (1), but while the group's resources are the entire membership, the committee is usually only a small, possibly elected, subset.

There's an interesting loop apparent in the diagram, and that is that the members choose the central committee (1), which chooses the membership secretary (2), which in turn chooses the members (3). Notably, this is a recipe for nepotism—i.e., the central committee manipulating who gets selected as members—and highlights the need for good policies, rules, and oversight, to ensure a level playing field for all candidate members.

The central committee also chooses the secretary (4), and empowers the secretary to manage the group's resources (5) as decided by the committee.

Ranks

Ranks are different to roles. While in both cases it's people who have roles and people who have ranks, a rank is tied to a person, but a role is not. A person might be the secretary of a group and have certain duties, responsibilities, authority, and even privileges; but when someone else takes over the role of secretary from them, they no longer have any of those duties, responsibilities and, especially, they no longer have the authority and privileges of that role. On the other hand, duties, responsibilities, authority, and privileges which come with rank stay with the person and are not transferrable.

A person's rank is usually related to their skill and ability, and it usually increases over time.

The process of increasing one's rank, or *promotion*, may be very casual. In a small group, such as a a group of bondage practitioners, someone who has been around for a long time, who has often showed they have a level head, and who has demonstrated

---

8 While it's arguably the case that the authority in a group comes from its members, once the central committee or council has been chosen or elected, the day-to-day *operational authority* comes from them.

9 This point is probably an excellent topic for vigourous debate.

their skill many times, will tend to automatically acquire duties, responsibilities, authority, and even privileges within the group. For example, they may be frequently asked to watch over new members or do training (duties and responsibilities), they may implicitly have the right and obligation to intervene if they see something going awry (authority), and they may end up getting first choice of new and luscious group members (privileges).

One often unspoken requirement for increasing rank is that the person needs to be seen to be both familiar with the standards and goals of their structured group, and be aligned with them. Regardless of their skill or ability, someone seen as a "loose cannon" in terms of the group's goals is less likely to increase in rank than someone who is seen to better fit the goals of the group.

In larger groups, in more formal groups, and particularly in groups which are geographically widespread, formal ranks are a useful way for someone to move smoothly from a subgroup in one location to a subgroup in a different location and not have to prove themselves again. In other words, once someone has reached a particular rank in one subgroup, when they go to another subgroup the people in that second subgroup will already have an idea of the person's skills and abilities by virtue of that rank. The person doesn't need to be re-evaluated by that second subgroup.

Promotion

Rank usually implies privileges on one hand, and duties and responsibilities on the other. It doesn't serve a group for someone to get privileges when they aren't up to handling the corresponding duties and responsibilities. To ensure that this doesn't happen, it's commonly the people who are already of a particular rank who make the choice about promoting someone to their rank. They have the most to lose—such as respect and privileges—and so are likely to act to ensure that only those who truly merit their same rank, and those who "will do it proud", are promoted to it.

At this point, it might be worth looking at some ranking systems that are more formally established in the community-at-large and then see how we can map this into structured groups in the BDSM world.

While so far I've been using a group who shares a dungeon as one of my main examples, some of the more common *coins of the realm* in the BDSM world are skills, talent, and experience. We might look, for example, at bondage skills, or the ability to serve, or the ability to handle and direct a slave, or the ability to take charge of a submissive.

The process of development of these skills involves natural talent, enthusiasm, practice, and study. We can split this development conveniently into three stages:

1. Beginner, apprentice, student
2. Practitioner, instructor, journeyman
3. Master, expert, trainer, professor

At the beginner or apprentice level, the person is learning. In the case of a structured group, such as a bondage group, the person might already have excellent skills at bondage, but still have much to learn about the group itself, how things are done in the group, the group's protocols, roles, responsibilities, etc.

The point is that at this level the beginner or apprentice still has something to learn to be able to function as an independent, fully-contributing member of the group. There's a good chance that they'll be under supervision some or much of the time, and they won't have the same privileges, or access to resources, as full members of the group.

Subsequently, at some point, once their training and experience has grown to warrant it, the student will get promoted to something akin to full membership of the group. They'll get recognition as a practitioner of the skills of interest to the group, and they'll be recognised as being able to do their thing without needing supervision.

Because they're now considered competent, they'll also be able to provide assistance to new beginners and students.

But merely being competent at what you do is not enough to make you an expert or a master. To use bondage [yet again] as an example, it might be that someone is really good at doing, say, suspension, but that doesn't mean they are any good at Japanese bondage or mummification.

To become a master at some skill, you have to go the extra mile and become more than merely competent at *all* aspects of that skill. For some people this will never be important. They can be happy and usefully-contributing members of a group or community without necessarily becoming experts at all aspects of what the group does.

Although it's mainly skill that we're talking about here, this might be only one part of what's needed by a group in order to elevate someone in rank.

As I've mentioned, rank comes with privileges, *and* duties and responsibilities. If someone has the skills—such as bondage skills, the ability to serve exquisitely, or the ability to handle a slave—but lacks the characteristics which would allow them to carry out the duties associated with a rank, then they're not going to get promoted to it.

For example, someone who is an absolute expert at taking control of and managing a slave, but who cares diddly-squat about contributing their time to helping teach or supervise juniors, is going to find that they'll be happily left to do their thing. Promotion and privileges will go instead to those who have the technical skills *and* who are prepared to shoulder the duties that go with those privileges.

Such a three- or four-tiered ranking system is common in society, and has been common for hundreds of years, wherever practical skills can earn benefits, and wherever these skills take time and talent to develop.

Sometimes called trades, we can see this sort of ranking appearing with chefs, carpenters, thatchers, plumbers, metal-workers, coopers, electricians, tinkers, blacksmiths, and so on. Likewise, in BDSM we can see the same sorts of skills and ranking, even if not formally labelled the same way, with practitioners of bondage, cutting, slave-handling, flogging, serving, corporal punishment, etc.

An interesting, if minor, complication in labelling appears when we consider that it's not just the people who tie the knots, or who wrangle the slaves, who can be ranked. Submissives, bottoms, and slaves also have skills, can require training, and can be called upon to train others of their ilk. Thus they too can have levels of rank based on their own skills. In the BDSM world it would be awkward to talk about a "master submissive", or a "master slave" or, indeed, "master master", so in some groups a neutral alternative to "master", such as "adept", is used to indicate the superior level of competence and expertise, and we get "master adept", "slave adept", and so on.

Finally, ranks only have meaning between people in the groups in which the ranks are used and recognised. For example, if I were in the army and happened to meet another army person with the rank of lieutenant, then their rank would be important to me because it would indicate where that person stands relative to me. But if I were in the army and met a *police* lieutenant then I wouldn't care too much because their rank is irrelevant to me. They aren't part of my group, and they aren't part of my hierarchy.

Rules

The last of the three R's of structured groups is *rules*. The smallest of groups will have rules, even if these are only implicit and unspoken.

When a structured group comes into existence, it does so to achieve one or more goals of the members. Rules which are designed to further attain those goals appear at the same time.

For example, suppose that a group of masters and slaves get together to learn from each other and to provide themselves with opportunities to interact and develop in a "pure" master/slave environment. A rule for their group might be that members must have mastery and slavery as their main interest. Thus, someone who is, say, primarily interested in bondage, or piercing, or corporal punishment, would not be encouraged or even allowed to join.

Rules and standards which define who can become a member and how they do so have to do with *exclusivity*, a common characteristic of structured groups, and how they protect the resources they share with their members. In the current master/slave group example, one of the resources which they protect is the purity of the master/slave environment which they provide to their members. Such an environment may have value to someone who isn't keen on many of the other activities of BDSM, such as piercing, etc., and who instead wants or needs to solely explore or participate in authority dynamics.

Some rules come into existence strictly to ensure the smooth-running and cohesion of the group. It serves no one if a group is created and resources pooled, only to have infighting, bickering, or conflict cause a rapid turnover of members, or to cause the group to break up completely.

For example, rules for this same master/slave group might have to do with how a master claims a slave, how they announce that they have done so to other members of the group, and how such claims are respected.

As mentioned above in the discussion of roles, as structured groups grow to the point where decisions can't be made by the entire membership, such as when there are too many members to do so, or when it's too hard to get them all together at the same time and place, some tasks of the group get delegated to individuals or subgroups. A usually unadvertised consequence of this is that from that point on, *only the delegates can perform that role*. For example, suppose it was the practice in a group that anyone could bring along a potential new member to a group. Once the role of membership secretary or membership committee is created, the original practice must disappear and any individual group member's right or authority to introduce new members similarly disappears. From then on, all new membership approaches must be made by or through the new membership secretary/committee. I.e, this becomes the rule.

In the same way that rules appear which govern the process of becoming a member, not far behind them come rules which determine when and how a member gets disciplined or, ultimately, gets kicked out of the group. Typically these have to do with behaviours contrary to the goals of the group, such as bringing along unauthorised strangers to gatherings, and acts or ways of treating others which aren't aligned with the goals of the group, or which tend to destabilise the group, or which diminish the value of the group to its members.

In smaller groups rules might appear more intuitive than intentional and, indeed, this is often the case. We all see this in our experience with being part of different groups at school, university, work, socially, etc. As a result we tend to automatically recognise "good behaviour" (that which helps the group) and "bad behaviour" (that which destabilises the group).

But as groups grow in size, the demands on the individuals, and the need for consistency, can exceed the simply-intuitive abilities of the group's members. Rules are created to give everyone the same base for their decisions and actions, and help to ensure consistency and predictability wherever and whenever group members act.

Subgroups

In a large enough group, it may become useful for members to create subgroups within the overall group structure.

Earlier, in the discussion on ranks, I mentioned subgroups in different locations. When the membership of a group becomes large enough, it may become worthwhile for members located close to each other to form a geographical subgroup, still operating under the rules and directorship of the main group, but mainly associating with one and other.

Even within a group, subgroups might form to reflect special interests. For example, in a bondage group, some members might form a Japanese bondage subgroup. They still operate within the structure and rules of the main group, but would focus more on their preferred aspect of bondage.

Master and slave as a structured group

It's interesting, at this point, to consider a master and a slave as a structured group in miniature. One of the defining characteristics of a structured group as compared to a simple social group, is the existence of different roles within the group. In a typical social group, each individual has equal rights and station within that group.

As we move towards a master/slave relationship and away from, say, a bondage couple where the person who does the tying and the person who is tied have equal and equitable say in what goes on, we see that the master acquires (and requires) executive authority over the direction of the relationship (i.e., the group) as a whole, not just over the slave herself.

The master becomes the custodian of the relationship, as well as the custodian of the slave, and his role becomes that of ensuring the growth and development of the relationship/group. To do this he'll utilise the skills and abilities of not only himself, but also of the slave, to achieve this.

We can see then, that the roles of secretary and central committee (appearing in the form of the master) become formally instantiated in a master/slave relationship.

Even further than that, we might also see in a poly-inclined master/slave relationship the role of membership secretary occurring. One person, i.e., the master, becomes primarily responsible for the selection and smooth-fitting of new people into the relationship, either just temporarily, such as in a quickie *menage a troi*, or for the long-term expansion of the *family*.

Structured groups create novel and unique contexts

A group having multiple members creates contexts and situations which don't or can't occur in relationships between two individuals alone. Importantly, this fact can be one of the reasons for a structured group to come into existence.

Continuity of context

It's common that one person—say a dominant, submissive, top, bottom, master or slave—will look for someone of a complementary ilk with whom to establish a relationship which will satisfy their mutual needs.

There's an important idea associated with this though:

- From time to time one or other of the two people involved will not be around, either because of some temporary absence such as work, sickness, business trip, etc.; or because of something more permanent, such as the relationship breaking up, one person moving away, etc.

Thus there is the implicit expectation that both people involved have to be able to cope on their own at times. Consequently, their surrender to the context and dynamic between them must be limited, i.e., they need to hold something back for the possibly-extended times when they're on their own.

Now let's consider what happens when people join a group of like-minded BDSM-inclined individuals.

If the two people are already a couple, then they are already a group of two with a focus on each other and this, to some extent, separates them from the group[10].

If, however, a single individual joins the group, then something wonderful can happen.

Let's consider the case where a bondage bottom joins a group of other bondage tops and bottoms. Her expectation may not be that she is going to find a partner there, shack up with him, and that only his ropes will embrace her body for ever more. Instead she may be seeing herself as part of a group and that *any one of the tops in the group*

---

10 Note the boundary issue here. I.e., there exists a boundary separating the couple from the rest of the group right from the start.

might potentially tie her up. Likewise, the tops in the group may not see themselves as necessarily partnered with any particular bottom, and will be expecting that they may be tying up virtually any bottom of the group.

This has an interesting consequence for continuity. Instead of having to keep something in reserve in case their one usual partner is absent, a group top or bottom can expect that should any particular bottom or top be absent, that someone with the same standards and inclinations will be available in their place.

The group ensures that bondage needs will be satisfied, that there will most always be someone available, and that there won't be awkward quiet times between relationships when needs must be suppressed or sublimated.

The existence of the group provides a continuity of the BDSM context beyond the simple availability of one partner, and also creates a new type of relationship where one person is no longer the top, bottom, master, slave, submissive or dominant of one other *person*, but is instead in a *relationship with the group itself*, with the awareness that it is now the group and not just one other person who is there to help them satisfy their needs.

In a similar way, a master/slave group ensures that a slave always has someone of quality to serve, and that a master always has someone to master.

If we consider that individual masters and individual slaves, rather than couples, join the group, then as long as the group is not purely social, but exists to allow the members to satisfy their D&s or master/slave needs, then the slaves will enter with the expectation of being mastered by masterly members of the group, while masters will enter with the expectation of there being slaves to master. Because each individual's focus is not towards other individuals with whom a long-term, possibly monogamous, relationship must be established, masters will be able to satisfy their needs with more than one of the the slave members (note the plural) of the group, having a continuity even if individual slaves come and go. Likewise, slaves will have a continuity of mastery, even if individual masters come and go.

This does not preclude that a master and slave may form a pair at some stage, thus possibly removing the slave from the pool of slaves available to other masters of the group, or limiting how she may be used by them.

A requirement for continuity of context to work is that the group's membership rules ensure a certain quality or standard of member. This standard will determine the degree of surrender possible by the members. For example, a bondage group whose only entry requirement is that members be enthusiastic about bondage is not going to be able to guarantee a context where serious, demanding (or even tight) bondage is going to occur between members. If this high standard happens to be what a member is looking to immerse themselves in, then their experience in this low-standard group is going to be patchy.

Exit groups, exit training, exit strategies

One of the advantages of a structured group or community of sufficient size is the *full immersion* opportunities it presents. Instead of having to maintain vanilla relationships, a large enough community of like-minded BDSM souls can create contexts in which the people concerned can be constantly supported in their BDSM-type lifestyle, attitude, and behaviours.

For example, imagine a submissive or slave whose friends are all *in the scene*, who works in a small office run by a dominant, and whose corner shop is run by a dominant/submissive couple. She would be in a position to largely live as a submissive or slave 24 hours a day, 7 days a week because the people with whom she works, trades, and socialises are all part of and supportive of what she thinks and feels.

It's important to be aware though that the more formal the behaviours and requirements of the community in which she operates, the less able she may become over time to fully function within a vanilla environment.

For example, if the community rules insist that she defer to the males she comes in contact with, then this is good while she remains strictly within the confines of the community, particularly as the community itself is likely to be structured to ensure that she is adequately protected and supported, and that her needs are met within that context. But once she steps outside of that environment which is cognisant of her condition and into the vanilla world, then she is greatly disadvantaged by the desires, needs, and habits of deferring to men when women are more-or-less expected to stand up for themselves and not defer.

We can see then that it's possible for someone to have been trained or conditioned to function in a BDSM context where:

- Her personal authority has been reduced by training, habit, or conditioning,
- She has been trained or conditioned in ways which would be disadvantageous in the vanilla world—such as being required to be sexually available to all males,
- She has had limited or no contact with the vanilla world for a long period of time, and
- Her personal or sexual boundaries have been reduced or minimised.

In such a situation, should circumstances be such that she leaves this context or community, then she'd likely require help un-learning some of what she learned within that immersive BDSM context, and to require help re-learning some of the forgotten or disused skills she used to have that let her operate in the vanilla world in which she finds herself again.

This is something which I explored in *The Control Book* where I wrote, in part:

> *Decision-making is a learned and practiced skill. If a submissive had been under the control of a dominant for a long period, then they may need time to relearn the skills and/or knowledge required to competently make their own decisions again. This isn't directly an issue of being or not being under control, but is a consequence of having been under control. As such, I would argue that it's part of the responsibility that the dominant acquired when they first took control of the submissive, to help the submissive regain these skills.* [MASTERS2006] (pp. 78 - 79)

Enter exit training, exit programs, and exit strategies.

These are all varieties of teaching or training which would help someone learn new behaviours and habits which are better adapted to the vanilla world, and how to recognise when their BDSM needs or desires—no longer satisfied within the group or community of which they were a part—may tempt them to return to behaviours which are no longer safe or productive for them, such as sexually deferring to a strong male, or deferring to a male who reminds them of people within their old group.

More than this, if the submissive or slave (or dominant or master, for that matter) have been "out of the loop" for an extended time, they may need to learn other day-to-day things, such as how to ride the subway (if it has changed), any new laws which may apply to them, new road rules, etc. They may also need help finding an apartment, finding a new doctor (because they may, for example, have been using a doctor inside the group who was understanding of caning marks), and may need help finding work (because they've maybe been in situation where they can't readily explain what they've been doing the last few years to future employers, and without a full work history many employers are wary).

This sort of training and support can be performed by someone:

- Who knows how the submissive or slave was trained in the first place, and who knows the context in which they existed,
- Who can recognise their behaviours,
- Who is careful not to assert or trigger any authority responses in the slave or submissive,
- Who can point out to her the inappropriate-in-the-vanilla-world responses she's not seeing herself, and suggest how she can avoid them or overcome them, and

- Who stands with a foot in both worlds—i.e., in the group the submissive/slave is leaving and in the vanilla community, and who maintains contacts in each.

A new market

Another example of a context or situation which comes into existence along with a growing structured group is a marketplace. The group, by definition, consists of many people with common interests and standards, and this concentration of people creates a single place where someone with something to sell can efficiently focus their efforts.

I'd like to briefly mention two possible markets which might emerge, or which might become viable:

1. Equipment
2. Training

Equipment

Group meetings, conferences, mailing-lists, or newsletters are an ideal place to market things such as rope, chains, collars, cages, crops, canes, slaves, etc. In large enough groups, the individuals doing the selling may be able to get quantity deals from their suppliers.

Training

With many people in the group, possibly with significant numbers coming and going, there may also be a need for newcomers to seek training. It may reach the point where training becomes an organised activity by a subgroup who are especially skilled at it.

Payment

Payment for services, such as training, or for equipment need not be in money. With many people around with similar interests and drives, barter might be just as useful.

The individual's relationships within the group

A member of a structured group has some notable relationships. Some of these are interesting just because they go beyond what exists in a normal social environment, and some are interesting because of their BDSM influence. As you're reading, please keep in mind what I talked about in chapter 9, *Relationships II*, because a number of these relationships are not with actual real people.

To others in the group

A member of a group necessarily has a closer connection to other members of the same group than to complete strangers. For one thing, they presumably share a common interest—namely, whatever it was which got them to join the group in the first place—and thus they will be aware of a boundary between the members of the group (themselves included) and the rest of the world in terms of this interest.

They, and the other members of the group, are also perceived to be part of the "haves", while the rest of the world are the "have nots" in terms of having access to whatever resources the group husbands and shares, such as a particular dungeon, a community of "quality" masters and slaves, and so on.

Because other members of the group have in some way earned membership of the group, a group member will trust them more than strangers. Partly this is because betrayal can have a price in terms of membership, and thus group members have something to lose should they let other members down.

Non-person people come into existence in structured groups, and individual members have relationships with them as well. The *secretary* is a good example. Each member is likely to have something to do with the secretary. But even though the actual person holding that office may change from time to time, the dealings each member has with the secretary have a sense of continuity of identity.

Likewise, if the group sponsors or creates other roles within the group—such as official trainer, membership secretary, counsellor, etc.—the individual members can have ongoing relationships with these *offices* even though the holders of these offices might change.

In a BDSM context, dominants, submissives, masters, slaves, etc., also can, to some extent, wear the office of community dominant, community submissive, community master, community slave, etc. Thus, others in the group might see another member, react to them, and deal with them, in terms of the duties which they fulfil in the group. This is particularly the case when membership of the group has its own obligations and duties.

For example, a slave may expect and be required to turn to a group master of a particular rank—any group master of that rank—when she has some need which must be fulfilled, and he is expected to deal with it. Likewise, a dominant may equally approach any community submissive when he is seeking to address his wants or needs knowing that they, too, have an obligation and duty to them.

In each case the individual slave or dominant may be seeing the other member of the group as someone with a role or duty to fill in the group (i.e., an *office*) as much as they may see them as a particular individual.

This may not be as formal and demanding as it sounds, but when you're part of a BDSM group and someone—who is also a member of the same group—respectfully comes to you saying, for example, that they are in need of a serious flogging, then you feel an obligation to at least consider their request. Certainly you will feel more inclined to support them than some stranger at a public BDSM play party.

To the group itself

Each individual will have a relationship with the group itself. This is not reflected in how they relate to particular individuals in the group, but does colour how they relate to *every* member of the group.

And, interestingly, one of the benefits of the group is that it provides a *continuity of context*, such as assuring a slave of a continuity of mastery, even when this mastery may be provided by more than one master over time. Thus the slave will have a relationship to that continuity itself. In other words, where the group provides a context in which some or all of the person's needs are met by the group as a whole, rather than met by a particular individual member, then they will have a relationship to that provided context (i.e., to this group-provided *Other*).

An example may be required here. Suppose that a dominant in a group expresses his dominance regularly with different submissives of his group. Over time, he may develop relationships with individual submissives, but he will also develop a relationship with an *image* of a group submissive[11], so that when he approaches any group submissive he will feel the same stirrings, have similar responses to them, and so on.

This idea of an *image* of a group slave, group master, group dominant, or group submissive, is an important one here. As we saw in chapter 9, *Relationships II*, we develop an image in our personal unconscious due to repeated exposure to the same or similar characteristics in a type of person. For example, we might recognise a common or garden variety top by the black leathers, the chaps, or the equipment hanging from his utility belt. Tied to this image is his behaviour, and we'll quickly learn to discriminate between a pretender and the real thing.

Likewise, in a structured group of masters and slaves, by virtue of the rules used to select members, and by virtue of the training, protocol, and behaviour rules of the group, we'll learn to recognise that particular set of behaviours, dress, etc., as being a *group master image* or a *group slave image*. And, as *Relationships II* showed, we can have a relationship with an image, as well as with a person. This relationship to an image is one of the forms of continuity a group can offer.

---

11 Particularly when the submissives all have the same standard of training or behaviour imposed on them.

Citadel complex

I've already referred to Diane Elise's excellent paper *Unlawful Entry - Male Fears of Psychic Penetration* [ELISE2001], and I'd like to use it as a basis to explore how gender may get involved with the defence of groups.

One thing we have observed so far in this discussion of structured groups, is that there is necessarily a boundary or divide between those who have access to the resources of a structured group and those who do not. This boundary is created along with the creation of the group itself. At the same time it becomes the role of the group and its members to defend this boundary. If just anyone were allowed into the group and to access the group's resources, then its value would be lost to its members.

Relatedly, it is common for members of a group to identify with the group itself. They may say things like, "I have been a member of the most worthy Ad-Hoc Tennis Club for fifteen years, and my father, and his father were members before me!" Being a member of the group can have value for a person and be part of their identity. They will not give it up easily.

But just as they will cling to the fact of being a member of the group, they will also strive to ensure that the value of the group—as they see it—is maintained. They will do this both because it ensures that they continue to get something out of the group, because they identify themselves with the group, and because they see any diminishment of the value of the group as a decrease in their own value as a person.

One way they may try to maintain the value of the group is by ensuring that the people allowed into the group as members maintain a particular standard (i.e., they try to keep the riffraff out).

We thus enter territory in which Elise's different gender responses to penetration can start to play a role. In the case of women, sexual penetration is the norm, and they know that their identity, or self, is not at risk by this penetration. Men, on the other hand, experience what Elise calls "The Closing of the Male Psyche" [ELISE2001] (p. 502), the creation of a barrier between them and the outside world. Penetration of this barrier risks destabilising the gender aspect of their identity. What is inside this barrier is their *citadel*.

Things start to liven up when someone or something starts to approach the boundary between their group and the outside world. By identifying with their club or group, and by extending their own fear of penetration to the group as a whole, men can see a highly personal and intimate threat. This differs from the female response which more intuitively recognises that penetration doesn't necessarily lead to harm to the group. This is, indeed, something we commonly see in relation to groups or clubs, with men—rather than women—typically playing the sometimes-posturing role of defender, say, of an exclusive golf or country club, even when there is no real threat.

In conclusion

- A structured group exists to collect or create, and manage and protect, resources on behalf of and for the benefit of the group.

- A structured group is one where roles with delegated authority exist to help or ensure the smooth-running of the group—such as *secretary*, as distinct from other roles such as top, bottom dominant, submissive, etc., which have no delegated authority.

- A master/slave relationship is a structured group in miniature.

- There are distinct and guarded boundaries between the group and the outside world.

- *Continuity of context* is an important resource which comes into existence with the creation of the group.

18. Analyses

At a hotel

Some years ago I went to a hotel frequented by gay and lesbian people with a friend to watch a show in which she was performing. For a while I happened to be standing on my own while she did her turn. Part way through a woman came up to me, said hello, and then asked, "My master was wondering if you were gay?" I replied no, and she walked back into the crowd.

Simple?

Not quite.

For a start, the master didn't approach me himself. For whatever reason he sent his slave. Maybe he would have felt awkward approaching me himself and it was easier to send his slave, or maybe he felt the need to exercise his masterly attributes over her, or maybe it was something else. In any case, he—the unseen executive of their two-person structured group—tapped into one of the group's resources, i.e., the girl, to solve this problem.

This, of course, involved me, someone not in their group. At this point we become aware of a boundary: the boundary between them, on the inside of their group, and me, on the outside.

At the time I was wearing jeans and a T-shirt—an outfit not suggestive of any involvement in master/slave activities, and so the issue of consent subtly enters the picture. In fact, the boundary I just mentioned was, amongst other things, a boundary of consent.

If I were innocent of such things, an approach by a woman who said that she had a master might have been seriously disturbing. As it was, I just found it mildly unpleasant

175

to have been included in their dynamic without my consent. That is, the two of them had agreed to be engaging in a master/slave relationship with each other, and to be doing various things based on that awareness. They had no way of knowing how I'd feel about it though.

This is worth considering because had this happened at, say, a BDSM party, then my consent to be involved would have been implicit. It would have been normal, nay expected, in such an environment, for masters and slaves to be running around willy-nilly, and it really would have been naive of me to have gone there thinking otherwise.

We can also separately see implicit consent here because, had I been at a supermarket or a parent/teacher evening at a school, a direct question about me being gay would have been inappropriate. As it was, I was at a gay/lesbian hotel, standing *on my own*, and thus there's clearly the possibility of being approached.

This issue of involvement with the couple has nothing to do with me pulling a whip out of my bag and launching into a heated exchange with the slave girl's back, or sending her off to wash my car and then bring me a drink when she's finished. Merely being approached as part of the master's exercise of his masterly will over the girl was enough. Likewise, had I been in a non-homosexual environment, raising a question about my sexual preferences may have been enough to cause me consider things I was uncomfortable with.

A better way of handling this may would have been for the man to approach me himself and ask if I was gay. Given the context—a gay and lesbian hotel, rather than a master/slave hotel—there would have been no issues. Indeed, knowing whether I was gay or not actually had nothing to do with mastery or slavery. Activating a master/slave context between he and his slave, and me, was superfluous on the face of it, but somehow was seen by the man as justified and valuable otherwise he clearly wouldn't have done it.

The Sad Man

I never met the Sad Man, but for a quite a while he was the master of a female friend of mine. Initially I only heard about him through her from time to time, but later he and I exchanged some emails before he and she went their separate ways.

I later discovered that he had devoted considerable time and effort over some years in trying to convince my friend that I was only interested in her to get close to the group of which they were both members. For many years I would telephone her and visit her regularly, and he somehow decided that it must be that I was doing these things because I wanted to get closer to his group. He had this belief despite him having never met me, nor in our correspondence having ever asked about my friendship with her.

Certainly, in the email correspondence I had with him, whenever there was even the slimmest opportunity for him to interpret what I wrote as an attempt to cosy up to him or to meet other members of his group, he grasped it unhesitatingly and chastised me about it.

While his group—however large or small it might have been, or however magnificent it might have been, is not the problem here—the two facts that: a) the group existed, and b) he was a member of it, were enough for him to use as leverage for his own unfortunate and suspicious ideas.

From the BDSM point of view this occurrence acquires more gravity because he was, and perhaps still is, a senior master within this particular group. If you consider the weight that many submissives and slaves often necessarily give to the pronouncements of their masters, and to the guidance and direction which they seek from them, the fact that he was prepared to interfere with and sabotage a close friendship of someone under his care, i.e., my friend, is, I think, a gross abuse of position. More so because it was based on a figment of his imagination.

But—and this is why I think of him as the *sad* man—with no evidence either way, he chose to believe that someone (i.e., me) would be trying to manipulate a person's trust, rather than be trying to build a friendship. To me—with my hopeful and optimistic soul—this is indeed very sad. I suspect that he thought he was doing the right thing, but the road to hell is paved with good intentions, and I think his intentions failed to match both his abilities and his awareness of the emotional baggage which he himself was carrying.

Had it been the case that he and my friend were not members of any group, then I think it's unlikely he would have been able to construct anything like the same sort of evil intent which he projected on to me. At worst, perhaps, he would have been able to imagine that I was trying to get my friend away from him and claim her as my own slave.

Correspondence canned

Some time ago I used to correspond via email with a slave many, many hundreds of kilometres away from were I lived. I never met her in person.

She was a member of a BDSM group which was large enough to have its own council, and we maintained our correspondence quite openly—both the council and her own master knew it was going on.

One day though, someone said something. I don't know what was said, or to whom, but it caused the council to order my slave friend and her master to stop communicating with me. My friend said she was unhappy with the order, but had to abide by it and contact stopped.

A few months later she left that group and resumed contact with me.

This particular group was, and possibly still is, one of the secretive types. Its council never contacted me, nor did I have a way of contacting them. As far as I know, I never had met any of the individuals on the council, but because they were a secret group I cannot be sure. I never knew what was said, whether it actually did involve me or whether it was just an order not to speak to outsiders, and I was never given an opportunity to appeal. The decision to order my friend and her master not to talk to me was given to me by my friend via email simply as a *fait accompli* (or done deal).

I suspect that because I was not part of the group, and had no rank in it, that the council could not see me. In other words, it might have been a case of tunnel vision. They knew I was there, but my existence was not significant in their decision-making because I was outside of their group, and that boundary prevented them seeing me as noteworthy.

Delegated authority

The above is an excellent real-life case where a master has delegated some of his own authority—namely his authority to choose with whom he can associate—to the central management body of the group to which he belongs.

This is an interesting consideration because we normally like to think of a master as being the epitome of the expression of authority, but in a structured group even he has to toe the line or risk being ejected.

The unpaid consultancy

A slave with whom I had been friends for a long time, and who I did know personally, was ordered by her master to ask me to fly down to where she lived. I didn't know until later that this request was ordered by him, or that it was actually a part of a project of his, or that she hadn't actually wanted to ask me to to be involved in it—i.e, to spend my own time and money flying to a distant city.

However, because she was a good friend, and because I didn't know about the project at the time, just the short message I got from her was enough for me to pack my bags and go.

This particular master was an executive in a secretive group. I have never met him, and I don't know what he was trying to achieve with this project. He never explained. There didn't actually seem anything for me to do during the visit—or certainly nothing to warrant my actual presence, and I soon left to come back home feeling rather dissatisfied.

While I was happy to spend my time and money to visit my friend, deviously being made to spend my time and money for a secret project of a master I'd never met is, I think, somewhat poor form. I only found out about his involvement after he and she had gone their separate ways, and I never received an offer from him to repay my expenses or to pay for my time.

Perhaps this particular master thought that as I was contributing my time and money because my friend had requested it—even though he was the one who ordered such a request be made to me—that this validated what he was doing.

This does prompt the question: where do you draw the line? If a master has a slave, how many of the resources which she has at her disposal can he call upon for himself? If she has the goodwill of someone, can he draw upon that for his own purposes? If she has money, can he spend it on himself? Can he drive her car? If opportunities come her way due to something she did before he came on the scene, how much should he be able to profit from that?

Token compensation

As I've noted above, some groups hide their existence from the rest of the world. They may do this for any of a large number of reasons, such as to prevent wannabes constantly knocking on their doors, or to avoid the gaze of the law. The point is that they become a secret, join-by-invitation-only, group.

But no man, or group, is an island, and they necessarily have interactions with the world outside their group. Perhaps their members attend public BDSM social gatherings, or maybe they play and participate in BDSM activities with people who are not members of the group. Perhaps they even scout the more public events looking for new members.

Sometimes the activities or goals of the group impact people outside of the group, but when this happens, and even if the outsiders are significantly affected, the group must remain hidden. Likewise, if the group, or some members of it, have some project which needs the assistance of an outsider, then they can either forgo the help, or get it, as we've seen above, through subterfuge.

Let's look at two scenarios:

1. Slave S meets master M at a BDSM party. To S it seems that M is an ideal master for her, and she puts in a lot of effort to make a good impression. Indeed, they seem to be getting along like a house on fire.

M is, though, a junior member of a secret group, and he happens to mention to some other masters in the group that he has started getting involved with S, who is not part of the group. These other, more senior, masters tell M that they have already been keeping an eye on S, and that they have other plans for her once she develops more skill and understanding. They insist that M ends his relationship with S, which he does.

M can't tell S the real reason why he is ending his relationship with her. S is understandably hurt and upset.

2. A master/slave couple (C) in a secret group have need of some particular form of assistance. It might be they need help with a problem in their relationship, or that they are looking to develop some particular skills. It turns out that there's no one in the group who can help, but someone else in the group has a friend outside the group with the necessary ability.

So the call goes out and this outside expert (E)—who knows nothing about the secret group—gets asked by his friend to help out. He does so, doing a favour for his friend, and the master/slave couple get what they're after.

In the first scenario, an innocent outsider, S, has been hurt as a consequence of the goals of the secret group. In the second scenario, the group arranged for expert E to unwittingly provide a service to the group by leveraging his friendship with someone in the group.

In both these cases the group may feel obligated to somehow make it up to the outsiders—to somehow compensate slave S for the hurt they have caused her to feel, even though their intentions were good; and to compensate expert E for his time and effort because even though he thought he was doing a favour for a friend, he was actually doing a service to a couple his friend barely knows but who happen to be part of the same secret group.

For slave S, the group might arrange that at the next few play parties she attends, that one or two of their members will clandestinely ensure that she has an *excellent* time. Likewise, for E the group might arrange through others of its members, that he receives unexpected opportunities or other boons.

On the face of it, this looks to be an equitable way for the group to deal with these issues and still stay secret, but there are two important factors which get overlooked in this sort of behaviour.

Consent

Consent is something which many in the BDSM world consider to be of vital importance. The fact that someone is properly informed and then agrees to engage in some particular activity beforehand is part of the creed of many BDSMers.

In both examples above consent is absent. In the first, S is not involved in any of the discussions between M and the other masters of his group. Even if she does agree to end the relationship with M, she isn't given the real reason, and thus any consent from her is based on false information and is invalid.

In the second example, E is asked by his friend to perform a favour. E is not informed about the real relationship between his friend and the master/slave couple and so his choice to help out is based on false information. Thus his consent is also not valid. He was agreeing to something which looked like one thing but was actually something else.

Recompense

When slave S gets her excellent times, or E gets his extra opportunities or boons through agents of the secret group, who is being benefited or compensated?

If E finds a $50 note on the street one day, is he going to somehow associate this with the service he performed for the master/slave couple? No? Then why should he associate any other unexpected opportunity with that same service? And if he sees no association, then it's not payment or reward in his eyes. It's just luck.

Indeed, with E being engaged as an expert, it's also up to him to set his own price based on the circumstances of his employment. In the example above, he doesn't set the price. The group does, and it may or may not be what he'd set.

Likewise, if some master treats S to a good time, unless told otherwise she might think it's her lucky night, but it won't take anything away from the hurt that she felt due to the break-up with M. No matter how lucky she feels, it's not compensation in her own terms.

So, if neither S nor E actually benefits from these *acts of compensation*, who does?

Answer: the secret group does. By making these "payments", the group, or the members of the group involved in what's happened, get to feel that they've appropriately compensated the outsiders involved. They can feel that they've made an effort to restore the balance, to pay their obligation to the outsiders.

This is an unfortunate and dangerous way of thinking for a number of reasons, including:

1. The group decides how much S's hurt is worth, how much E's time and effort is worth, and how the group is going to compensate them for it. This is akin to the buyer deciding the price to pay, and the terms of payment, rather than the seller. A problem with this is that there's actually no way for the group or its members to determine what's fair payment. The group

may think that something is fair compensation, but S or E may actually think that it's far less valuable than the group does.

For example, we've seen that E is an expert who gets paid for his time. What happens of the group decides to recompense him by providing him with a business opportunity? More specifically, what happens if he has sufficient work and isn't interested in any more? The business opportunity might look quite valuable on the face of it, but have no value at all as far as E is concerned.

2. It is, as I've already mentioned, completely non-consensual.

3. It provides a framework, which I've seen formalised in at least one group, where taking advantage of, using, or causing problems for outsiders, is sanctioned by the group though established procedures for providing compensation for the outsiders. This is unfortunate because it tells the group members that: 'you can do these things to outsiders because if you follow the compensation rules then it's all fair.'

If we look further at the example of S, it might be the case that S gets a bucket-load of good times secretly from the group to make up for them taking M away from her. But if this experience happens a few more times, then it doesn't matter how many good times S has received, she's likely to pack up and leave the BDSM world feeling very disillusioned because the masters she expresses interest in seem to keep going away.

If she's already had a couple of painful experiences with other masters, then even if the group only does this to her <u>once</u>, it might be that this one time is the straw which breaks the camel's back. In this case, the actions of the group would have directly precipitated her departure and ultimate disillusionment.

One of the points here is...

One of the points here is that structured groups create their own authority and their own new contexts. These are as open to misuse or abuse—such as being used as a basis for justification or rationalisation—as any other situation, be it in the world of BDSM, or be it in white-bread land.

A structured group may define, for example, what is acceptable behaviour for its members, and usually this is for the purpose of allowing the group to achieve whatever goals it has, such as ensuring standards of skill or honour. It is, therefore, entirely reasonable for a group to have rules and procedures. It is, however, sometimes tempting to use this rule-making authority beyond the bounds of legitimacy.

The present example of token compensation is a case in point. While members of a group implicitly or explicitly agree to be bound by its rules, there is no such agreement from people not in the group.

The group gains legitimacy and consent from its members to act for them. This sets a clear boundary of where and how the group can act. This won't necessarily stop the group trying act outside these boundaries however.

Just because a group sees a problem, doesn't mean that an arbitrary solution it comes up with is fair. It can say that something is fair us much as it likes, it doesn't make it so however. But the fact that the group has said so lends an air of legitimacy anyway, at least to its members.

Looking at it another way, there's actually nothing stopping me authorising the U.S. Navy to launch an amphibious assault on Tasmania. However this is unlikely to get very far because the US Navy wouldn't recognise my authority. It's clearly and obviously way outside any possible legitimacy I may have.

However, if the council or central committee of a structured group authorises some form of behaviour that is outside its area of legitimacy *but not obviously so* (such as the present example of token compensation), then the members of the group may accept it at face value and believe that they have been *legitimately* authorised to behave the way the council says. Unless they have a full appreciation of the consequences of their actions, then the "authority" granted by their council may be enough for them to proceed full speed ahead.

We can see this sort of issue to do with boundaries of legitimacy in the earlier example of *Correspondence canned*. The group concerned didn't form to regulate its members' social lives. It formed to create opportunities for better and more profound master/slave experiences. It's unlikely that my friend, the slave, and her master joined the group thinking that the group's council would decide who they could be friends with. It was probably never mentioned to them when they joined, didn't appear in the group's manifesto, and it certainly wouldn't have appeared in any glossy brochure which the group might have distributed to potential members. But the council attempted to claim that authority anyway. This is well beyond its legitimacy, and is akin to the committee of a bowling club trying to tell its members which dentist to use. It rankled, and it contributed to my friend leaving the group.

We can thus see that boundaries involving legitimacy don't just have to do with who is, or is not, a member of the group; but also have to do with how much authority is granted to the group by its members, and how that authority is used.

Common factors

Distancing

In much of the above we can see the factors which can lead to the executive or management of a structured group becoming "out of touch". This is a common problem in clubs and other groups, often with the rank-and-file feeling that the executive is no longer acting in accord with the needs of the members of the group.

When a group becomes large it's often impractical for the entire membership to be involved in the decision-making. Thus a management council or committee is formed, and this committee acts through other members of the group, such as the secretary. This creates the situation where the committee decides, but someone else acts, and this places distance between the executive and the consequences of their actions.

This occurs perhaps even more so when the structured group consists of masters or dominants who are more inclined to want to tell others what to do than do it themselves. In other words, because exercising their authority and control over their submissives and slaves is actually a goal and a source of pleasure and satisfaction for them and their partners, they are more likely to do this—even when it's *not required*—than vanilla counterparts in a non-BDSM structured group.

There may be other factors contributing to this use of slaves or others to ensure distance between a decision and the consequences. Many people try to avoid conflict or contention, and use of a slave or other messenger can be an effective way to achieve isolation. The person or group with the authority may not even realise that they're doing it.

Thus, authority may be exercised when it'd be more appropriate not to do so. We saw this in the *At a hotel* example above where the master, through activating his slave in my regard, created a potential consent issue. It would have been safer to approach me himself.

Likewise, when the council in *Correspondence canned* decided that two of its group members, namely my friend and her master, should no longer communicate with me, the council too was creating distance between their decisions and the consequences by not communicating with me directly.

We've seen earlier that one of the outcomes of BDSM can be derealisation, the detaching of someone from reality. While in many cases this can be related to a submissive or slave who is long-term immersed in, say, a service relationship with her master or dominant, the same sort of distancing from reality can be created by the executive of a structured group—be it a single master, or a council or committee—by virtue of their choosing to operate at more of a distance than required.

Indeed, the fact that group structures existed created the opportunity for what I consider its misuse in each of these cases.

Citadel Complex

When we consider the Sad Man we can see another opportunity for misuse of structured group environment. By potentially identifying closely with the group, and attributing to the group a very high value in his life, the master could imagine that I thought being a member of the group was more valuable than a long-term friendship. This is Elise's *Citadel Complex* [ELISE2001] in action—namely in his eyes that I couldn't just be standing near the walls of his citadel; I had to be trying to get in.

Tunnel vision

One general problem of structured groups is a tendency towards tunnel vision. This can be exacerbated when the group is exclusive or secretive—which some BDSM groups tend to be as a way of preventing the great, and possibly voyeuristic, unwashed from beating on their doors.

This tunnel vision takes the form of a reluctance or inability of the group to look outside its own borders. Part of this is perhaps a human failing. If the group itself is looking to resolve a problem, its sphere of influence ends at the boundary of the group. Therefore it's easier and more certain to use people, actions, or resources which can be activated within the group to resolve issues, rather than reach out to the world outside its borders where the group has much less control.

But another part of this tunnel vision can be forced upon the group if it uses secrecy or obscurity to protect itself. For example, if the group is invitation-only, or if it includes high-profile members who want their privacy maintained, or if the group's activities or resources might seem extremely attractive to voyeurs or to the excessively libidinous, then for the group to act outside its own boundaries might attract undesired attention or publicity.

For all of these reasons, a group's preferred solution to a problem, even if it's not the best solution to the problem itself, may well be the one which doesn't expose the group to the outside world.

There are a few potential issues here:

- Internal solutions to problems involving the world outside the group are often less than optimal. Indeed, the larger the involvement of the outside world in the problem, the less optimal a purely internal solution is likely to be.

- Where the group is secretive or deliberately obscure, then people outside the group may be disadvantaged by the group's solution without even being aware of it.

- People outside the group may get involved unwillingly. This brings up the matter of *consent*, a common and important ethical discussion topic in the world of BDSM. In particular, how can a secret group solve a problem involving the outside world without letting the outside world know that it's doing so? What can the people outside do if things go awry, and how can they be recompensed if it costs or harms them in some way? And especially if they don't know that it's the group's actions which caused it.

Conclusion

So, when we look at BDSM activities and recognise that there are people for whom some activities might not be suitable—such as play rape for a previous victim of real-life rape, or caning for someone abused by a teacher at school —we can also note that even being a member of a structured group can be consciously or unconsciously misused by someone predisposed towards paranoia, arrogance, or *dom's disease*.

19. Types of authority

I'd like now to spend a little time looking at different types of authority, their place in the world of BDSM, and how they operate. This is something I looked at incidentally in the context of one person controlling another in *The Control Book* [MASTERS2006], and I refer the reader to that book if they're interested in the actual mechanics of control-taking. Authority is one step *before* control-taking. It establishes the right to take or assert control in the first place.

This is a very large area, and I will be doing no more than scratching the surface here. For further information, I also refer you to these excellent texts:

- *Authority* [WATT1982]
- *Ethics of Coercion and Authority: A Philosophical Study of Social Life* [AIRAKSINEN1988]
- *The nature and limits of authority* [DEGEORGE1985]

Authority of office

One of the first kinds of authority we come across in our lives is authority of office. This relates to the role someone performs in our lives, rather than the actual identity of the person. A teacher or child-minder is a good early-life example. Both have authority over us in particular circumstances—the teacher has clear authority while we're in school but little authority should we meet them outside of school, and the child-minder has authority only during the time they've actually been charged with our care by our parents. Should we fail to do what we're told by these people when their authority is active, the wrath of minor gods, the state, or our parents will fall down upon our heads.

The office of The President Of The United States Of America is another example of this type of authority. The office itself is clearly differentiated from the person who holds the office, and the authority is due to the office, not to the person holding the office. Ex-president Jimmy Carter might be a very nice guy and all that, but he is an ex-president and none of the authority he gained by becoming president stayed with him when Ronal Reagan took over.

Sheriffs and police officers have authority of office which we recognise due to the uniforms they wear. In the case of teachers and child-minders, we are introduced to them and told their role. Police, fire-brigade officers, and members of the military are unknown to us until they appear in front of us in uniform, and we recognise their authority due their office by virtue of that uniform.

In the world of BDSM, particularly if we're of a slave or submissive disposition, we might recognise the authority of a master or dominant by their clothing or uniform. However, this recognition will be tempered by context. If we're at a leather bar we're more likely to attribute authority to the person wearing the uniform than if we see the same uniform at a vanilla fancy-dress party.

In my previous discussion about structured groups I also mentioned some roles or offices which come into existence at the same time as the group. The office of *secretary* and *membership secretary* are two good examples. The secretary has authority over the resources of the group, and the membership secretary can decide who gets into the group.

In all cases, the authority of an office is limited. Teachers can't tell us what to become when we grow up, child-minders can't tell us how to invest our superannuation funds, presidents can't tell us what hobbies to pursue, a police office from France can't tell someone in Idaho what to do, and group secretaries can't tell us who we should be partnered with. The boundaries of each office's authority is clearly defined and we generally know what is included and what is excluded.

It's worth noting that I have not been talking about personal attributes, skill or ability. These are largely irrelevant in regards to authority of office. They may be relevant to how well a particular incumbent carries out the duties of the office, but don't affect the authority of the office itself.

For example, we may have an idea in our minds of what being a master or slave entails, and this actual image isn't affected if we see someone claiming to be a master (i.e., to hold that office) and they're particularly incompetent at it.

As I've noted, authority of office is transferrable. Presidents, teachers, police, and child-minders come and go from our lives, but the office remains the same. Just the person or people occupying that role change, and how well they do it.

Technical authority

This form of authority is associated with someone who is an expert in a particular field. While we might do what a nice police officer says just because he's a police officer, should a bomb-disposal expert tell us to start running then we do it because he's an expert and there's a very good chance that what he's saying is good advice.

Technical authority is about expertise. There is no office associated with being a technical expert, nor is it a transferrable type of authority. Expertise cannot be passed from one person to another.

To give a BDSM-related example, we might be at a play party engaging in some challenging form of bondage with a luscious member of a very interesting gender, when a well-known bondage expert tells us that we should loosen a particular knot. He has no rank or office, and is just another guy at the party, but we recognise his *technical authority*—his expertise in the field—and very seriously consider what he says.

Technical authority is important when someone is deciding whether to engage— in BDSM terms—in some activity with someone. This is what some bottoms and submissives will surrender to. Not to the dominant or top themselves, but to the expertise and to the knowledge that the dominant or top will be able to carry through whatever activity is involved.

Sometimes there is an overlap between authority of office and technical authority. This is related to rank, which I'll talk more about in a moment, where someone is awarded a rank (or office) based on their ability.

Personal authority

This is perhaps the most important and rewarding form of authority in master/slave and dominant/submissive relationships. In such relationships, it is often how personal authority is exercised which is important. Whether a master is tying up his slave, or sending her to get him a cup of coffee, or is fucking her senseless—it is his use of authority within these activities, not the fact that he does them, which is often important.

There are a few important requirements for personal authority:

1. The desire, need, and hunger to command,
2. The fully-aligned surrender of self to commanding,
3. Having a goal to achieve through that command.

If any of the above three are missing, it pretty much puts the kibosh on the whole exercise of personal authority. Note my use of the word "command" in each of the three requirements. It is through command that personal authority is experienced by the master and by his slave.

Desire, need, and hunger

A master or dominant needs a desire, need, or hunger to command and to *feel* that command being exercised. It is no use to simply issue commands without any feedback or feeling of the consequences of those commands. This would be like simply speaking the words into an empty void—while they might be truly excellent commands, they would go nowhere and give no satisfaction.

It is also the need or hunger to command which communicates itself to the slave or submissive. This can, and perhaps should, be at a primal or visceral level[12], and is what gives the command, and the authority backing it, the ability to deeply satisfy.

Desire, need, and hunger also contribute to making command and its exercise just a natural part of life, allowing the master or dominant to automatically make it part of how they interact with their slave or submissive.

Fully-aligned surrender

As I've noted elsewhere[13], our upbringing and various other factors can interfere with our ability to freely express our true selves, and to seek what our true selves need. Learning to recognise our true selves, and to recognise the nature of the conflicts which we experience, allows us to pursue ways of overcoming these conflicts. Ultimately, this can lead to the situation where all of our energies are focussed towards satisfying our needs; rather than having to devote some of them, for example, to overcoming perpetual guilt (a favourite of some religions).

In terms of personal authority, we can best satisfy the need to express it by surrendering to it. That is, by embracing and accepting the hunger—by conscious acceptance, by ferreting through our social and familial conditioning and weeding out the bits that conflict, and by creating personal circumstances which allow rather than deny the hunger—then we fully-align ourselves with its satisfaction.

If we aren't fully aligned, then our ability to express that authority will be dulled, and likewise our satisfaction.

Goal

Personal authority must be activated by a goal. As masters, slaves, dominants, and submissives are generally looking for an experience of power or authority which lasts for longer than a simple BDSM scene, a more substantial goal than a super-dooper

---

12 See *The language of the collective unconscious* in chapter 4, *Conscious and unconscious.*

13 Such as in chapter 5, *Identity maintenance, management, and role-play.*

orgasm is usually called for. This may be, for example, the construction of a personal service-based relationship, an extended training relationship, or the development of some master-driven project (such as the establishing and running of a BDSM nightclub).

Delegation

It is possible to delegate some forms of authority.

We saw the example of delegation in the case of the child-minder. Our parents delegate some of their authority to the child-minder for the duration of the exercise. Likewise, a president may delegate authority to their vice-president while they're on holidays or unavailable, and a master may delegate some of his authority over his slave to another master for a while—such as when he says, "Here. Take care of my slave while I'm out."

Delegated authority is always implicitly or explicitly limited. For example, a child-minder doesn't get to adopt out the kids in her care. And in all cases the person who makes the initial delegation at the very least keeps the authority to rescind the delegation, such as when the master returns and claims his slave back.

Technical authority can't easily be delegated, but if a bomb-disposal expert tells you to watch a panel, and then run like the wind and take everyone with you when a particular light comes on, then you have acquired a limited technical authority due to your new training.

Rank

Authority can be vested in an office, or it can be awarded due to some attribute or characteristic of a person—such as a skill. The advantage of authority being vested in an office is that there's no need to demonstrate any particular skill before people let you exercise that authority.

It would be extremely burdensome if a police officer had to demonstrate their expertise at policing each time they tried to move people on, calm down two street antagonists, or enter someone's house to check for burglars. Instead, we rely on their uniform or badge to recognise their authority to do these things.

In effect, a rank is a recognition that someone has earned the right to exercise some form of authority. We recognise that a police officer has earned that rank by their uniform, and this generally speeds up the work of policing immensely. The big benefit is that when we call the police and a dude shows up in the right uniform with the right badge, we don't need to validate their skills and knowledge ourselves. It is de facto done.

Some BDSM groups—particularly groups which might be geographically dispersed, or which have many subgroups or chapters—use ranks to allow members to move smoothly from one subgroup to another without having to demonstrate their skill or ability each time they get to somewhere new. I mentioned this when talking about promotion in chapter 17, *Structured groups*.

Where all the groups, subgroups, and chapters concerned have similar interests and standards, then ranking can be an effective way to enable the exercise of authority and roles within the groups as smoothly as possible. This *portability of rank* can be highly valuable.

Awarded authority

Authority can also be awarded. Often this is on the basis of personal skill or examination, and bears some similarity to rank. However, where a rank is awarded by peers, an awarded authority comes from an institution. A diploma or certificate from a technical college or university is a good example of this.

Often such an award comes as a result of completing a particular course of study. This differs from a rank where personal attributes or characteristics are taken into consideration in promoting someone. Diplomas and certificates can be awarded to complete assholes.

Awarded authority is like *technical authority*, but isn't based on proven skills. Instead, it is an artefact of the authority the granting institution has to make a recognised judgement or evaluation.

Physical superiority

In the BDSM world this form of authority can make an appearance where physical strength is used, or where one person out-thinks the other. It is where some inherent characteristic of one person is superior to that of another. Using physical strength to manipulate, control, or restrain a submissive can be a very powerful experience, for example (and can be a form of penetration, of course).

This type of authority is, naturally enough, not transferrable. Indeed, it may not even be able to be exercised where, for example, a particular submissive is significantly stronger or smarter than the dominant they're with.

Many hats

It's often the case that people have many forms of authority at the same time. An attorney general will have at least: a) the authority of the office of Attorney General, b) his own legal expertise, c) authority awarded to him from the university which graduated him in law, etc.

Likewise, the secretary of a BDSM group carries the authority of the office of secretary, their own personal authority, authority due to their rank in the group, and any technical authority they have in their particular BDSM area of interest.

Not authority

BDSM frequently includes some elements of authority in one or more of its many forms. Often this is viewed in terms of one person being subservient to, or obeying, another. This can be due to a constructive use of authority, but obedience and subservience can be due to other factors which don't have any healthy relationship with authority.

Coercion

This can be the use of force, constraint, or restraint, to get someone to do what another wants. For example, if one person manipulates circumstances so that the other has only one option, then this is coercion.

Threat

Threats involve suggesting that dire consequences await a person if they don't do what's wanted from them. It can be difficult to draw the line between threats and the reasonable use of punishment to direct a submissive towards a goal.

The difference can be that reasonable use of punishment can be part of a whole structure in which the submissive is being directed towards a larger goal they wish to achieve. It becomes a threat when the goal is one which they do not wish to achieve.

Fear

While coercion and threat are imposed from the outside to get obedience or compliance, fear can be imposed by a person on themselves. For example, a common theme is that one partner is afraid that if they don't do certain things to please their partner that their partner will leave them.

This type of fear is different to that of, say, a "mind fuck" scene where the fear is used as productive component of penetration.

20. Training

Everyone must leave something behind when he dies, my grandfather said. A child or a book or a painting or a house or a wall built or a pair of shoes made. Or a garden planted. Something your hand touched some way so your soul has somewhere to go when you die, and when people look at that tree or that flower you planted, you're there. It doesn't matter what you do, he said, so long as you change something from the way it was before you touched it into something that's like you after you take your hands away. The difference between the man who just cuts lawns and a real gardener is in the touching, he said. The lawn-cutter might just as well not have been there at all; the gardener will be there a lifetime. Ray Bradbury, Fahrenheit 451

I have been formally trained as a trainer. I have a certificate on my wall to attest to this, and have a lot of practical experience to back me up. I hasten to add that this isn't a BDSM qualification. It is instead an internationally-recognised training qualification which took many years, much study, much hard work, and much practice to attain.

Lots of people really don't need to see any sort of big training picture. They feel happy and complete, and have generally pretty good lives without understanding all the ins and outs of training. If they don't need to know it—if they're not seriously trying to train people, and if they're not being seriously trained—then not knowing about training is cool.

But, some people would benefit from an understanding of training. Sometimes bad training is worse than no training at all. Hence the existence of this chapter. What you are going to read in this chapter are the views of yours truly wearing his trainer hat reflecting on this aspect of BDSM.

This isn't a how-to chapter though. Instead I just want to talk about the sorts of things you can learn, and maybe how they are taught. If you don't have it already, by the end of this chapter I want you to have a good appreciation for the role of training in BDSM, and to have some idea of the sorts of things you can be trained in.

I'm going to divide this chapter into three sections:

- Play: some discussion about skills and experience that are most useful during play (as in dungeon) sessions,
- Service: in this section I'll talk about training and abilities that are most useful in the context of one person serving another, and
- Training and trainers: here I'll be writing about what's involved in training and learning, about being a trainee and about being a trainer.

Play

The sort of play that I'm going to be writing about here is the type of play that you typically find in a bedroom or dungeon-type environment. This is play that has a well-defined start and finish, such as a bondage session, or a flogging or cutting session. You can pretty easily tell when it has started and when it has ended.

Many people define training solely in terms of play. For example, a recent correspondent of mine mentioned that she had had "basic training". I asked her what she meant and she replied, "By basic training i mean spanked, whipped, bondage (light), gagged, golden shower, orgasm control, breast bondage, ..."

Let's talk about this sort of training.

For the bottom

At first glance you might think that there's not a lot of training involved in, for example, being spanked. You pull down your knickers, bend over, and then the top does the rest. What more is there for the bottom?

In fact, there's a lot more for the bottom.

How someone will react to a BDSM activity—both during the scene and in the hours and days afterwards—is something they don't really know before they've tried it.

So, the first thing each bottom needs to learn are their reactions to these new experiences. Here are a few reactions which can be confusing or surprising the first time they happen:

- Sub-space. I've already spoken about this, but it bears re-explaining. Also sometimes just called "space", this is a state of mind which is very relaxed and usually passive. Often someone in "space" will have trouble verbalising, and might not be able to say when they're in distress or difficulty. They might lose awareness of their own pain, not realising they are experiencing pain, or not being able to respond—such as use their safeword—when they are being actually harmed (as opposed to just being hurt). A safeword is a pre-arranged word, phrase or action (such as saying the word, "red," or dropping a ball which the submissive has been holding) to indicate to the dominant that the submissive is having problems or is in distress.

- There might also be a phase shortly after play where the bottom seems to come down from a high induced by the play, and where they hit a brief depression or sadness. This is sometimes called "sub-drop".

- Unexpected tears or emotion. For various reasons, play can sometimes see a release of emotion[14], or an unexpected reaction in the bottom. This can be crying and tears, anger, yelling, screaming, or even unexplained laughter.

- Bruising, marking and tenderness. Of course, physical play scenes involving caning, flogging, or bondage can lead to physical marks. Bruising, redness, tender pink bits, or welts are not uncommon. These may be a surprise for a firth-time bottom.

Following the first few play sessions, most bottoms—as well as many tops—put a fair number of neurones to work as they think through how they felt and reacted to what happened. They need to learn the mental skills or postures that best and most productively allow them to absorb what happens to them in play. Instead of becoming physically or mentally tense, for example, they need to learn how to stay relaxed and immerse themselves[15].

There are also physical skills which a bottom might need to learn. If bodily orifices are involved, then they might need to learn about muscle control, lubrication, orgasm control, and so on. If you're going to be tied up in one position for a long time, then muscle control is important to help avoid cramps and numbness.

For prolonged sessions, such as long flogging or bondage sessions, there's more. They probably need to learn about going to the toilet well in advance, and about problems with getting thirsty halfway through the session. Body temperature control can become an issue, e.g., becoming cold as their metabolism slows down, or becoming hot if sealed in cling-wrap. What to eat (or not eat[16]) in the minutes, hours, or days

---

14 See also *Catharsis* in chapter 10, *Motivations*.

15 See also the discussion on fully-aligned surrender under *Personal authority* in chapter 19, *Types of authority*.

16 Lentils anyone?

beforehand could be important depending on any bodily orifices involved—such as if an enema will be used—or if the bottom will be upside-down.

When a bottom is planning on taking part in a play session, they need to think about the physical signs of play. An underwear model, for example, is probably not going to want to do any heavy flogging or caning on the day before an important photo shoot. And red marks on your neck from a rope can be difficult to explain at the office the next day unless it's winter and you can wear a polo-neck sweater.

Training for play then, involves getting familiar with the different activities, and learning your own reactions and feelings, and how to deal with them *post factum* (which means, "afterwards", he says, showing that he knows at least these two words of Latin).

These are all things that the bottom can learn, or be assisted with, by their top or by a more experienced bottom. They can also pick up other tips—like which salves or ointments to use to help get rid of bruising, and how to better handle sub-space—along the way. The top can help by starting off slowly and giving the bottom time to get used to what's happening, rather than throwing the bottom (metaphorically speaking) into the deep end straight away.

Part of the work though, the integration side of all this—the acceptance, processing, and finding of a place for these reactions and feelings—is up to the bottom themselves. Talking with other bottoms can help.

Finally, good training lets a bottom tell (or show) a new top what to expect from them, and what they can or need to do as part of play.

For the top

Tops, on the other hand, tend to have more to think about during a play session. They are usually the more active partner, and are mostly the ones making the moment-to-moment decisions.

In the practical skills department there's a whole raft of things which the top needs to know or have. Here are a few lists:

General top skills

- Be able to manage and work with the bottom while they're in sub-space,
- Respond usefully to any communication problems which might appear during a session,
- Know how to get a bottom out of sub-space if they seem lost or confused and can't recover on their own,

- Be able to recognise signs of distress, or signs that the bottom is losing touch with what's going on,
- Know some basic first-aid skills, and
- Be level-headed and not prone to panic.

Bondage

- Know how to tie knots,
- Be prepared to cut free their bottom if there's an emergency, such as if the bottom passes out,
- Know where to place knots so they don't press on any of the bottom's joints or nerve bundles,
- Know how to recognise circulation problems, or when part of the bottom becomes numb perhaps due to pressure on nerves,
- Recognise when the ropes or chains are too tight,
- Know how to untie knots,
- Have spare keys for padlocks,
- In long scenes they might need to have water available if the bottom becomes thirsty, and
- Blankets and fans need to be available in case the bottom becomes cold or hot.

Impact play - flogging, caning, etc.

- Know where to hit, and to have a good aim,
- Know where not to hit (e.g., not on joints, not on the head, and not near major organs),
- How to choose the right implement,
- How to control the pace and strength of blows,
- Knowing what implements will cause what types of pain (e.g., sharp, dull, heavy impact but little pain, etc.), and
- When and how to do a warm-up.

Cutting and piercing

- Have a good understanding of hygiene, have clean and sharp equipment, and have a generous supply of antiseptic on hand,
- Know where major and minor arteries and veins are located,
- Know where significant structures, like muscle groups and nerves, are located when they're close to the skin surface, and

- Not faint at the sight of blood.

And, on top of the above, the top needs to learn how to immerse themselves in the experience so that it is rewarding and satisfying for them too, while still being alert for problems.

Service

One common theme in dominance & submission, and in mastery & slavery, is service. But what is this service?

If we were to make a first cut at defining service in a BDSM context, we might delve into the dictionary and come up with something about the submissive doing work for, or being of assistance to, their dominant. However, if we're going to consider the idea of training someone for service, then we need to take a closer look.

Just because a submissive shows up on our doorstep to be trained, doesn't mean we can just start them on some standard regimen and end up with a perfectly-adapted service boy or girl. We need first to look closer at *their* world of service and get an idea of its shape. After all, for example, it'd be meaningless to get a girl some specialist oral sex training when she's doing it just because she loves sucking cock. Teaching her to please the cock's owner better isn't a high priority for her and she's likely to not be very interested.

I have an excellent book on butling [FERRY2003]. Butling is what a butler does, and it's quite formal personal service stuff, though it doesn't generally include the sexual side which we see in BDSM.

To my mind, the skills and abilities of a good butler epitomise the sort of standard you'd expect for top-notch personal service. Even if a book on butling doesn't include how to perform sexual gymnastics, it does cover a lot of the personal service ground which a submissive or slave might be expected to tread—such as serving drinks, preparing meals, unobtrusively smoothing out the bumps in master's life before he even sees them, cleaning house, organising small parties for master's friends, shopping, making the bed, etc. What submissive or slave wouldn't want to be the absolute best at these things that they possibly could be?

In reality, most of them probably don't care diddly-squat about such levels of skill. If you left a book on butling on the table, most would walk past and barely give it a second glance, let alone open it and read it. Indeed, many dominants and masters don't care about this either, and the book would end up with a thick coating of dust.

Why?

To answer this question we need to look at why submissives might want to serve their dominants in the first place. Let's look at three types (and please also consider these in terms of the relationships I described in chapter 9, *Relationships II*):

1. The "do-me" submissive,

2. The reflexively service-oriented submissive, and

3. The directly service-oriented submissive.

1. The "do-me" submissive

There are many submissives for whom the actual feeling of being submissive is the bee's knees. Curling up at their dominant's feet, getting him a drink, sucking his cock, or being dragged to the dungeon by the hair, or being tied up and flogged, are all ecstasy without equal.

It's very likely that their dominant is also having a great time, too. With a cunt on-tap, and someone always available as an outlet for his sadistic tendencies, it means that he's getting his jollies as much as she is.

But where does service enter into this?

If sucking her master's cock sends her into paroxysms of pleasure, is she really serving him? Or is he serving her by giving her the, er, "tool" to achieve her own pleasure? Or are they both serving each other?

If she gets all warm and gooey by bringing him a drink, is she actually serving him, or is he serving her by letting her do it?

On the surface, of course, he is getting something out of what his submissive does—be it a blow job or getting him a drink—but underneath it can be that she is being equally, or perhaps even better, served by what's happening.

The "do-me" comes from the need of the submissive to have things done to her, and opportunities created for her by her dominant where she can get her needs met.

This can make more sense if we look at what she needs in terms of penetration. What she is looking for is the immediate experience of penetration and it needs to be provided by him.

2. The reflexively service-oriented submissive

When the dominant isn't around, can the submissive still get her jollies? Is she still going to serve?

If the submissive's enthusiasm or drive rapidly fades away when the dominant leaves the room, then we can probably safely say that we are talking about a "do-me" submissive.

If it doesn't—and she keeps on making the beds, doing the shopping, and cleaning house when the dominant's not around—what's keeping her going?

Well, maybe she actually is service-oriented. Maybe the service itself gives her a buzz, and she's more than happy to do it under the authority and command of her dominant.

There's a good chance she also likes to get her regular floggings and to orally explore her master's appendages when he's around. But the fact that she also keeps on serving and being useful in his absence, suggests a genuine service orientation.

- If he's not there, then who is she providing this service to?
- What is she getting out of it?

You can get some idea of the answers to these questions by seeing how well she responds to correction. Is she keen to perform to her dominant's own standards? If he indicates a preference for the way she should do something, is she quick to do her best to embrace it?

Or is she stubborn and continues to do things her way?

If she insists on doing things her way, then she's probably serving herself (or an image of her ideal dominant) rather than her actual real dominant.

3. The directly service-oriented submissive

While a reflexively service-oriented submissive serves *her way*, and thus shows that she's using her dominant simply as part of the picture in which she's pleasing herself, the directly service-oriented submissive actually does aim to please her dominant or master, and he is an integral and active part of the service relationship in which she's operating.

The big clues that this is the case is her attention to his standards and rules, and her readiness to adapt to his changing needs and desires for her.

Criteria—who sets the standard?

Before you consider any sort of training for a submissive, it's important, to know why, and in what circumstances, they serve.

There are a few tests you can perform to determine the shape, or nature, of a submissive's service:

1. Determine what tasks they'll perform on their own, for how long, to what standard. For example:

   (a) Preparing meals,

   (b) Washing and ironing clothes,

   (c) Making the bed,

   (d) Shopping,

   (e) Gardening, or

   (f) Getting the car serviced.

   Try telling her how to do each task, and vary how to do the tasks each time, and see how well and enthusiastically she adapts.

2. Do they get "hungry", horny, or aroused when serving?

3. Give them reading material, or find a course, on some aspect of service which they do perform for their dominant. How do they react?

Training and trainers

How do you become good at the practical skills of BDSM? How do you become good at skills such as commanding someone, recognising limits, handling, and managing pain and hungers? How do you become safe and competent tying someone up, or flogging them, or piercing them?

Training isn't just a matter of books and practice. Nor is it simply a matter of copying what someone else does. There is far more to it than that, and particularly when we start talking about serious training in a BDSM context, we're getting into authority dynamics, control, surrender, and other very interesting topics.

In this section I want to present a view of training from the inside. In line with the general theme of this book, I want to talk the *why* of training, rather than the *how*.

Being a good trainer is far more than simply demonstrating what to do and giving some useful tips on safety. I am sometimes dismayed when I come across people whose idea of training is little more than flogging someone until they learn to like it.

Certainly a good flogging can be a path to something more profound, but if a well-meaning teacher simply helps their student to learn to absorb or tolerate the pain the way they themselves do, without recognising that the student is capable of a much more profound surrender or submission if guided differently, then they are, I think, doing a disservice to their student. The student ends up at a dead end which, while possibly extremely hot and all that, isn't where the student's potential could actually take them.

Going further, there's a big difference between learning to make a cup of coffee and learning the Japanese Tea Ceremony, and between learning to kneel and learning to serve. The former, in each case, is a mechanical skill; the latter is a life-changing transformation possibly taking years.

When a trainer is involved in such a transformation, their role becomes reminiscent of the quote which began this chapter. To be able to act as guide and companion in this life-changing journey, the trainer also must have a high level of self awareness, have some knowledge of the journey already, and know when to step in, and when to step out of the way.

Three types

I like to think of the people who do teaching and training as being one of three types:

1. Doers. These are the people who simply do, but don't necessarily know why. They can demonstrate what they do themselves and may be able to show you how to do it yourself. I refer you to *The scarcity of why*, and my discussion of magic in chapter 1, *Introduction*, for more about this.

   The fact that they can only show you, and perhaps teach you, what they do is significant. There's no guarantee that this is right for you.

2. Instructors. These are the people who make it their business to be able to teach a wide range of practices well and safely, even those they don't necessarily do themselves. They may do this because they have adopted or acquired the role of trainer within their particular group, or because they simply like helping people out. It's likely they put in extra time to get the skills in the things they aren't personally keen on but still want to be able to teach.

   Go to them to learn how to tie a particular knot, how to do piercing safely, even how to kneel, make a martini, or suck cocks like an industrial vacuum cleaner.

3. Masters. These aren't the BDSM-type masters, but instead are master trainers. Not only are they good at what they teach, but they also know why things are done and can explain them. Beyond just teaching individual skills or practices in isolation—which is what instructors do, they teach the whole shebang in the context of the development of the particular student they have in front of them. From a master trainer answers like, "This is the way it has always been done," or, "Because I say so," or, "I will explain it to you when you have more experience/understanding," are never acceptable.

The latter of the unacceptable answers above deserves a bit of clarafication. It may genuinely be that case that a student asks a question, or seeks training, in an area in which they don't yet have the understanding or skill to be able to proceed. It's not the job of the trainer to fob them off, or alternatively to try to teach them anyway knowing that such efforts are either doomed or will be fatal to the student's development. The better sort of answer at these times is to explain or demonstrate a path to the point where the student *is* able to be taught what they're asking about.

One of the ways in which you can differentiate between an *instructor* and a *master* is that instructors can deal well and with confidence with usual cases but typically not with unusual cases. For example, bondage with a two-armed person is straightforward. With a one-armed, or a no-armed person, other problems appear. What are they and how do you deal with them?

Instructors are often excellently suited to students who simply want to learn a particular one-off skill and that's it. For a student who is looking for long-term development, a master trainer will better be able to look at the whole picture.

It can be tempting to consider these issues of training in terms of tops, dominants, and masters, the types of BDSM practitioners who are typically associated with the "doing" of BDSM. But training is equally applicable to bottoms, submissives, and slaves because there are important skills for them to learn, as I mentioned above.

A bottom may need to learn skills to do with pain management, medical issues to do with bruising and welts, disinfection, etc. A slave may need to learn about service and management issues.

A doer or an instructor will often simply be limited to teaching one particular skill or practice. For them what they're doing is simply presenting what they know on that particular subject and then they move on to someone else. A master trainer instead must surrender to the path of the trainee. In other words, a master trainer can't simply teach what they like or focus on what they know best. To do the best for the student a master trainer must adapt themselves completely to the nature and the path they see for the student. This is surrender, and it is the power of the master trainer.

More than this, the path they see for the student must be the student's real path, not a projection of the master trainer's own desires or needs for the student. Thus, the master trainer must be fully actualised. There must be no ego, no conflict.

This differs from the role of instructor where they will teach a particular skill, and possibly teach it very well. But this will be in isolation, rather than placed in the context of the larger development of the student.

Making it concrete

I'd like to give, perhaps, more concrete examples of what I mean by these definitions.

The doer

If you see a doer doing something like directing his slave, or tying someone up, and you ask him about it, he may be happy to show you. If you're a submissive or slave and see another doer slave or submissive perhaps engaged in some particular type of service, they can share what they do with you in detail, and even demonstrate and help you learn how they do it.

If you ask a doer about something that's outside their own personal realm, then they don't know and aren't particularly interested.

The instructor

The instructor, on the other hand, has his or her own repertoire of skills, and is also suitably knowledgeable about a range of other activities. They may prefer bondage themselves, but they've also done courses, attended workshops, or have done training in other aspects of BDSM, perhaps because they—or someone else—sees the need for this sort of expertise in their group.

They can sit down with you for an afternoon and discuss, or run a workshop on, the things they know and teach others the important ins and outs.

The master trainer

The master trainer, on the other other hand, can take a student—say a student master, or a trainee slave—and begin teaching them the skills, knowledge, and attitudes they need. For the skills that the master trainer is not themselves able to impart, they find someone who can, but the master trainer directs the whole development of the student.

An important part of this is that the master trainer will go through three important phases with their student:

- In the first phase they will be instructing and leading their student, sensitive to the developing nature of their student, finding and adapting their teaching to the particular predisposition and skills of their student.

  This is an important difference to the doer and the instructor. Both of these may be able to expertly teach some particular isolated skill, but they are not called upon to evaluate which particular skills a student should learn and what direction a student should travel.

- In the second phase the master trainer will no longer be leading their student, but will instead be accompanying them, travelling alongside them. In this phase the student has gained an awareness of the direction they may need to take, and instead of being led all the time by the master trainer, they direct more than lead, but still require the training and skills that the master trainer teaches them. They tap into the expertise of the master trainer, rather than just let him guide them.

In both the first and second phases, the ability of the trainer to empathise with the student is important.

Indeed, it may be the case that an experienced slave can serve as a trainer for a master better than another master. In many cases she is likely to be able to sense his needs and help him learn to articulate them even before he is aware of them himself. This sensitivity may well be, after all, what inclines her to be a slave in the first place.

Similarly, a master may serve best as a trainer for a slave because it is his sensitivity to the condition of a slave which compels him to be a master in the first place as well. While another slave might teach a trainee slave the mechanics of being a slave, a master is perhaps the best one to draw her out.

- In the third phase the master trainer acquires the role of *respected elder*. The trainee "graduates", but still may seek guidance and continuing lessons from their master trainer. The trainer is now a peer, and must relinquish any residual authority (other then technical authority) which they asserted over their student during training.

Let us consider the development of a slave by a master trainer in terms of these phases.

In the first phase, the trainee slave looks to their trainer for guidance, for authority, and for lessons. This *authority* aspect is important here, because even if the master trainer is a slave herself, she must exercise authority over her trainee to direct her.

Indeed, during this phase the trainer must, at times, function as a master or mistress for the trainee to serve. Beyond the practical skills, the trainee slave must learn to respond to a master *as a master*. To do this she needs to be confronted by someone who is a master to them.

At the same time though, the trainer needs to be seeing the training in terms of the trainee herself. She must empathise with the trainee and sense what is right for her.

In the second phase this empathy becomes more important as the master trainer needs to travel alongside their trainee and, as well as continuing practical lessons, needs to be able to share stories and experiences which the student will find useful.

Thus the trainer needs to embody both master and slave to be able to, in one instance, lead and be a master to which the student slave can respond, while in another instance be able to be a technically-authoritative slave companion.

In the third phase, the trainer needs to be able to step out of the way and let their student travel on without them. It is tempting for a trainer to attempt to continue guiding or training someone *ad infinitum*. But there comes a time, the right time, when the student must follow their own path and be released by the trainer.

If the student stays tied to the training of the master trainer then they can, at best become a shadow, never exceeding the master trainer. But once free to develop beyond where the master trainer can take them, they are free to excel at being the very best they can be.

21. Abuse

The topic of abuse comes up pretty regularly in BDSM circles. Almost as regularly the topic ends with no clear conclusions reached. It's a difficult subject much of the time, and even professional counsellors and therapists can have problems with it.

The common view

If we're not talking about BDSM then it's fairly easy to spot and to label abuse:

- If person A hits person B, it's abuse.
- If Person C yells at Person D, it's abuse.
- If Person E ties up Person F, it's abuse.
- If whips, canes, or handcuffs are involved, it's abuse.
- If Person G grabs Person H by the scruff of the neck and pushes them roughly to the floor, it's abuse.
- If Person J is cruel to Person K, then it's abuse.

In BDSM none of the above are necessarily abuse though. In BDSM we might find some or all of these actions in a genuinely healthy relationship.

So how can we understand what abuse is when ropes, whips, striking, and handling someone roughly, can no longer be our guides?

Definitions

I looked up *abuse* in a dictionary [OED] and found that it is:

- Wrong or improper use, misuse, misapplication, perversion,
- To take a bad advantage of; to misrepresent, colour falsely, or
- To make a bad use of, to pervert, or misemploy.

Some examples might be the abuse of drugs—using them to get high instead of to get healthy, or taking advantage of and fucking a bondage bunny who signed on strictly and only to be tied up.

These definitions are useful and they're a good start, but I've come across enough abused people to know that there can be long-term, even lifelong, effects of abuse, and the dictionary definitions don't say anything about these.

I then thought that I would look through laws dealing with abuse and see how they define it. After all, laws are created by our elected representatives, and maybe when they grappled with the problem they came up with something usefully concrete.

It was confusing. Various laws define abuse in various ways, and often in conflicting ways. What I did find though, were three factors which kept showing up:

1. The abusive action or series of actions, or what was done to the victim,
2. The intent or purpose which the perpetrator had in mind at the time, and
3. The consequence or consequences: what happened to the victim, or what they experienced (physically, emotionally, etc.) as a result of the abuse.

These factors seem useful.

The first factor, the abusive action, was common to all definitions I came across, even the dictionary ones. Many laws mentioned the intent of the perpetrator, but some laws said that intent was irrelevant (i.e., the fact that some abusive action was done—such as striking someone—was enough to establish abuse). Some laws instead said that intent was highly relevant. A few laws mentioned consequences, though mostly for determining how severe the abuse was rather than whether something was abuse or not.

Let us look more closely at these three factors:

The abusive action

Some abusive actions are well-defined within the community-at-large. Here are some common and well-accepted standards. Keep in mind that I'm not specifically talking about BDSM here yet:

- Hitting someone is physical abuse.
- Taking advantage of someone—for example, when they're drugged or unconscious or can't otherwise give their consent—is abuse.
- Using physical force, or overpowering someone, is abuse.
- Intentionally terrorising, frightening, or scaring someone is psychological abuse.
- Locking someone up, or depriving them in some way of their liberty to move around, is abuse.
- Yelling at or insulting someone is verbal abuse.
- Using fear, threats, or violence to coerce someone is abuse.
- Deceiving someone to achieve a personal or private goal is abuse.

You will probably have noted that most of the above actions occur in everyday BDSM. In BDSM someone might get the caning of their life and be full of joy and glee afterwards. Or someone could be insulted and humiliated in punishing detail and come away feeling cleansed and refreshed. Or a guy might have pins stuck in his dick, or a woman have needles pushed through her nipples without any attempt at anaesthetic and be happy to come back for more once the wounds have healed. Or a person might have usually-private bodily orifices painfully stretched and penetrated in front of a whole crowd of people and then later be having a few drinks with the person who did it to them saying how well it went.

In fact, any of the actions I listed above as abuse can be necessary to reach a positive and productive outcome in BDSM. It's clear then that the actions on their own are not necessarily indicators that abuse is occurring... at least, not in the world of BDSM. I will come back to this a little later.

The intent

The intent behind abuse is often that the perpetrator gets some benefit which they wouldn't ordinarily have. This could be:

- Getting some otherwise-unobtainable sexual gratification,
- Taking out their anger on someone,
- Compensating for feelings of inferiority by beating someone else down or manipulating them, or
- Conning someone out of something.

The consequences

Generally, in cases of abuse the consequences are negative and include things like these:

1. Fear,
2. Grief,
3. Anxiety and stress,
4. Shame and humiliation,
5. Low self-esteem or impaired self-respect,
6. Inability to relate to others in a healthy way,
7. Issues with trust,
8. Eating disorders,
9. Drugs, smoking, alcohol, gambling, or other types of addiction,
10. Various physical symptoms or illnesses, or other health problems,
11. Poor, excessive, or otherwise inappropriate responses to others,
12. Inappropriately coloured perception of circumstances, e.g., always being suspicious of the motives of others, or
13. Reinforcement or creation of negative self-opinions, behaviours, and attitudes.

Just as with my list of abusive actions earlier, the picture is less clear when you are talking about BDSM. Sometimes the initial consequences or results of the actions, i.e., the reactions of the "victim"—such as intense fear, humiliation, and physical injury (like bruising or bleeding)—are also necessary and normal for a positive outcome in a BDSM context.

Let's now take a few paragraphs to look at each of the above list of consequences with an eye to BDSM.

1. Fear

You'd hope that a dominant or a submissive would look forward to coming home from work to meet up with their partner. In an abusive relationship this anticipation can be replaced by fear. Perhaps the dominant sets excessively high standards for the submissive, or looks for unjustified excuses to punish, beat, or yell at her. Or maybe the submissive applies pressure on the dominant to perform and causes him to feel inadequate. Either way, joy is replaced by fear.

2. *Grief*

Grief usually comes from a sense of loss. In BDSM this could be from loss of sexual innocence or from a violation—like the example given earlier of a bondage bunny being fucked when she had only agreed to be tied up. It could also be from a loss of identity or self-worth when someone—submissive or dominant—has surrendered so much to their partner only to see it thrown away or treated lightly. And it can also come from a sense of lost time or opportunity, from investing a lot of time in a relationship that turned out to be be based on deceit.

3. *Anxiety and stress*

Most people need a good foundation for their lives. These can be solid anchors which provide constancy and give them a sense of security. Some behaviours from a partner can intentionally or unintentionally remove this security. For example, any of the following can lead to uncertainty and anxiety:

- An unpredictable or wildly impulsive partner,
- Appointments made, like lunch meetings, and then not kept or changed at the last minute,
- Obligations not met, or agreements not kept,
- Chaotic behaviour, and constant unplanned changes, or
- Constantly changing requirements or standards.

All these things can leave someone, dominant or submissive, not knowing what's going to happen (or not happen) next. They might be left holding the bag for their partner so much that they run out of time to do the other things they should be doing.

4. *Shame and humiliation*

Someone from a very conservative or catholic background can be shamed and humiliated by reminding them of how "bad" they are by being involved in BDSM. It doesn't matter if they consciously know that what they're doing is OK, a lifetime of conditioning by the church or by their family is not easy to dismiss.

It's a great way to manipulate someone, dominant or submissive, because it's a difficult-to-escape vulnerability that can be used at the whim of the abuser.

5. *Low self-esteem or broken self-respect*

I like to think that BDSM offers an opportunity to grow, and to explore, discover, and improve one's self. One partner though might be constantly critical, or constantly demanding. They might even uses subtle ways to imply or suggest that their partner is not up to their role, such as making obvious shows of boredom or lack of interest during scenes.

If so, this "failure" can cause their partner to doubt themselves or their ability. The partner could shrink instead of grow, or hide from future discoveries for fear of the consequences rather than seek them out. And they might even avoid meeting others for fear these supposed "inadequacies" will be revealed.

6. Inability to relate to others in a healthy way

If someone treats you an a bad way, making excessive demands of you in a BDSM context, then maybe you'll have trouble behaving or responding well when you encounter that same situation with someone else.

For example, an innocent submissive whose dominant "trains" her to be sexually available for all his friends, is going to have trouble behaving appropriately in more respectful dominant company.

7. Issues with trust

If you have a history of not knowing what's going to happen next, or have had lots of experience at being disappointed or being lied to, then it will be hard to trust the next person who comes along. This can be particularly so if this next person who comes along wears the same label—e.g., "dominant" or "submissive"—as the person who let you down.

8. Eating disorders

Eating disorders are common ways of reacting to stress (eating too much, or eating unhealthily), and of dealing with poor self image (bulimia). We've already seen how BDSM abuse can lead to stress, and thus eating disorders are a possible consequence of this stress.

Because many BDSM activities (like bondage, flogging, etc.) are done with few or no clothes, self-image can easily become an issue. For someone susceptible, a few carefully selected words about their body shape in the middle of a scene can easily lead them into self-doubt. This can put them but a hop, skip, and a jump away from an eating disorder.

9. Drug, smoking, alcohol, gambling, or other types of addiction

Again, indulging in drugs, alcohol, and the like, are common responses to stress, anxiety, and fear. We've seen how these feelings can occur with BDSM abuse. These can be hard to address, and can be made harder if there's no one who you can talk to about them who'll be understanding of your interest in BDSM.

10. Various physical symptoms or illnesses or other health problems

Even if there's no obvious stress or physical damage, there can still be physical effects. Ulcers and other ailments are well-known in this territory. Elevated blood pressure, poor digestion, bad sleeping patterns, etc., also might show up.

11. Poor, excessive, or otherwise inappropriate responses to others

Victims of abuse often tend to react poorly to situations or to people who remind them (consciously or not) of the abuse or the abuser. The reactions can be psychological, emotional, verbal, or physical. They can occur when situations or actions are similar to those in which the victim was abused. Or they can occur when there's just the potential for something similar to arise.

For example, a submissive might respond with fear when a dominant enters the room, or when she sees a particular type of implement, if past experience with a dominant, or with one of those implements, badly hurt her somehow. This might happen even if the dominant or implement is not the same one. This reaction would be entirely inappropriate if the dominant is someone she hasn't even met yet, or the implement is just on show and is not intended for her.

Also, a dominant might freeze up if a new submissive responds in some way similar to someone who has been cruel to him on the past.

12. Inappropriately coloured perception of circumstances

Someone who has had a lot of bad times in a dungeon is not going to walk into a new dungeon feeling bubbly and full of anticipation. Anyone with a consistent abusive history in a particular situation might not be able to put aside their past experiences, and might see what's happening now in terms of what happened in the past, even if there's absolutely no relationship. You could maybe call this, "loss of innocence".

13. Reinforcement or creation of negative self-opinions, behaviours, and attitudes

Abusers often choose, and play on, a weakness of their victim. Any existing self-doubt, bad habit, or physical or mental shortcoming, can be fair game in their eyes. Combine that with the difficulty that some people doing BDSM might have in finding a way to talk with someone more experienced, and you have a great way for self-doubt to be planted or fostered by an abuser.

Good intent, but bad consequences

At this point it's possible to see that there could be negative consequences for the best-planned and best-executed scene should the head-space of one or other of the participants go astray. A top could react badly with guilt at the sight of the bloodied and beaten body of his partner after a prolonged flogging or whipping scene, even if his partner is delighted with the head-space they themselves achieved. Or, equally, a submissive could find that a new activity triggers repressed memories of something bad from her past and leaves her cowering and terrified. Or a bottom with marginal self-image problems could be pushed over the edge by being undressed in some new circumstance, or by some innocent remark.

The point is that when we look at abuse, we need to recognise that determining it has occurred solely on the basis of the consequences experienced by someone is not sufficient. That doesn't diminish the fact that there are consequences, and that these consequences might take a long time to fix or overcome.

Because the actions commonly associated with abuse in the vanilla world are standard fare in the world of BDSM, we need to be careful to recognise that oftentimes these same actions are not enough to justify a diagnosis of abuse in a BDSM context even when we see the consequences I listed above.

Long-term consequences

It seems then that the actions themselves aren't the problem, and neither are immediate consequences—such as a bloodied back or a feeling of terror. But if abuse has occurred then there must be some effect of it. There must be a negative or unproductive consequence for something to be called abuse.

I think that the idea of *long-term* is important here. Fear, for example, can be a consequence of some types of BDSM scenes (i.e., "head fucks" or "mind fucks"), but like roller coaster rides and throwing one's self out of an aeroplane with a parachute, the fear should be relatively brief.

> *Where there is a negative or counterproductive effect, such as any from the list of consequences above, of some action or series of actions, and this effect remains long-term then abuse becomes a candidate cause.*

Looking at it like this, it doesn't matter what the person who caused the consequences had in mind. It might however be relevant what the victim *thought* the intention was because this will change how they feel about it all; for example, how deeply they may feel violated.

Indeed, just the simple fact that there are long-term consequences like the ones listed above is a call to action. The victim needs some form of help or therapy to overcome them.

The role of intent

At the beginning of this chapter I mentioned intent as one of the factors of abuse. How does it enter into the picture? Is it abuse if there was no malicious, hidden, or dishonest intent by the person who performed whatever actions were involved?

I think that deliberate intent is required for there to be abuse. Most definitions I came across in my research talked in terms of deceitful, malicious, or dishonourable motivations.

However, I think that it's important to realise that exactly the same set of consequences can occur to someone even if there is no evil intent. The experience which creates a negative consequence is strictly what is perceived by the person to whom it happens.

Unequal power

Abuse is generally done by way of deceit, manipulation, fear, threat, or physical violence. For these to work there must be an unequal power relationship between the victim and the perpetrator. Here's a short list of what might give the perpetrator this advantage:

- The perpetrator is smarter or physically stronger than their victim,
- The perpetrator knows something which the victim doesn't know,
- The perpetrator has something which the victim wants or needs, or
- The perpetrator is able to trigger a reaction or fear against which the victim cannot defend themselves.

I'd suggest then that where there are long-term negative consequences, such as those listed earlier, and where there is a deliberate and selfish use of power then we have abuse.

I'd argue though, that where someone has deliberately and selfishly tried to use power to their own advantage—regardless of whether there were negative consequences for someone else or not—then this perpetrator is in need of some counselling, treatment, or punishment to help them see the error of their ways.

Instances of abuse

With the above definitions in mind I'd like to look now at some ways that abuse occurs in a BDSM context. I have split some example statements or attitudes into two categories: deceit and manipulation. For each statement, I have written some comments putting them more clearly into their abusive context.

Before I start I like to say that it's easy to imagine a dominant taking advantage of a submissive, maybe by offering a simple bondage session when he actually intends to give his dick a workout once she's tied up and helpless, but a submissive can abuse a dominant as well. We'll see this below.

Deceit

Using lies, omissions, or exaggerations, to influence how someone behaves:

1. "Real submissives can take more pain than that."
2. "All the dominants I have known have demonstrated their confidence by taking me without a condom."
3. "It's OK to use a cane on my joints and testicles."
4. "I know I'm bruising, but it's OK to continue—really! I'll tell you when I need to stop."

1. "Real submissives can take more pain than that."

Well, maybe some submissives or bottoms can take lots of pain; but many submissives don't respond positively to pain at all, except possibly in a training context as correction or reinforcement, and maybe not even then.

There aren't many submissive who like being dangled by hooks through their tits either, and just because you don't like it doesn't make you any more or less submissive.

Trying to compare someone to a "real" anything suggests that they are less than they ought to be. This is coercion by playing on their inexperience or self-doubt.

2. "All the dominants I have known have demonstrated their confidence by taking me without a condom."

Again, this is a submissive trying to coerce a dominant by comparing him to other— maybe non-existent—dominants.

As far as dominance is concerned, it is—in your humble scribe's opinion—more dominant to be guided by your own values in the face of attempted manipulation than to yield.

3. "It's OK to use a cane on my joints and testicles."

Well, no, it's not OK. This is playing on someone's ignorance—in this case the ignorance of a top who doesn't know any better. Outright lies can be difficult sometimes, such as with someone who wants to do breath-play who says they're not asthmatic when they really are. But, some things can be avoided by, for example, studying up on caning and whipping before you attempt it, and by spending time getting to know someone well before you do any risky play with them.

4. "I know I'm bruising, but it's OK to continue—really!"

Maybe this is using someone's desire to please—in this case the top's—to get them to go beyond their limits. This word "limits" is the key here. The top has limits just as much as the bottom. If the top says, "Stop! I have reached my limit and I'm not comfortable hitting you any more," then the bottom needs to respect that. Manipulatively pushing the top beyond their limits is just as abusive as a top pushing a bottom beyond theirs.

Manipulation

This is using someone's ignorance, fears, doubts, desires, or needs, to cause them to behave other than they normally would:

1. "If you were a real dominant you'd use the bigger cane on me and hit me hard enough so that it really bleeds."

2. "You are my submissive and I don't want you talking to other submissives without my permission. If you do then I will release you and you'll have to go."

3. "You're going to have to tie me tighter than that if you want me to fuck me."

4. "You're not very submissive if you use your safeword when all I've done is X."

5. "You obviously don't trust me very much if you have a safe call."

6. "I won't have sex with you if you insist on a condom. I don't like them. They rob me of feeling."

1. "If you were a real dominant you'd use the bigger cane on me and hit me hard enough to that it really bleeds."

This is plainly an attempt to take advantage of any ignorance or self-doubt that the dominant might feel. This would be most effective, I guess, on a relatively new dominant who hasn't yet discovered his own boundaries. The perpetrator here, the submissive, might have an unhealthy self-destructive drive, or might have a need to be punished that overrides any consideration of the well-being of the dominant.

2. "You are my submissive and I don't want you talking to other submissives without my permission. If you do then I will release you and you'll have to go."

This is an attempt to manipulate the reality of the submissive. The dominant is creating a situation where they can convince the submissive what is right and wrong by taking away the options for a submissive to talk to others about his or her feelings. I.e., the dominant puts themselves in a position where they can invalidate what the submissive believes to be their own limits. By insisting that the dominant's way of doing things—no matter how wrong it might seem—is the right way often enough, the dominant might be able to create enough self-doubt in the submissive that they'll go beyond where they should.

3. "You're going to have to tie me tighter than that if you want me to fuck me."

This is an example of offering someone a reward for going where they don't want to go. Someone desperate for a fuck (read: guys) might get sucked in by this one.

4. "You're not very submissive if you use your safeword when all I've done is X."

This is another play on someone's self-doubt or inexperience. Safewords are about taking responsibility for yourself. They might be entirely appropriate in a scene when you think you are approaching your limit. After all, it is your limit, not the dominant's, and you are the authority on it.

5. "You obviously don't trust me very much if you have a safe call."

And perhaps this lack of trust has been entirely justified by this one phrase from the dominant!

6. I won't have sex with you if you insist on a condom. I don't like them. They rob me of feeling."

This is, of course, blackmail.

Physical outcomes

So far I've been focussing on long-term psychological or emotional consequences of abuse. There can also be, of course, physical outcomes of abuse.

Bruising and bleeding are sometimes expected outcomes of BDSM activities. Typically these are superficial. Great gushings of blood or deep bruises on the other hand are generally not desirable.

More permanent injuries—such as organ damage, loss of feeling in a limb, and infection because implements weren't cleaned properly—are often signs of carelessness, poor education, or assumption. They can also be the results of abuse.

Carelessness and neglect

Someone so keen or arrogant to whale into a submissive with a flogger or cane without taking the time to learn where, and where not to, hit; or to play with rope without learning where to place knots, or who plays at piercing without learning something about disinfection and the location of major veins and arteries is, perhaps, stupid and careless. Someone who knows they are ignorant and still tells the submissive that, "I know what I'm doing," is abusing the submissive. They are coercing the submissive into participating via deception.

Neglect, when the perpetrator should or does know better, can also enter here as a form of abuse. For example:

- Leaving someone alone who is tied up or otherwise unable to take care of themselves, or
- Not providing adequate aftercare following a scene.

In fact, in a BDSM context we also have the situation where not hitting someone can be neglect or abuse. For example, where a submissive joined up with a dominant because she likes being caned or manhandled, and then he refuses or can't be bothered to cane or manhandle her any more.

A note about the perpetrator

Usually, people talk about abuse in terms of harm caused to the victim. But, here I'd like to consider the perpetrator.

When it is the intent of someone to use deceit to be abusive—for example to lie to get into bed with another someone, or to hunt up a pain slut to beat with a flogger or cane while unhealthily imagining that the pain slut is actually someone against whom the abuser bears a grudge—the consequences for the victim, because of their ignorance of what's really going on, aren't clear.

Indeed, there might not be any negative or unproductive consequence for the person we'd normally call the victim. Maybe she ends up having the greatest orgasm the galaxy has ever known and she goes away with an amazing feeling of contentment, or maybe the pain slut goes away thinking what amazing staying power and strength the abuser has.

But there still is a victim here. The victim might actually turn out to be the perpetrator themselves. When their attempts at deceit and manipulation have been successful, they have been gratified and rewarded for antisocial behaviour. Their behaviour involving not being open and honest with others (and, possibly, with themselves as well) has been reinforced. This is certainly a negative outcome and has unproductive implications for their self-esteem, self-respect, and their ability to deal well and fairly with people.

It's worth recognising that BDSM does provide a subculture or context in which one person, be they nominally dominant or submissive, can enact abuse with a partner while their partner suffers no ill consequences from this:

- Someone with poor self-esteem, or who has a self-destructive component in their personality, could seek out someone who will humiliate them, piss on them, or abuse them verbally,
- Another person who was physically abused or hurt by someone close to them may seek to return to that closeness by looking for someone who will also hurt them,

I quoted the following earlier in this book from DSM-IV:

> *When Sexual Sadism is practiced with nonconsenting partners, the activity is likely to be repeated until the person with Sexual Sadism is apprehended.* [DSMIVTR] (302.84) (p. 573)

In the same way, as long as an abuser gets rewarded for their abuse, and as long as their strategies of deceit or manipulation are successful, they will tend to continue until someone catches them out.

Recognising abuse and abusers

Here are three important points about abusers:

- More than likely, you're not their first victim,
- More than likely, it's not something special about you. It's their lifestyle. It's what they do, and
- More than likely, they've been doing this for years.

If you're a more-or-less normal, level-headed type of person then you don't have the practice or the skills to pick up on most abusers. Sure, you might spot the really obvious cases—such as the recurring fucked bondage bunny example—but long-term manipulations, snide remarks, subtle put-downs, non-obvious threats, and deceptions can be hard to recognise. Abusers often have entirely plausible excuses for everything they do. They might even be able to make you think that you're the crazy one.

Remember, they have way more practice at being abusers than you have at detecting them. They are abusers 24 hours a day, seven days a week, and probably have been for years. They might be the first one you've ever come across. Who has the edge here experience-wise?

Because of their subtlety and skill, the best indicators that you're dealing with an abuser are you and your reactions. If you're experiencing any of the consequences I listed earlier and you're confused about why, then it's time to step back and have a close look at what's going on. Maybe talk to your friends or a professional counsellor about it.

Also keep in mind that an abuser might not be doing what they do consciously or deliberately. It could be subconscious. It could be something they've learned as a strategy for getting their way and they apply it without thinking. Regardless, the consequences can be very real, and very damaging.

Wrap-up

Abuse is about actions, intents and consequences. In a BDSM context, the actions and short-term consequences are not necessarily a good indicator of abuse. Instead, the long-term consequences should be considered.

22. Conclusion

One conclusion we can draw from all of the above is that the world of BDSM is a truly rich environment, and is one in which new and unusual contexts are created which normally do not and cannot exist in the wider community.

For those who are enthusiastic, open, and careful, these new contexts provide opportunities for profound self exploration, learning, and even ecstasy.

However, this same richness also provides new opportunities for those who are predisposed towards harming themselves or others. BDSM isn't alone in this, of course. Almost any human activity can be abused, and humans seem remarkably adept at ferreting out opportunities to do so. I have attempted to mention at least some of the ways this can occur in BDSM, but certainly there are many more.

We can see that the world of BDSM is not one where masochism and sadism exist in their true sense—i.e., where pain is an end in itself—but is instead where pain can be a means to an end, be that end catharsis, penetration, intimacy, an uncovering or discovery of self, or mere(!) recreation.

But inasmuch as it can be about penetration, there are many forms of penetration, and there are—correspondingly—many barriers and boundaries to penetrate. This helps us understand why there are so many different BDSM activities—namely because there are so many different ways to penetrate someone and, therefore, many different horses for many different courses.

We've also looked at ways in which BDSM can be differentiated from other relationships and activities, such as fetishes. We've looked at how the *Other* fits in, and how images and ideas of our ideal partners and relationships play their role in giving us a sense of continuity in our real relationships.

As part of our examinations, we've seen the role of our partner in all of this, and thus why BDSM clubs and parties aren't replete with automatic whipping machines or with other devices to do the pinching, poking, and loving infliction of pain. Even where there are machines, they are never automatic—there's always another person controlling it.

We've also looked at the role of authority in BDSM—its different forms, its use, and even its abuse. Authority and power are important in BDSM, and often the disparity in power between two partners is key to how penetration and other activities play out. Control is authority made manifest, and it is the fact that each partner has different control which is one of the characteristics which defines BDSM.

We've looked at BDSM as something more than an activity which is strictly between two people, and have seen how it is shaped by the culture in which it exists.

On top of that, one of the goals of this book has been to consider BDSM, not just as a range of behaviours or activities, but as a culture between people, and to that end I have considered its anthropological basis, its cultural underpinnings, and the microcultures it creates.

I have also looked at the role of groups, both social and structured, in the nature of BDSM, and have noted how groups create their own unique and exploitable contexts for making BDSM more varied and more profound for its participants.

Another point is that BDSM isn't done in isolation as some researchers might try to lead us believe, and nor is it done simply in some private context of, say, a bedroom or BDSM club. BDSM is shaped both by the human and personal needs it satisfies, and by the culture in which it operates. This latter is very important. Looking at BDSM as merely a personal weirdness takes it away from its true nature. While it is an intensely personal experience, it occurs in the context of a much wider culture, and this culture strongly effects how our own personal BDSM is enacted.

Travel this road with care and I believe there is much joy to be had.

I wish you well on your journey.

Bibliography

[ABELHIRSCH2006] - *The perversion of pain, pleasure, and thought: on the difference between "suffering" an experience and the "construction" of a thing to be used*; Nicola Abel-Hirsch; pp. 97 - 107; Chapter 5 from *Perversion: Psychoanalytic perspectives/perspectives on psychoanalysis*; 2006; Editors Dany Nobus and Lisa Downing; Karnac Books; ISBN 1855759179

[AIRAKSINEN1988] - *Ethics of Coercion and Authority: A Philosophical Study of Social Life*; Timo Airaksinen; University of Pittsburgh Press; ISBN 082293583X

[ANTHONY1995] - *Thy Rod and Staff - New Light on the Flagellatory Impulse*; Edward Anthony; 1995; Little, Brown and Company; ISBN 0316906670

[BARLEY1986] - *The Innocent Anthropologist - Notes from a Mud Hut*; Nigel Barley; 1986; Penguin Travel Library; ISBN 0140095365

[BAUMEISTER1994] - *Shrinking the Self*; Roy F. Baumeister and Joseph M. Boden; pp. 143 - 173; Chapter 5 from *Changing the self: Philosophies, techniques and experiences*; 1994; Editors Thomas M. Brinthaupt and Richard P. Lipka; State University of New York Press; ISBN 0791418677

[BAUMEISTER1997] - *Sexual Masochism - Deviance without Pathology*; Roy F. Baumeister and Jennifer L. Butler; pp. 225 - 239; Chapter 12 from *Sexual Deviance: Theory, Assessment and Treatment*; 1997; Editors D. Richard Laws and William O'Donohue; Guilford Press; ISBN 1572302410

[CALIFIA1994] - *Public Sex: The Culture of Radical Sex*; 1994; Patrick Califia-Rice; Cleis; ISBN 0939416891; (reference found in paper *Working at play: BDSM sexuality in the San Francisco Bay area*; Margot D. Weiss; 2006; Anthropologica; ISSN 0003-5459; p. 232)

[DEGEORGE1985] - *The nature and limits of authority*; Richard T. DeGeorge; 1985; University Press of Kansas; ISBN 0700602704

[DSMIVTR] - *Diagnostic and Statistical Manual of Mental Disorders - Fourth Edition - Text Revision*; American Psychiatric Association; 2000; ISBN 0890420246

[ELISE2001] - *Unlawful Entry - Male Fears of Psychic Penetration*; Dianne Elise; 2001; Psychoanalytic Dialogues, ISSN 1048-1885, Vol 11(4), Aug 2001, pp. 499 - 532

[FERRY2003] - *Butlers & Household Managers - 21st Century Professionals*; Steven M. Ferry; Imprint Books; ISBN 1591093066

[FORDHAM1991] - *Introduction to Jung's Psychology*; Frieda Fordham; 1991; Penguin Books; ISBN 0140135685

[GEERTZ1973] - *Deep Play: Notes on the Balinese Cockfight*; Clifford Geertz; pp. 412 -; Chapter 15 from *Interpretation of Cultures* by same author; Basic Books; ISBN 0465097197

[GHENT1990] - *Masochism, Surrender, Submission - Masochism as a Perversion of Surrender*; 1990; Emmanuel Ghent; *Contemporary Psychoanalysis*, ISSN 0010-7530, Volume 26, Number 1, 1990, pp. 108 - 136

[GRANDIN1992] - *Calming Effects of Deep Touch Pressure in Patients with Autistic Disorder, College Students, and Animals*; Temple Grandin; 1992; *Journal of Child and Adolescent Psychopharmacology*, ISSN 1044-5463, volume 2, number 1, 1992, pp. 63 - 72

[HILL1996] - *Individual Differences in the Experience of Sexual Motivation: Theory and Measurement of Dispositional Sexual Motives*; Craig A. Hill and Leslie K. Preston; *The Journal of Sex Research*, ISSN 0022-4499, volume 33, number 1, 1996, pp. 27 - 45

[HOFF2003] - *Power and Love: Sadomasochistic Practices in Long-Term Committed Relationships*; Gabriele Hoff; Dissertation to the Faculty of the California Institute of Integral Studies; February 2003

[KRAUSS1987] - *The Effects of Deep Pressure Touch on Anxiety*; Kirsten E. Krauss; 1987; *The American Journal of Occupational Therapy*, ISSN 0272-9490, volume 41, number 6, 1987, pp. 366 - 373

[MASTERS1998] - *Understanding Submission*; Peter Masters; 1998; http://www.peter-masters.com/understanding_submission/undersub.html

[MASTERS2006] - *The Control Book*; Peter Masters; 2006; Rinella Editorial Services; ISBN 0940267098

[MESTON2007] - *Why Humans Have Sex*; Cindy M. Meston and David M. Buss; 2007; Archives of Sexual Behaviour, ISSN 0004-0002, volume 36, number 4, 2007, pp. 477 - 507

[MORRIS1978] - *Manwatching - A Field Guide to Human Behaviour*; Desmond Morris; 1978; Triad/Panther Books

[OED] - *Oxford English Dictionary*; Oxford University Press

[PLATOCRAT] - *Cratylus*; Benjamin Jowett; http://www.ac-nice.fr/philo/textes/Plato-Works/16-Cratylus.htm (retrieved 11 Jan 2008)

[STEVENS1994] *Jung*; Anthony Stevens; 1994; Oxford University Press; ISBN 0192876864

[TAYLOR1953] - *Sex in History*; G. Rattray Taylor; 1953; Thames and Hudson

[TOYA2001] - *Subspace - The Journey of a Submissive*; Toya; 2001; Whisper Enterprises; ISBN 0473075725

[WARREN1994] - *The Loving Dominant*; John Warren; 1994; Rhinoceros; ISBN 1563332183

[WATT1982] - *Authority - International Series in Social and Political Thought*; E. D. Watt; 1982; Croom Helm; ISBN 0709927428

[WINNICOTT1955] - *Clinical Varieties of Transference (1955 - 1956)*; Donald W. Winnicott; *Through Paediatrics to Psycho-Analysis - COLLECTED PAPERS*; 1992; Brunner-Routledge; ISBN 0876307039

[WINNICOTT1960] - *Ego Distortion in Terms of True and False Self (1960)*; Donald W. Winnicott; *The Maturational Processes and the Facilitating Environment - Studies in the Theory of Emotional Development*; 2006; Karnac Books; ISBN 0946439842

About the Author - *Peter Masters*

www.peter-masters.com

Peter Masters is five feet ten inches tall, and is not unique in that respect. He is the author of two well-reviewed books on sex and BDSM, namely *Look Into My Eyes* and *The Control Book*, and spends the majority of his time when away from the keyboard fending off the advances of horny and amorous women (he wishes).

Since puberty he has been both an active explorer of the kinky side of life, and a passionate devotee of power and authority dynamics. For the last decade he has also been researching and writing about BDSM.

He is an experienced trainer, runs workshops and classes on things straight and twisted, and for a number of years also ran a discussion group on dominance & submission.

He lives in Sydney, Australia, rents a nice apartment near a fire-station, and is a devout heterosexual. Highly attractive young women with large assets should not hesitate to contact him via email.

If not apparent so far, he also enjoys writing about himself in the third person for the "about the author" page of his work, and perhaps doesn't take it as seriously as some might wish.

Peter Masters is also the author of:

- *Look Into My Eyes - how to use hypnosis to bring out the best in your sex life*
- *The Control Book*

Both books are available at Amazon.com

CPSIA information can be obtained at www.ICGtesting.com
Printed in the USA
LVOW011726261211

261108LV00016B/206/P

9 781934 625682